Teachers Abroad Mysteries

#1 Revolution Revenge
#2 Oasis Assassin
#3 Turkish Delight Gone Sour
#4 Singapore Fling

Turkish Delight Gone Sour

Phyllis Wachob

This book is dedicated to all English teachers who love to travel.

I would like to thank my mother, Betty Lou Hylton Wachob, for her support and help during the writing of this book.

Preface

Although some of the places in this novel are real, for example, the village of Goreme, the morning balloon rides, the Open Air Museum, Pidgeon Valley, and Love Valley, most are fictional. The real places of Cappadocia are easily found in literature in guide books or on the web. However, there is no Aladdin's Cave or the Perfect American English Academy. In its essence, this is a work of fiction. Names, characters, places and incidents are either the product of the author's imagination or are used fictitiously, and any resemblance to actual persons, living or dead, businesses or establishments, events or locales is coincidental.

Cast of Characters

Barbie Falcon – English teacher at the Perfect American English Academy

Recep – manager of the PAEA

Ayse – Recep's wife

Bunyamin – Recep and Ayse's son

Aygul – Recep and Ayse's daughter

Kemal – owner of Aladdin's Cave

Penelope Watson – Barbie's friend and former colleague

Georgia – English teacher at PAEA

Geoff – English teacher at PAEA

Ted Baxter – English teacher at PAEA

Charlene, Maureen, Colleen – aka the 'eens – teachers at PAEA

Mrs. Ted Baxter – Ted Baxter's wife

Faruk – owner of the quad bike shop

Hakan – Faruk's assistant

Chapter One: The Balloon Ride

The knock came heavy and insistent. "Balloon ride!!!"

Barbie sat up, bewildered and angry. "Balloons? Where?" Then she understood and pushed her way through the bedclothes and into an upright position. Swiftly throwing on jeans, long sleeved shirt and grabbing her jacket, she was out the door in less than five minutes. She swiftly caught a look at her blond, curly flyaway hair in a window and reached for her hat which was the remedy for many a bad hair day.

Inching down the wooden staircase, feeling her way around the corner which she knew was there but could not see in the dark, she saw the other teachers huddled in a group in the lobby of their pension, Aladdin's Cave. The group whispered in the darkness and Barbie noticed that the two kids, Recep's youngsters, had been left behind. She wasn't sure how many had forced themselves to get up, but at $150US a person, if you paid, you went. Kemal, the owner of Aladdin's Cave, urged them out the door and into the van. They piled in, finding seats wherever they could. The three 'eens' sat on each other's laps, and Recep's wife demurely sat in the back beside him. Barbie caught sight of Georgia's flaming red hair and blank, sleep-deprived expression.

Barbie stared out the window, trying to make out the shapes of the Fairy Chimneys that surrounded the pension and saw that the sky had turned just the softest shade of navy blue in preparation for the dawn. Kemal barreled down the narrow streets and out into the wide main square of Goreme, then headed out of town. Barbie was confused and had no idea which direction they took. She turned back to count the other passengers. Recep and wife, the three 'eens', Georgia, she counted, and then she saw Geoff in the front passenger seat. And herself.

"Ted Baxter, where's Ted Baxter?" she asked. Then, when no one answered, she turned and asked Kemal, "Did we forget Ted Baxter? Did you wake him up?"

Kemal shrugged and kept going. Geoff turned around in the front seat, "Don't worry Barbie, Ted Baxter is an adult, he can fend for himself. If he didn't set his alarm, too bad. I, for one, can do without him this morning. And after last night, I'm not surprised that no one else cares about the missing Ted Baxter."

"Yeah, you're right, "Barbie answered. "But I would be really ticked off to have missed this!"

Kemal braked and bumped into the parking lot of the Kismet Balloon Tours parking lot. "All right, breakfast here, then off you go! Enjoy yourselves."

The group of teachers from the Perfect American English Academy in Ankara milled around with tourists from all over the world. Coffee, tea and pastries were available. Assignments were being made. Barbie was pleased to find that the group of eight was assigned to the same small balloon. The total of ten passengers were directed to another van which quickly sped away. Barbie noticed that dawn was not far away and the pure air of Cappadocia meant that the color of the sky smoothly faded from one shade of navy blue to another with a small elongated dome of yellow and orange where the sun would appear within the next half hour.

Before they realized, they were in amongst the balloons. Multicolored behemoths lay on their sides; vividly colored pillows of silk gradually becoming fatter and fatter. The noise of the flames, along with the intense colors made a mysterious, otherworldly scene. Among the fairy chimneys, here just large lumps of striated rock with occasional holes barricaded shut with wooden doors, the balloons looked out of place and yet, Barbie knew, they had begun to define the 'experience' of Cappadocia for the world.

As they were introduced to their captain, Barbie thrilled to see the huge balloons on either side, gradually fill and begin to jerk upright, pulling their baskets to an upright position. The captain, a young blonde with a long ponytail, spoke authoritatively, "Yes, I am Damla, the captain, please to board carefully. You must climb, like this" and she adroitly leapt into the basket. The rest boarded the same way, the 'eens' helped by eager young Turkish assistants' hands as they missed their footing on the sides of the wicker basket. Recep cautiously pushed and pulled his wife with her long coat into the basket while Barbie tried not to laugh, smothering her giggles in her gloved hand. She left herself for last and gave a whispered wish to do it at least as gracefully as the fully covered Ayse.

"Give me a hand Geoff," Barbie called out above the roar of the flames as the basket tightened against the ropes that held it to the ground. Geoff pulled, Barbie lifted her leg as far as it would go, and just as she felt a hand on her bottom, she popped in. The ropes slackened and within seconds, they were aloft. Quickly they rose above the fairy chimneys, and the scene spread out before them. It seemed as if a hundred balloons rose with them, the roar of their flames gradually softening with the distance, just as the sun peeked above the horizon.

Then, the roar above their heads stopped, and the stillness that invaded the empty space thrilled them. They just <u>had</u> to squeal and exclaim with delight. Barbie took a cautious look at Damla, the captain in her navy-blue sweater with small gold epaulets on the sleeves, who smiled involuntarily. She must have done this so many times, Barbie thought, she must know exactly how all of us will react. But nothing was going to spoil it for Barbie, as they silently floated over the village of Goreme. Around them, balloons floated and occasionally they could hear snatches of conversations, exclamations and demands for photos interspersed with roars of the flames as the captains turned on and off the flames to make the balloons go higher and lower.

"Look, Aladdin's Cave!" said one of the 'eens', pointing excitedly downwards. The pension was easily recognizable because of the terrace on the second floor where they would eat breakfast, a small space set with tables and surrounded by blossoming flowers. Just outside the front door was parked the gray Mercedes van and Kemal's little motorbike. Little streets and roads snaked off into the other parts of town and into the neighboring desert. Barbie looked out and the whole of Cappadocia seemed spread before her, now lit by the strong dawn light.

Desert punctured with giant fairy chimneys, low hills folded into perfect neat rolls whose shape and color changed with each slight movement of the rising sun caused a slight 'oh' of appreciation to emerge from Barbie's throat. The still clear air meant that the landscape below revealed rich colors of browns, grays and black and the deep shadows hid more textures and colors. If Barbie turned her head and seconds later turned back again, the scene had changed, more details revealed, shapes morphed into one another, concealing one detail, but exposing another. Away to the horizon, all around her, Barbie saw fantastic Cappadocia: the chimneys, the hills melted into surreal shapes, the small towns gripping the base of hills, the rocks punctured with doorways and windows, the small farms with withered plants and trees, and the ribbons of roads and paths. All dry, but the myriad shadings of colors startled the imagination.

Now she glanced down. They were higher than before, the flame was silent and a fear gripped Barbie. Nothing was below her, she hung in the air with nothing but an extremely flimsy basket between her and what seemed a thousand feet of pure air. With an anguished look, she turned to Damla, the supremely confident pilot. "Could we go a little lower, please???"

Damla laughed and waited for a couple of heartbeats as the basket floated down almost imperceptibly. "We can go low, but not too much. We need to be high, catch the wind, move away from Goreme. We want to go there". She pointed to the north, towards Avanos, a small town in the distance to the north. "But now, we go low, for you." She smiled mischievously at Barbie.

They drifted with the wind, surrounded now by almost a hundred balloons as they moved towards the open fields to the north and west where they would land an hour from takeoff. The 'eens' giggled as they pointed out familiar landmarks around the town. Then, just as one of the 'eens' screamed, "What's that?" Barbie saw it as well. A man lying, arms outstretched, in a ditch, wearing a bright blue jacket. The color of the jacket was unusual, so incredibly intensely bright, with a red stripe over the sleeves. They all recognized it. "Ted Baxter," whispered someone.

"What is he doing there? Sleeping in a ditch? Why didn't he come with us? Maybe he has been there all this time." Geoff spoke for all of them. The questions, the bewilderment that he didn't come with them this morning. Overslept, in a ditch, or did someone steal his jacket?

Barbie made a quick decision as she pulled out her phone from an inside pocket. Do phones work up here, she wondered. She saw the familiar bands of connectivity, but noticed that her battery was low, again.

"Kemal", she said as the phone was answered immediately. "Where is Ted Baxter?" she asked hurriedly.

"Good morning, my friend Barbie. Have you landed already?"

"No, but I need to know if Ted Baxter is there!"

"Why do you need to know? I think he is there with you?"

"No, he is not here in the balloon with us. But we think we can see him, down below."

"Okay, I am knocking his door now." Barbie heard a number of loud thumps through the static on the line. "He is not answering. I will open door with my key."

Barbie waited as she noticed they had drifted away from the figure below. She called out to the group, "Find out where that spot is!"

"No one here, Miss Barbie. I don't know where is Ted Baxter," Kemal replied.

"I think I do," muttered Barbie into the phone as the roar of the flame drowned out her words.

Chapter Two: What to do about Ted Baxter

All of the teachers who had come to Goreme for the national holiday, with the exception of Ted Baxter, gathered in the lobby of Aladdin's Cave. They had spread out across the lobby sitting on chairs set in front of the office and the wooden chest opposite. The 'eens' had taken two chairs from their room as it was adjacent to the lobby. Ayse had taken the children to their room upstairs and had settled them down with a favorite computer game and now descended the small narrow staircase to sit quietly beside her husband Recep. The police had come and gone. Kemal, as the pension owner, had given them Ted Baxter's passport, allowed them to search the room and now sat sadly staring at the locked door just in front of him.

Barbie spoke quietly. "Recep, what do we do now? What are the protocols with the police? Do we need to do anything? I don't know about the rest of you, but going on with the holiday seems a bit callous, but going back to Ankara and leaving Ted Baxter here seems even more callous. What happens now?"

Recep stared and Barbie recognized his typical thoughtful pause. Recep's English was good, he was very intelligent and it did not seem necessary for him to pause so long. But Barbie knew from the last few months working with him that he never said anything unless he had thought about it before he opened his mouth. It was a quite refreshing method of communication considering that many of her countrymen were far too quick to spew out thoughtless comments without the forethought that this gentle Turkish man had. On the other hand, waiting for Recep to speak could require a long wait. Barbie noticed his bald head covered in sweat and the heavy growth on his face. He had not had time to shave yet this morning. As the Director of the Perfect American English Academy's branch in Ankara, he was the dead man's boss, and so had been with the police as they removed and identified the body, collected his identification papers and searched his room at Aladdin's Cave. Recep had been with them all morning and had had nothing to eat since the meager tea and pastry at 5 am.

The rest had gone upstairs to the open-air lounge and stuffed themselves with cereal, fruit, cheese, olives, fresh bread, tomatoes and cucumbers. They had eagerly attacked the honeycomb and gouged great holes out of it in their attempt to capture honey and bits of beeswax comb to go on their bread. Numerous cups of coffee and tea had washed down the breakfast. Most had felt the caffeine necessary after the events of the morning that had started far too early. Now cups of coffee and tea were scattered amongst them as they contemplated the future.

"We must stay here," Recep said at last. "We cannot leave Ted Baxter here. We are responsible for him."

"Speak for yourself," muttered Charlene, the shortest and decidedly the plumpest of the 'eens.' "There is no way that anyone is going to talk me into accepting any responsibility for that jerk."

"Hush," said Georgia, her face going as red as her hair. "Even if you didn't like him, he was one of our group and we can't just up and leave. He was a *colleague*, for heaven's sake."

Charlene bent over and her bust bumped the table as she hissed at Georgia, "A colleague and a jerk."

"Of course, we stay," declared Maureen, the tall thin 'een'. "But do we have to go into mourning? Can't we just go about our business here?"

Recep again went thoughtful. They waited. Kemal heaved a sigh of troubled anxiety.

"Recep," Barbie intervened. "What did the police say he died of? When? I mean, it was just a terrible accident or sudden illness, wasn't it? I mean, what can we do about it? I know, it must seem just a wee bit unfeeling to continue with our vacation, but if we were just demure…and…didn't call attention to ourselves and not laugh too much." She hesitated and looked around, checking to see how her suggestion was being received. The 'eens' all nodded vigorously, Georgia looked neutral, Geoff sighed like Kemal did. Recep looked at his wife, who sat stoically. Barbie thought she was pretending not to understand English again. What a tricky situation.

"Well, we don't know how he died, so that is not the issue here. The real question is whether we can pretend one of our colleagues is just not here with us and continue on as planned. Maybe…" Recep's voice drifted off.

"We quietly go about our vacation." Geoff's voice cut through the soft words and unwillingness to commit to a course of action. It was a suggestion that was noncommittal and could cover a multitude of attitudes and activities.

"In that case, I'm going to take a nap," and with that Colleen, the third 'een', got up from her place and headed towards the room just a few steps away that she shared with the other two 'eens'.

A yawn formed on Charlene's face, then was infectiously caught by Maureen and the other two of the three 'eens' left.

Ayse leaned over and spoke quietly to her husband Recep who also got up and then they too headed upstairs to their room. Children's voices could be heard and sharp steps pounded across the floor upstairs. "Bunyamin, Aygul, please be respectful of other's privacy!" shouted Recep.

Barbie laughed and said to Recep's disappearing back, "The eternal English teacher, speaking English to his four and six-year olds!"

"Well, they will learn the language, unlike so many of our students," quipped Geoff as he got up and disappeared upstairs as well.

"Cynic", said Georgia shaking her head, making the red curls bounce in her exuberance.

"Ladies will drink tea!" Kemal, the ever-helpful host said. It was not really a question, but a statement. Kemal, along with other Turks, was constantly offering tea and to refuse was bad form. He got up and disappeared into the office.

"I missed my run this morning, I think I'll go now. Wanna come?" Georgia asked Barbie casually, as if she expected a negative answer.

Barbie made a face. Georgia's athleticism was almost a joke at the school and among her friends, and Barbie, who occasionally walked and swam at least three times a week, heaved a sigh much like the others. "Too tired, I guess. Where would you go? Don't forget what Kemal said about the dogs."

"All the more reason why milady should come with me!" Georgia grinned and tossed her head again. Kemal warned them the evening before about the dogs of Goreme. Most were not nasty, but there were a few Kangal dogs around, at least partially feral, that were known to be vicious. Kangal dogs were sheepherding dogs, about the size of their charges, and could be very scary due to their size. Hairy, huge-mouthed, possessing an awful roar that went for a bark, they could stand taller than their owners. Householders in rural areas of Turkey were fond of them as guard dogs, but the proliferation in urban areas was something to which many foreigners objected.

Barbie thought of the first time she had seen a Kangal, the lead dog of a small gang that burst from the shrubs as she had waited for a bus at Kizilay in downtown Ankara. She was shocked that a pack of dogs would wander around the busy downtown streets, and even more shocked that no one else besides her seemed to notice. She stared and tried to act normal and soon the small pack disappeared as quickly as they had come. Now she thought of the long legs and slobbering mouth of that dog and shivered with the remembrance and the fear that the hound had instilled.

"Maybe after lunch and I want to go hiking, not running. I want to see what there is, not watch it speed by. I'll catch you later, I guess." As Georgia got up, slinging her running jacket over her shoulder, Barbie burst out. "You remember, this morning, when we were at the ditch and we saw Ted Baxter's body? And the blood and the rock… You saw the rock, right? Well, did you…?" Barbie stumbled and her brain searched for words. She looked at Georgia's face and stopped. Something funny in her expression stopped Barbie from saying any more. It was as if Georgia saw and knew more than Barbie and did not want to talk about it. "Yeah, right, go for a run. See you later."

Georgia dashed upstairs and within two minutes was whipping out the door at a double time step. Kemal appeared from this office with two cups of tea. "How many sugars, two or three? And some Turkish Delight?"

"How about one sugar, Kemal. I am trying not to get to be a fat middle-aged woman. Middle-aged I can't help, but please, help me out a bit here!??" Barbie laughed as she said this and Kemal joined her. He placed the two tiny glass tea cups on the table along with a small bowl filled with squares of Turkish Delight. The candy, made from various flavors of fruit, was basically sugar and starch with a few pieces of nuts. The pieces were dredged in powdered sugar to keep them from sticking together. Barbie actually liked the stuff, called 'lokum' in Turkish, but today she shuddered at the thought of the sweetness.

She poked a pale pink piece with her finger. "Kemal, the Turkish Delight has gone hard, stale, just like this holiday, which has gone sour." She paused and sighed. "So, what do we do about Ted Baxter, Kemal?"

"Ah, I have done what I was asked. I gave the police the passport and they will call his wife in America and…"

"Wife!" Barbie interrupted. "I didn't know he was married?? Who knew about this? The way he behaved was not like a married man. That rat, that scum, that dirty, filthy, cheating, lying… Ooh, I wish I had put my paws around his neck before…" Barbie stopped as Kemal looked at her strangely. "Ok, ok, I didn't like him much, neither did anyone else, he was such a jerk. He was always saying things about people and sometimes I wondered if they were true or not. But a wife, wow, that puts a new spin on things. Are the police going to do anything before she gets here? Oh, being a wife, I guess she would come and get him and take him home. That's what a good wife would do. What are <u>we</u> going to do about Ted Baxter?"

"I think," Kemal said slowly, "that the police will not do very much. You know it is the holiday and they will just wait until Ted Baxter's wife arrives. And they can use this to do nothing. 'We must wait', they will say. And then, they will have their holiday with their family and they will not look any more."

"What do you mean, 'look any more'? What are they looking for now?"

"You know, you were there, they are looking more bloody rocks. Or maybe something else." Kemal looked away as he said this.

"More bloody rocks? Do they think that he hit himself on more rocks? I mean, it was a bit of a mess, that whole scene. Vomit and scuffle marks everywhere, like a herd of elephants, and then the rock. Oh, that was terrible, like it jumped up and hit him, instead of him falling on it. That seemed a bit strange." Barbie drifted off into thought, while Kemal slurped his tea, making loud noises as he cooled the hot liquid through his mouth.

They sat silently as Barbie carefully lifted her miniscule glass by the edges and tried a tiny sip. She always found herself the last to finish her tea if among Turks, as they had truly mastered the technique of drinking hot tea.

"Maybe they are looking more. Maybe the festival stops them, but they want to look more."

Barbie peered at Kemal's face, trying hard to fathom what he was implying. "Are you saying that they think there is more to it than just a heart attack or accident or something? Are you saying they suspect something, or someone else? Is that what they think?"

"Maybe, maybe." He slurped again.

"So maybe it is not a case of what should we do about Ted Baxter, but what we should do about this mess that involves us?"

Silence filled the space where Barbie expected an answer. "There is more, isn't there Kemal?"

Again, she was met with silence as Kemal turned his head away. He stared at the Anatolian kilim hung on the wall opposite. The strings at the ends had become faded in the light; too many people and backpacks had rubbed against it and had created dirty spots and smears. "Maybe, maybe. My wife can wash this and make it clean." He looked at the floor, avoiding Barbie's stare. "Maybe, maybe we can just forget the bad things, dirty carpets and dead guests, busy police and left wives. Maybe if we are quiet, they will become clean and no one will bother us anymore."

Barbie for once was unable to find an answer, or in fact, anything to say, to this series of disjointed thoughts. She looked at Kemal and tried to figure out what he was trying to say. Even though she had met him online almost six weeks ago and in person yesterday, she had felt as though she could communicate with him easily from the first. She had been an English teacher now for almost twenty years, living and working all over the world, student of many languages, master of none, and she thought that she was able to communicate with almost anyone with almost any level of English. But this rambling incoherence stumped her.

"So, what you are saying is, we have to wait and see what happens? There's nothing we can do now? Right?"

Kemal looked tired suddenly as he slumped forward and then heaved himself to his feet. He had been up since before they got up and had had not a moment's rest since. When Barbie had called him this morning, he immediately notified the police on duty and they had designated an old van as a temporary ambulance. Following Georgia's directions, they had driven out of town along the roads the teachers had seen that morning. It had taken less than half an hour to locate the blue jacket-clad body of Ted Baxter lying in a ditch. Discovering that he was dead, they left the body where it lay, in hopes of preserving enough of the scene to decide what had happened. By the time the regular police chief arrived, the rest of the teachers on the balloon ride had arrived. They gathered around and watched as the police had walked around and around the body, bent over it, felt for a pulse, turned it over, picked up the bloody rock that lay near the body. They picked up some of the vomit that was there and sniffed at it. To Barbie, it was NOT the way a crime scene should have been treated. On TV and the movies, more care would have been taken. Where was the crime scene tape? Where were the photographers? Where was the magnifying glass and the footprint analysis? But as she watched them, she thought they had a different concept in mind. Barbie then had thought that she watched too many cop shows on the TV in her apartment. Maybe she should give up the cable subscription and forget about following 'Bones' and The Closer and the BBC gruesome murder shows. But now, with Kemal's remarks buzzing in her head, perhaps she needed to rethink. Were the police just inordinately incompetent and didn't want anyone to know? Or perhaps they thought it was just a tragic accident and so no 'crime scene' existed, but now had changed their minds.

In any case, the body had been moved into the makeshift ambulance and it had been driven slowly away in the direction of Nevsehir, a bigger and more important city nearby. What was the truth? Did the police suspect anything like 'foul play' or not? Was it 'misadventure' or malicious?

"What are you trying to say, Kemal? Do the police think it is not normal, that something else happened?"

"Maybe, may…"

"Good morning, everyone. Good morning. Are we ready? Are you ready for the day of your life, seeing the spectacular fairy chimneys, painted churches, underground cities and dovecotes of the world-famous Cappadocia? Zoom around among the most stupendously wonderful scenery the good life has to offer? Ah, beautiful lady, are you ready?" Faruk grinned widely and took both of Barbie's hands in his. "Yes, beautiful lady?"

Barbie stared, her mouth falling open. She felt it, that stirring, that animal attraction.

Kemal turned and headed towards the office, presumably looking for another glass. "Good morning, Faruk, how are you?" Kemal was handsome and friendly and everyone was his 'special' friend. Until Faruk arrived. Then all eyes went towards this incredibly handsome, black-eyed, black-haired youthful man with an intensity that wearied his friends.

"Faruk, when did you get here? Where have you been? Did you hear our awful news?" Geoff asked.

Barbie tilted her head and looked at Faruk.

He stared at her, open-eyed, with crinkles on the edges of his eyes that gave the impression that he really meant what he said, that it was not a fake smile or a fake emotion. Barbie thought that this was what charisma was like, when someone made you feel as though you were the only one in the room, or at least the only one that mattered. And Faruk had charisma. And sex appeal. It wasn't just the 'beautiful lady' comment, it was the spark, the heat, the fire, that he said it with. It made Barbie want to find out what those strong rough hands could do to her. She felt herself involuntarily melting under that heat and fire.

"Ah, yes, the man we have lost. Such a good man, so devoted to his job, his colleagues, such a wonderful teacher to his students… We have lost a great man." Faruk smiled at Barbie and accepted a glass of tea from Kemal as he sat next to Barbie.

"You didn't even know him," Barbie answered hotly, momentarily casting off the spell that Faruk had woven around her. "How can you spout such drivel? None of his students liked him, neither did his colleagues. How can we even be sure that even his wife liked him?"

"Ah yes, the wife. Poor thing. What are you going to do about Ted Baxter? Will you leave now, or stay and have your vacation? Will you all gather round and mourn him?" Faruk smiled again, but this time without the crinkles. He kept hold of Barbie's hands in an intense grip and looked deep into her eyes.

Kemal interrupted the little love scene by placing a glass of tea at a place opposite Barbie and with a nod, invited Faruk to sit there. "No plans are made, yet. We are waiting the police and the wife. We will be quiet, but we will continue our vacation."

Faruk laughed and Barbie noticed the muscles flexing under his long-sleeved T-shirt. "Good, we can still play with our quad bikes today then? You will come, won't you my beautiful lady? You will sit on the seat of my most deluxe quad bike and let your blonde hair stream away into the breeze. You will laugh so gaily as we zoom round, up and down the mounds of red hills. Rounds of mounds like your beautiful body." Faruk laughed again, the special laugh just for Barbie as he pointedly assessed her feminine rounds and mounds.

Barbie smiled back, then remembered. "Thank you, handsome man, but I don't do quad bikes. Too dangerous for someone of my advanced years. As I was telling everyone last night, a friend was badly injured on a quad bike and I swore then and there that I would NEVER get on one. Besides, they are noisy, they disturb the peaceful quiet of this beautiful place and they pollute the atmosphere. Ask the 'eens', they'll take you up on it. They like things like that, and they like YOU." Barbie flirted.

Faruk rolled his eyes appreciatively at the mention of the 'eens'. "Such lovely YOUNG women. They don't have the mature sensibilities that you have. Ah, was it Benjamin Franklin who advised the young man to take a mature mistress? She would appreciate it so much more!"

Barbie gritted her teeth and rolled <u>her</u> eyes, "Don't think that was necessarily a compliment." She tried to talk herself out of liking this man; he had the capacity to make women act foolishly and Barbie had been known to be foolish in the past.

Faruk and Kemal exchanged some quick words in Turkish, Barbie catching a reference to the 'eens' and Geoff and 'quad bikes.' Also, to the afternoon.

Then Faruk switched to English. He asked Kemal what had been happening with the police and the question of what to do about Ted Baxter. Kemal very noncommittally made a reference to the religious festival and waiting.

"Oh well, I guess we have to wait. No use pushing the police, but do let me know. I don't want to get into trouble by angering them with my business. You know, owning a quad bike business is really welcomed by the tourists, they love being able to rent them. But some complain. I don't know, what am I supposed to do? I mean, who knew this Ted Baxter? Why do we have to go into mourning because of his stupid drinking and wandering off in the middle of the night? Forget it! Enjoy ourselves!" Faruk looked from one to the other with a twisted sad smile. He turned and batted his large, long eyelashes at Barbie.

Barbie fluttered her eyelashes back at him. This silly flirtatiousness had just come over her and she wondered where it had come from. She oftentimes fell into her role as a 'Barbie'. Curly blonde hair, sweet face, glittering smile, nice figure and her parents had named her 'Barbie', what could she do about that? Live the life that is given to you!

"Iyi gunler," Faruk called as he leapt out the door. Barbie heard the growl of the motor of his vehicle and then the noise faded as Faruk went on the prowl for more beautiful ladies to rent his quad bikes.

Barbie stared at the space Faruk had vacated. "Gosh, he speaks really fluent Turkish for an American."

Kemal laughed, "He's not American, he's Turkish. Very Turkish, I know."

"And I am an English teacher, been one for twenty years. I know that no one can speak American English like that and not be American. Not unless he spent a lot of years as a youngster in America. He has perfect grammar, perfect pronunciation and the gestures, perfect!"

"No, no, his Turkish is so perfect. He is from Malatya, I can tell. Maybe he spent some time in America, but no, no, he is perfect Turk."

Barbie and Kemal looked at each other, stubborn looks on both faces.

"I know that I have just met him, but how long have you known him?" Barbie asked cautiously.

"He came here three months ago and bought the quad bike business. It was my friend's business, but it is a difficult one, as he says. I don't know anything about him. But his accent is Malatya, or near that region. And I know he likes girls!"

Barbie asked, "What kind of passport does he have? American or Turkish?"

Kemal shrugged, "I don't look at passports! And I don't know much about him; that is true. But he is from Malatya."

A racket broke out over Barbie's head as two small children dashed out of an upstairs room, hurled themselves down the stairs amid screeching from both. "Minor problem today." Barbie mumbled.

Recep's short figure appeared after them. "Children, children, please, this is not a bad thing. Nothing to do with us, don't worry. Please, children."

The two youngsters stopped at the open door of the pension, staring outside as if they had seen a goblin lurking there. Recep arrived and touched both of them, pulling them into a hug. He looked over their heads at Kemal and Barbie. "I had to tell them, but it frightened them both. They think someone else did this, that someone…killed…poor Ted Baxter. And now they are frightened." He turned to both children and murmured in Turkish to them. Recep's wife had materialized at his side and bent over her huddled family. Coos sounded from her throat, which Barbie thought sounded like a pigeon pecking at her food. It made the children quiet down, though.

As the family mounted the staircase, Barbie thought that the day was deteriorating. It hadn't started well, but Ted Baxter was dead and no one could bring him back. But now, the kids thought he had been murdered. Faruk was planning to coerce them onto quad bikes and disturb the peace. And they still didn't know what to do about Ted Baxter.

Chapter Three: Lunch at the Blue Moon Café

It seemed as if the participants in the fall break teacher's holiday were suddenly awake, rested, eager to go and all appeared in the lobby.

"Lunch at the Blue Moon Café?" Barbie suggested. "I was told the gozleme were exceptional."

"Great," murmured Georgia. "Grease, carbohydrates, and no vitamins to speak of. Sounds perfect, let's go".

The 'eens' trouped out the door single file and Geoff joined them. As Recep and his wife Ayse walked reservedly down the staircase, the two children leaped from step to step, making the entire building rattle with every thump on every step. Barbie glared, but couldn't help herself from laughing. Kemal poked his head out of the office and noticed the exodus. "We're off to the Blue Moon Café," she said to him.

"They have good gozleme," he replied. "The best in Goreme. You should be sure to get the potato ones. Very delicious."

"Georgia is prepared to be delighted with the nutritional content. Listen, if Faruk comes by, please don't tell him where we are. If someone wants to ride a quad bike, they know where to find him."

"Oh, don't you want to see Faruk? The very handsome, smiling Faruk?" Kemal's eyes twinkled as he gave Barbie a crooked smile. "We clean your rooms now, okay?"

"Bye, see you later, alligator!"

"After while, crocodile!" Kemal answered. They both laughed. Barbie had taught Kemal this silly exchange the night before and she was delighted that he had remembered. She told herself to remember to emphasize the 'awhile' not 'while'. She prided herself on being always 'on' as an EFL teacher. Her motto was to emphasize form, communication and practice in equal parts; appeal to the brain and the heart and exercise them both. Hey, she reminded herself, two out of three is not bad.

She gingerly picked up her foot and placed it over the worn wooden lintel of the door and stepped down two narrow concrete steps to the street level. On a slight rise, Aladdin's Cave looked out over the town of Goreme. At least from upstairs, Barbie could see down to the bus station, and could follow the line of twisting streets to the south as they climbed to Sunset Point above the town. The fairy chimneys, towers of soft volcanic tuff, some with caps of hard basalt, were scattered about the town. To the east, the road snaked between two enormous chimneys towards the UNESCO Open Air Museum. To the west, a line of deeply eroded folds of rock ended in a winding canyon. "Pigeon Valley," Barbie reminded herself. Then she jumped down from the last step and scurried to catch up with the group, who were now at the end of the short street, waiting for Barbie's directions.

The fall 'getaway' for teachers at the Perfect American English Academy in Ankara had been a tradition for years. But this was an excellent year as a five-day holiday fell at the appropriate time. Usually it was a Sunday outing, but this year, the big boss in Istanbul gave his permission for the whole staff to take off. Although not everyone had wanted to come, enough had done so, and Barbie had suggested Cappadocia. Only five hours from Ankara on a luxury bus and the lucky find of a whole pension they could book for the four nights they planned to be here, made the trip very appealing. Barbie undertook to make arrangements and felt so lucky to have happened upon

Kemal. He assured her that everything was possible and he would make all the phone calls necessary. 'No problem,' he assured her again and again. And, except for the incident with Ted Baxter, he had kept his promise. Barbie reminded herself that the Ted Baxter problem was not really his. She felt very satisfied with her arrangements so far and was glad to have done some research into restaurants and activities she could suggest. Actually, she was the newest hired teacher at PAEA, but felt as though her superior skills as an organizer were the reason that everyone else let her take the lead on this. Even Recep and his family were happy to follow her. Like a Pied Piper she said to herself, leading her charges to the most fun places to go and things to see.

The group waited for her and Barbie smiled as she remembered the first time she had met the 'eens'. They introduced themselves one after the other and then squealed together, "The 'eens'!!!" American Maureen was tall, willowy, friendly and had brown hair. Colleen, also American, four inches shorter, but the same weight as Maureen, was also friendly and had brown hair. Charlene, on the other hand, was British, from London, and although she too weighed the same as the other 'eens', was at least four inches shorter than Colleen, eight inches shorter than Maureen. She was plump, also friendly and had light, reddish-brown hair. Approximately the same age, within a year of one another, all had obtained their teaching qualifications at about the same time and had arrived within two weeks of each other at PAEA. Maureen and Colleen had done their course together and had applied at the urging of the other. Not particularly good friends when they left the US, they had clung together when they arrived in Ankara. Two weeks later, when they were introduced to Charlene, they looked at one another and smiled delightedly. They could never remember which pointed out the 'een' connection, but within an hour of meeting, they had become the 'eens'. They now shared an apartment in Ankara, and a hotel room in Goreme. They were unrelentingly jolly, playful and full of laughter. It was hard to find anything wrong with the 'eens'. They were wonderful teachers and their students loved them; a series of practical jokes had started in the academy that involved them and their students. Although Recep could have put a stop to all the nonsense, he was unable to think of a good reason to quash the good humor. Even when the three of them showed up one day with electric pink hair, disrupting the routines of the office and the school, no one could find a fault with them. They were too good to be true.

Geoff arched his eyebrows at Barbie as she joined them and led them to the Blue Moon Café. Geoff was a good pal, Barbie had thought when she first met him. He was the kind of teacher that she had met so often in her many jobs as an English teacher. He said he had become a teacher because he wanted to travel and see the world. Although a cliché among EFL teachers, it was true for most of them. He was tall and slender, with the beginnings of a middle-aged paunch and he had begun wearing his belt just a tad below his waist, to give room for a little round belly. He sported a discreet reddish-brown beard, had freckles sprinkled across his face and his comb out revealed a receding hairline. Barbie had not heard much about him from himself, but had learned a little from the other teachers. He'd been at PAEA for a year and a half and had come from Slovenia, and before that Poland and before that Thailand and before that… Typical EFL teacher. Known as a rather stern teacher but also as knowledgeable, his students went to his classes and learned English.

Today, though, Geoff had seemed a bit subdued and hadn't said very much at all, only answering when directly addressed. Barbie wondered if Ted Baxter's death had disturbed him. Had they been close? Did he know what had happened? Barbie wondered who the last one left was with Ted Baxter last night at the Meeting Point Café. They had gathered for dinner together and Recep and his family had left early to put the youngsters to bed, but the rest, all singletons, had stayed. Barbie had left with Georgia, but then Georgia had begged off going all the way back to Aladdin's Cave saying she wanted to buy something. Maybe Geoff knew more about what had happened to Ted Baxter.

"Did you stay with Ted Baxter last night, till he left?" Barbie asked Geoff.

Silence greeted this question. Then Geoff turned to face Barbie, his eyes holding menace and perhaps hidden meanings. He asked reluctantly, "Why do you ask?"

"Well, we don't really know what happened, did he drink too much or…"

"Probably. He usually did, didn't he?"

"I mean, why was he so far from the pension, and the restaurant? How did he get all the way out there if he was drunk?"

"Barbie, this really has nothing to do with you!" Geoff's voice fell to a gruff low whisper. "I know that you have taken on the burden of what to do about Ted Baxter, but I really think that it is just not your job. I think doctors and police and officials whose job it is will get on to it." He smiled thinly at Barbie as he added, "Butt out! Give yourself a break."

Barbie stared at Geoff, but unable to hold her garrulous tongue, kept up the pestering, "But don't you want to know? What if he met with 'foul play' or whatever the Turkish is for someone hitting him on the head, not him falling and hitting his head. Aren't you afraid, or maybe aren't you afraid for others? What about those big Kangals Kemal has warned up about?? Maybe he met with a pack of them and ran and fell and…"

"Did you see any dog bites? Any signs of that sort of thing? Didn't think so. I've heard you talk about other 'misadventures' you have been involved in. But I really, really think that this is just a case of old Ted Baxter having too much to drink." He turned away from Barbie and cheerfully addressed the rest of the group, "Wow, here we are. The Blue Moon Café! Who knows why it is called that? What is a Blue Moon, anyone?" Geoff laughed, a gentle soothing teacher's laugh, the one a teacher uses when s/he wants to let the students know that if they don't know the answer, it is not because they are really stupid, but that it is a challenging question.

The waiter appeared and then ensued the choosing of where to sit, the shuffling, the bringing of more chairs, and the handing out of menus. Barbie announced very loudly, "Eleven of us." She looked around, then took a breath that caught in her throat with a hiccup. "No, only ten, sorry."

"No, eleven," Faruk appeared unexpectedly, pulled up a chair and sat beside Barbie.

Startled, Barbie blubbered, "I know we were eleven, but now Ted Baxter…" Impishly, she changed tracks, "Will you come to Ankara and fill in for him with his lessons? I'm sure Recep could use a native speaker now that... one is gone!"

"Native speaker? Is that all it takes? Am I a native speaker? What do I have to do? What would I do with my business in Goreme? I've never thought of being an English teacher before. Do you think I could do it? Maybe I can open a branch here in this little burg. Recep, what do you think? Balloon rides, horseback riding, quad bikes and English classes. Sounds doable to me. I should look into that. Thanks for the suggestion." Faruk leaned back and grinned happily at Barbie, who found herself blushing back, looking directly at him.

Bunyamin, six years old, bespectacled and quite fluent in English (although he often pretended otherwise), only glanced at the menu. Slyly he leaned in towards Barbie just as Faruk had done, "Do you know why they are gozleme?"

Barbie humored him. "I know that 'goz' means eye, but they are waaaaay too big for eyes, maybe elephant eyes??"

"No, no. When you cook them, they have little eyes on them. You will see," he smiled sweetly at Barbie.

"Thanks for the lesson; I can't wait to see the eyes."

"Actually," Recep intervened, "'goz' also means a cavity or hole." He pointed to his eye. And gozleme have a hole or pocket where the filling is placed."

Barbie laughed, "I kinda like Bunyamin's explanation better. Little eyes all over it. Bring on the cheese, the spinach, the potato, whatever!"

The group ordered a variety of gozleme, drinks and some small mezzes to dip fresh bread into.

As soon as the ordering was accomplished, Bunyamin started on his next project. He began by straightening the place settings near him, his own, his father's, Barbie's. He tidied the forks and knives, the placemats, the salt and pepper pots, and the 'nar' pomegranate and vinegar jars. As soon as all those within his reach were straightened and squared, he bounced out of his chair and began the rounds of the table, brining order to chaos. Barbie looked at Recep, who tried to catch his son's attention.

"Bunyamin", he hissed. The little man ignored the parental attempt to curtail him and continued around the table until satisfied with the arrangements. Then he sat.

Seated at a large table near the sidewalk, it seemed as though their conversation and those of the other tourists blended. Everyone strained to keep the conversation light and Barbie overheard Geoff explaining the 'blue moon' in his 'teacher's voice'. Barbie noted slyly to herself that although Geoff's words were neutral enough, the tone was too oily and self-important to her ears.

"Popularly known as the second full moon in a calendar month, an unusual occurrence, hence the expression, 'once in a blue moon'. But where do we get the idea of a 'blue' moon. The moon doesn't really change colors, so it comes from the old term 'belewe' which means 'betrayer'. If you have an extra moon, how do you know what the real calendar is? This extra moon can 'betray' you into thinking it is the proper moon for that month. So people called that extra moon, the 'belewe', pronounced just like 'blue' moon. So this café is a very unusual and special place. And I see they have decorated appropriately." On the walls were photos of beautiful moons above the fairy chimneys of Cappadocia, some drawings in which the moon was blue and one of a fairy of a particular bilious color of blue poking her nose out of a hole in a fairy chimney, while a leering 'man in a blue moon' looked down.

"Memorable, wonderful, great expression 'once in a blue moon," came from the 'eens' who had circled themselves around the end of the table. "Turkish lessons and English lessons in one day," they chortled together.

"Recep," Barbie leaned over Bunyamin's head and whispered, "Do we know anything more about Ted Baxter, about what happened? What we need to do, or not do?"

Geoff overheard and his angry retort startled the whole table. "Barbie, leave it. Why can't we just have lunch, pretend everything is normal? We can't do anything anyway." Geoff stared hard at Barbie, who felt the intensity of his words and his reluctance to discuss the situation.

Startled by this outburst, Barbie glowered at Geoff and thought he might have had something to hide, something he knew, but didn't want to come out. Taking a deep breath and exhaling slowly, Barbie pulled up her shoulders, turned to Geoff and smiled her 'dumb blonde' sweet smile. "Of course you are right. Turn off the old spigot Barbie, listen to Geoff. Don't say another word about our poor dearly departed colleague." She caught Geoff's eye and gave him a withering glare. "Poor. Ted. Baxter!"

Two huge platters arrived from the kitchen piled high with gozleme cut into squares. Bunyamin and Barbie looked at the little round eyes created when the bread dough met the hot oil from the grill. "Eyes, you are right!" Barbie noted.

Quiet reigned around the table for some minutes as they tucked into their favorite filled gozleme, then the chat started. Barbie felt that English teachers were so vocal and erudite because they had studied language, in all its aspects, and they could joke, explain and provide examples with consummate skill. Meetings of English teachers took forever because they spoke so eloquently. And they could also argue. Engaging in an argument with an English teacher without due preparation was a perilous exercise. Today the chat was more subdued than usual, and they began to talk about Ted Baxter, even if it were not by name.

"So what did he have planned for today?" one of the 'eens' asked.

"Quad biking," answered Faruk immediately. "It's all arranged."

Barbie looked sharply at Faruk. "But I arranged things, and quad biking wasn't on my list," she murmured. "Who arranged this?" she asked the table.

"Oh well, we want to do the best, most wonderful things in Goreme," Faruk answered easily.

"Well, I think we want to go," Colleen answered brightly.

"My children are too young," Recep commented. "Why would he arrange this?"

Georgia and Geoff gave each other quizzical looks. "So how much is this 'wonderful' ride going to cost us?" Georgia asked.

"Come to the stand after lunch, it is only over there," he pointed to the corner just across the street from the bus station. A small kiosk sat at the busiest intersection in the town with a sign for the bikes.

Georgia stood up and craned her neck to see the small office, "Oh, you've got bicycles too, don't you?"

Faruk smiled and hesitated before answering, "Yeeees, we do, but they are…"

"They are healthier, for humans and the environment! Aren't you in favor of healthy living?"

Faruk answered Georgia's inquisition with an evasive grin. "So," he turned to the 'eens', "You are coming today?"

"Yeah, but we want to do some shopping first," said Maureen. "We were going to do that this morning, but… well… we got caught up in other things. I mean, it would have been a bit unseemly, or what's a better word, precipitous, to just walk off and ignore the poor man."

Geoff smiled and chuckled. "As if you really cared about him!"

"She is just thinking about how it would look. You are right, did any of us really love the guy?" Charlene spat back. "But I think we care that we don't seem to be gleefully dancing around. He was human after all."

Georgia snorted. "As in belonging to the species, yes, but I think, well, never mind." She got up and grabbed her bag, turning to the waiter and asking for the facilities.

"Hypocrites, all," Geoff said sotto voce.

Colleen interrupted the unpleasant conversation, "Look, we did this last night at dinner when he was actually here with us, do we have to do it again today? I mean, he seems to have come back from the grave, well, at least from the dead, and made it again an unhappy meal. Here's my share, I'm going to go look at those scarves next door." She stood up, slapped some bills on the table and left.

They asked the waiter for the bill and suddenly there was money flowing from pockets and purses while Geoff counted it up. "More than enough," he announced. "For once."

Barbie turned around to look for Faruk, but he had slipped away again. He did that last night, she thought, leaving abruptly and perhaps not paying his share. A small doubt crept into her head. How foolishly she had been acting.

She straightened up and looked around at everyone. "Well, did I or did I not choose a good place to come for our holiday?" Barbie asked no one in particular.

"Oh, but you didn't choose this place," Recep answered. "He did."

"No, it was my idea," Barbie insisted. "I volunteered to arrange everything, don't you remember? In the meeting just a few weeks after I got here?"

Recep looked at her and smiled. "He was good at that, manipulation. No, Ted Baxter suggested it first and then you answered 'yes' immediately and volunteered. But originally it was his idea."

"What a dreadful thought," Charlene said, "He wanted to come and then, tragedy strikes."

"Forget it, let's go," said Maureen. "Leave the miserable man in his grave."

"He's not buried yet, so where is he? Do you know where he is, Recep? Are you responsible for the arrangements?" Barbie asked, turning away from the topic of who had made the suggestion to come to Cappadocia.

"Normally, you know, in our cultural tradition, we must bury someone within a day of their death, but he was not a Muslim and his family isn't here. I pointed this out to the police and they were content to let it wait. You know, it is the holiday, and they are happy to stay at home and ignore this problem. Please, everyone, you are not to worry about this. This is for the police now. Please, enjoy your holiday." Recep pleaded with the group as they began to grab their belongings and scatter.

Barbie sat and asked for another glass of tea. The day was warming up, a soft breeze whirled dust in the street, and Barbie tried to take Recep's words to heart.

"Tell Georgia she owes me eight lira, would you please?" Geoff called over his shoulder as he left Barbie sitting alone at the table. Barbie noticed that Georgia hadn't come back yet, and saw her shirt sitting on her chair.

Barbie sighed and scrutinized the street scenery. It was even more wonderful than she had thought. Small, two-storied buildings lined the street, colorful scarves waved in the wind in the shop next door, carpets covered the front of the shop across the street, some even hung from the rooftop, creating an amazing riot of color along the street. Barbie could see beyond the scarf shop next door up the street where colorful signs welcomed tourists to sign up for balloon rides. Other signs showed a whirling dervish in a spooky, low-lit hall, colorfully clad dancers in local costumes, a singer crooning into an old-fashioned microphone and others advertising restaurants with pictures of local cuisine. And looming above them were the tuff formations called 'fairy chimneys.' Less than a hundred yards away, one stuck up among the shops and restaurants, balancing a 'hat' of basalt. Not more than twenty feet above the ground, a hole had been made in the rock. The opening appeared to be an entrance into the second story of a house, but perhaps it had once been a church as a square cross had been carved into the soft stone and painted red. Above that was another story, this one consisted of a set of small round holes, each outlined in white paint. Dovecotes, Barbie knew. Was it a house or a church? Or had the inhabitants been very religious, carving a cross on their doorstep or a small room as a chapel? More likely, Barbie thought, she was looking at a multipurpose house. These fairy chimneys had been used for hundreds of years, and some people still lived in them, so why couldn't this one have been used as a church, a house and a place to keep pigeons?

"God," Georgia sighed as she plunked down in her chair.

"Are you okay," Barbie asked. "You were gone a long time".

Georgia laughed uneasily, "No, I'm fine, just wanted to wait until the hordes left. I am a little tired of all of them and the chat about you know who. And that Faruk. Did he pay his share?"

"No, well, I don't know if he snuck out without paying. I guess we can be a little generous. Tell me this," Barbie demanded, "Was this trip my idea or…his?"

"His, silly, don't you remember that day? None of us objected, did we though? He suggested it, and then you jumped in with your resounding 'yes,' letting you take over all the responsibility for the hotel and the money and everything. You got suckered, lady! I sat there and watched that little smile on his face and thought, Barbie will learn one of these days."

"Well, this girl has learned, but it is too late for this trip!"

"And you know something else strange about this. Faruk. He's pretending that we all signed up for his stupid quad bikes. But NO one ever said anything about it. I don't think anyone but the 'eens' want to go. I think that Ted Baxter and Faruk had it all figured out."

"But I made all the arrangements and no one, not even he, ever said anything about the quad bikes or Faruk. And you just met Faruk last night. And Ted Baxter didn't know him either, I am sure of that…"

"Oho, that's the idea, huh? No, no, no. Ted Baxter and Faruk go way back. They've known each other for years. There is something there."

"No, I'm sure they just met. I was right there when they met, I'm sure…"

"No sweets, they have history, those two."

"Well, how do you know that?"

"He told me." Georgia grabbed her shirt, slung it over her shoulder and walked out.

Chapter Four: To the Scene of the Tragedy

Barbie lay on her bed, inventorying the furnishings. Twin beds with covers of local embroidery, fake kerosene lamps, or were they fake, she thought. Electricity could go out here like anywhere else, maybe even more than in Ankara. They had had outages at least three times in the last few months, so, maybe they were real kerosene lamps. She was in a room on the second floor, just outside the staircase to the second floor rooms as well as the balcony on which breakfast was served. But even then, her room was carved out of the soft tuff. It was a 'cave room.' There was one small window that opened onto the hallway, but all the rest of the light was by electric light. The walls were rough and the marks of the chisel were seen easily. In a few places, the rock had been smoothed out and paintings of flowers or other designs had been done as decoration. Kilims lay on the floor, bright red with bits of blue, green, yellow and brown and done in designs from Cappadocia that showed off the local handiwork. Rough-hewn furniture completed the room's décor. The drawers were hard to open, but the details of flowers and curling vines carved into the fronts made up for this inconvenience. What was not inconvenient were the bathrooms. Fitted with bright white tiles from floor to ceiling, they were outfitted with the latest modern conveniences. The hot water was quick to get hot, the towels generous and fluffy, the soap locally made from olive oil with twigs of aromatic herbs and the wide mirrors spotless. Funky local with mod cons, what a perfect find.

Next door to her, Geoff's room was a mirror of hers, and was next to the balcony. That did not mean it was lighter as it too had just the one small window. Across the hall were two rooms that Recep had reserved for himself, wife and the two children. They were 'arch rooms' as they had been constructed from blocks of tuff. The feeling inside was similar, but each room had two small windows that looked out over the street and therefore let some sunlight in. The rooms downstairs were in somewhat the same configuration. The office was directly underneath the breakfast balcony, next to it was the 'eens' room. It was also a cave room, but had three beds in it, and next to it was also another cave room that Georgia had taken. Across the hall were two more arch rooms. One was empty at the moment and the other had been Ted Baxter's. The hallways were decorated with some whimsical paintings by former guests and an eclectic assortment of farm utensils, butter churns, wagon wheels, saddles, jugs, evil eyes, carrying bags for horses and donkeys, embroidered pillow cases, as well as a local tablecloth on the table completed the eclectic decor. It was homey in a way that attracted foreign guests. The view from the balcony was as spectacular as Kemal had promised and Barbie anticipated watching the balloons from there early the next morning, just as they had looked down on their hotel this morning.

Okay, she told herself, I cannot even close my eyes, let alone nap. She got up, put on her hiking shoes, grabbed her water bottle and a jacket, and tucked a few TL into her small shoulder holster. Kemal still had her passport, but other vital items were always carried with her. Barbie was a very experienced traveler and found it was a good idea to keep these things close at hand. She gently opened the door and listened. Why she didn't want to let anyone know where she was going was not the uppermost thought in her mind, but that is what she intended to do. She crept down the staircase, carefully watching each step as if by watching she could make it quieter. Barbie was notoriously clumsy and it would be just like her to fall down the stairs, giving away her presence, but also possibly putting her in the hospital. Please Buddha, Jesus and my personal guardian angel, she prayed, let me just get down these stairs quietly.

Her prayer effective, Barbie reached the outside door rapidly. Neither Kemal nor his number one son were in the office, so it appeared that she had left without anyone knowing. She stepped down the two steps, and turned to the left, heading rapidly out of town.

Barbie strode purposefully, quickly raising her heart rate as her breath came with a labored huffing and puffing. It was quiet, that time of afternoon when many retreated to bedrooms or back rooms to get out of the sunshine and to rest. Even though the autumn sun was not hot, siesta was still a tradition and hard to break.

But Barbie wanted to put as much distance as possible between Aladdin's Cave and herself at this moment. It was not difficult to follow her instincts at each turning of the road as it left town, rapidly disintegrating into dirt roads that were rarely traveled. She kept to the left at each turning, passing the fields planted with grape vines, many in a sad state of neglect. Other fields had orchards and these were better, but the trees looked as though they were not well-cared for, if not actually neglected. Within ten minutes she arrived.

It was just off the road, down into a ditch that would fill with water when it rained. The exact spot was hard to see from the road, unless you were looking for it. There was nothing there. No one watching, nothing on the ground, just nothing. Barbie was sure this was the spot; she could see the tire tracks of the cars and the 'ambulance' (van) that had come to take away the body. What was she expecting, 'crime scene' tape or a uniformed officer telling her she could not look on the scene of the calamity? This was just the scene of an accident, a tragedy, not a crime. So Barbie had to ask herself, why was she here? What had brought her back to this place? She stepped down into the ditch and stood where she thought the body had laid sprawled on its face. The bright blue jacket had been a giveaway; if it had been brown or off-white or other more natural color, no one would have noticed for hours, even a day or two maybe.

She shifted to where she thought the body had lain, exactly. It was hard to pick out the outlines of anything given all the footprints of the scores of people who had been here. Was it just eight hours ago? Barbie bowed her head in acknowledgment of the misfortune. A man, not so young, had died here. He wasn't a nice person, but he did not deserve to die like this. Alone, at night, drunk (so they said) and sick. Sick, that's what she wanted to see. They couldn't have collected all the vomit, if there was much. It was not the sort of thing you needed all of anyway.

She dropped to her knees, and placing her hands in front of her, examined the ground very closely. She sniffed as she carefully turned over the soil. First she concentrated on the slight depression that she had remembered from this morning. She dug gently into the soil by using her hands as a brush. Sweeping the top bits of soil aside, she went from the core of the depression outwards, telling herself to be careful to preserve what she had uncovered. Then she overturned something dark. It was damp and brown colored, not the color of vomit. But what is the color of vomit, she thought, it could be anything. Maybe he was vomiting up blood? Barbie took it between her fingers and spread it out with her opposite hand. She brought it to her nose and took a deep whiff. Metallic. Not vomit, but blood. Barbie searched some more and found other traces that had been covered up.

But, she thought, this is to be expected; they said he had died by hitting his head on a rock. So, being a head wound, of course there was blood. But the absence of any vomit made Barbie think. What was here? Some blood, no vomit. How did he hit his head here? Barbie tried to think what she had seen this morning. She saw the body only a few minutes before the officials had arrived. The group from the balloon had been pushed back, but they stared mesmerized at the scene. Barbie closed her eyes and tried to visualize it as if she were taking photos, each frame of film a separate scene, a little slide show on a screen in her head. She imagined the scenes that Kemal, Recep and others reported to her as well as what she remembered.

During the phone call from the balloon, Kemal had knocked on the door of Ted Baxter's room and had gotten no response. He had used his key to open the door and discovered no one there. The bed had not been slept in and it did not appear as though Ted Baxter had come back the night before. He then called the police and told them what had been reported about the balloonists' seeing a man lying in a ditch.

After spotting what they thought was their colleague, those in the balloon had immediately demanded to return to Aladdin's Cave. In fact, it took nearly another half hour to come to a clear place and descend. They had skipped the traditional champagne celebration, climbed into the waiting van and demanded to be driven back to the pension. Kemal greeted them and had warned them that this had better not be a hoax, but he, too, was puzzled at the disappearance of Ted Baxter.

The three 'eens', Georgia, Geoff, and Barbie had gotten into the Mercedes van and directed Kemal out of town. Geoff had proven to be the most observant from the balloon, but Georgia insisted that the original road they took was wrong and directed Kemal in another direction. Barbie felt turned around and fell silent as Georgia and Geoff argued. Maureen had snatched the front seat and it was she who screamed at one turning, "This way," as she pointed to the left. Geoff and Georgia did not contradict her as they swung onto the dirt road. "Slow down!!" screamed Maureen. Kemal scrunched on the brakes and slowed. Everyone looked over to the right side of the road where a blue jacket flapped in the slight breeze. Kemal eased to a stop just beyond the prone man.

As they piled out of the van, Kemal called the police again. They were in the vicinity and promised to arrive shortly. In those few minutes, the group had approached the man and immediately recognized it as Ted Baxter. Georgia had been brave enough to approach closely to him and bend over to feel the carotid artery just behind the ear. She touched the skin and immediately jumped back. "He's cold," she said and then placed her fingers again on the artery. "No, he's gone. Dead."

Barbie looked at the ground. The dirt and gravel around the body had been disturbed everywhere. There might have been a herd of buffalos through here, or a herd of sheep. Feet had scuffed up the ground, human and/or animal, and nothing seemed at all clear. Ted Baxter's chest was on the ground, his right arm underneath, and his legs in a V shape behind him. The face had been turned slightly to the left towards them, facing the road. There was blood on the back of his skull, mixed into his hair. Just beside his head lay a rock with blood on it as well. Barbie looked at the rock, the bloodied head and mentally took a clear photo.

Just as Barbie inched closer to have a better look, the roar of vehicles behind her forced her to turn away from the gruesome sight.

Sharp orders came in Turkish and there was no mistaking the meaning. "Get back, keep away." The group of teachers backed off and the group of emergency crew and police took their places.

Enthralled, Barbie sneaked as close as she dared and watched the proceedings. She saw the emergency crew turn Ted Baxter over and feel for a pulse. There was a half-hearted attempt to do CPR or give oxygen, but that was rapidly abandoned when the crew realized that they had a corpse on their hands and not an emergency. The body was rapidly put into a body bag, zipped up and shoved into the van that doubled as an ambulance. One of the police noticed the bloody rock and hastily put it into the bag as well, just as the zip covered his face. The police stood around; the senior man speaking rapidly, looking around the ground. He fired a few questions that Kemal answered just as rapidly and then he climbed into the car that had brought him and was driven away.

Kemal and the six teachers from the PAEA stood still, looking at the ground, looking at the sky, looking at the road, the ditch, the surroundings, anywhere but at each other.

Kemal announced, "We go home now."

"But wait," Barbie said. "We still don't know what happened here. We don't know how he died."

"The police say he drunk too much, fell down and hit his head. You see the rock? That finish him. He fell down over it, or didn't see his way in the dark. He was drunk."

"He did smell of alcohol," Georgia interrupted. "Real stinky, kind of like vomit or spilled drink. A nasty smell."

"But did anyone see him last night? When did he go home? Did he really have that much to drink?" Barbie was oddly insistent.

"Barbie, sweets," Geoff leaned over her. "Ted Baxter drank every night, far too much. This is frankly not surprising. We need to leave it at that. Tragic, tragic. And in a man so young. And to go like this."

"We must go back to Aladdin's Cave," Kemal insisted, looking over his shoulder as if the police were still in attendance. They had climbed into the van and left.

Now, Barbie found herself with a lot of questions. Maybe the police could tell her, but they hadn't given any information. She had found blood, but no vomit. What did Georgia mean by vomit? Had he vomited as well? That would make sense if he were drunk. Barbie returned to the slight depression surrounded by sand, light colored, some of it almost white in color and studied it again. Using her hand, she began gently to scrape aside more sand. She used a crab-like walk and a sweeping motion around in an arc away from the place where the body had been found.

She felt it before she saw it, another patch of blood. The sand covered it, but the dark brown liquid had not completely dried up, nor had it seeped into the sand. Less than eight ounces certainly, it created a pool that Barbie carefully measured and noted in her head. She also noted that it was about eight feet away from the place where she had remembered the body lay. Did he fall and hit his head, get up and then fall again? That might explain why there was not a lot of blood where he lay. But why was the rock there? If he had fallen here, why was the rock near the body? Carefully Barbie spread sand over the rapidly drying patch of brown blood. Then she stood.

The sun was high in the sky and intensely bright as only it can be in the desert or the mountains far away from the air pollution of the twenty-first century. She shaded her eyes as she looked around the area. She thought of her sun glasses stuck in the outside pocket of her pack at the pension. Squinting against the brightness, Barbie backed up and scanned the wider area.

She thought now of the other times she had faced cruelty in death, more obvious than this. The Egyptian Revolution had brought out the worst in human behavior. It was seized as a time to settle scores and hide the evidence. It was in Cairo where one person's inhumanity, without morals and scruples, had robbed another of life. She stepped backwards onto the road and then took in the whole scene. The body had been found in the bottom of a slight depression, like a small ditch, just fifteen feet from the road's edge. Barbie recalled how the body lay, parallel to the road, as if he had missed his footing and rolled down the side. Beside the head lay a rock, now taken away by the police. From here, Barbie looked at where she had found the pool of blood, further from the road. In a six-foot circle around the place where the body had lain, there were scuff marks and disturbed ground. Also, the ground was disturbed from the road to the place. Elsewhere, it was relatively undisturbed. Except for one spot, just beyond the pool of blood.

Barbie climbed easily back down to the 'spot' and outward towards the now covered pool of blood. Standing close to the blood, she looked outwards again. From this perspective, it was difficult to see the line between disturbed and undisturbed ground. But now convinced she knew what she was looking at, Barbie once more dropped to her haunches and looked more closely. She again began the gentle sweep from side to side, trying to catch anything that might have remained here. Half defaced foot prints, scuffle marks, dips and ridges that told her nothing, ruffled out in front of her for another few feet. She became less careful as she went until meeting a large rock. Looking to the right and to the left, Barbie could no longer see the area that was disturbed from what was not.

She squinted as she looked harder at the ground. She closed her eyes and looked away, letting them rest. When she opened them again, the brightness made her flinch. She gazed out onto the scenery around her. No buildings could be seen, although she knew there were houses, corrals for horses and shacks in the fields. No vehicles could be seen, in fact nothing and no one had passed her since she left the village of Goreme. From the road, which Barbie felt sure ran basically north to south but here made a gentle turn towards the west, there was a gentle slope upwards. The short hills to the west of the road were startlingly white, with gentle gullies that had been grooved into them by the centuries of rain. A field of neglected grape vines lay between the road and the hills, only a few yards deep. The road, once paved, but now degenerated to dirt, seemed to lead from the town to the fields beyond. To the east was the small gully where Ted Baxter's body had lain and beyond that some thin fruit trees, now with their fruit and leaves gone. The landscape beyond that was undulating fields and small ridges in shades of brown and gray. Small bushes and a few trees gave hints of green, but otherwise, the landscape lay dry, brown and seemingly dead. Barbie could just make out the pink ridge line that marked the end of Rose Valley. She felt so close to civilization, yet also dominated by the natural features around her. She pointed her nose to the sky and breathed deeply. The sky here was azure, from one horizon to the other; totally blue without a single cloud to mar the completeness of the color.

She looked down at her feet. The rock that lay here was the boundary. It was obvious that beyond this nothing was to be found. She kicked at the rock. To her surprise it moved slightly. She bent over and with two hands picked it up. It was smooth and surprisingly light. She dropped it and turned it over. Dark stains marred the underside. Barbie bent down and examined its belly. She took her finger and felt the stains. Nothing came off on her finger. She leaned further forward and sniffed. No odor. She tried to scrape some of the stain off and the soft tuff yielded the stain along with crumbling rock.

Barbie sat back with annoyance. She looked at the place where the rock had lain, undisturbed? She heard a 'click' behind her.

Heart thudding, she turned towards the sound. A bright light flashed into her eyes, causing her to squeal with painful annoyance. She became quiet, trying to listen to any other sounds that might be out there. She thought she heard the sound of retreating footsteps just as a gust of wind brought sand stinging into her eyes. She heard panting and sounds of sand sliding. A human.

Chapter Five: A Hike in Pigeon Valley

Barbie stood and listened. She held her breath and closed her eyes, letting her ears tell her about her surroundings. She heard the distant sound of a breeze rustling in the tree branches behind her. In the distance she heard sounds of quad bikes, the uumph and yoouum of the engines. Cars or trucks speeding on a well-paved road were also in the distance. Nothing near. Then the hee-haw, hee-haw of a donkey in the mid distance and the twitter of a small flock of birds closer. She opened her eyes and looked carefully in the direction of the small hills across the road. Nothing disturbed the tranquil afternoon.

Barbie needed to think. She looked at the rock on the ground at her feet. It could tell her nothing more. Maybe the police could learn something from it, but not she. Get out of here, go for a walk, think in a quiet place. She thought that going back to Aladdin's Cave would not provide her with the quiet she needed. She stuck her hand into her jeans pocket and pulled out a folded piece of paper given to her the evening before by Kemal. It was a map of the town, and on the opposite side, a map of hiking trails in and near Goreme. Knowing that she was on a side road between the highway to Avanos to the north and the main road between Goreme and Uchisar to the south, she looked at the small line of white 'cliffs' facing her across the road. Just on the other side of this, she thought, she should hit the road. And then I will come out just to the north of the pension, and won't see anyone. She scanned the landscape and saw a modest track through the grape vines that headed to the cliffs.

She took it. Walking rapidly, she soon reached the end of the field and saw the thin trail that goats or sheep had made twisting up the cliffs. It was steep but walkable and soon Barbie found herself on the top of the miniature mountain range. From there, the curving road lay before her, and just opposite where the trail from this side joined the road to Uchisar, another road, like a town street, led off towards Pigeon Valley. Moving rapidly, and concentrating on watching her feet in order to not slip, Barbie reached the road and headed into the town along the quiet street. The locals lived in houses with the back parts, garages or storage sheds, dug into the cliff. Everyone here made use of the landscape and the meager places for building houses. She headed up the street, then topped a rise and saw Pigeon Valley.

Steep hillsides clustered into, then expanded outwards from a road, which deteriorated into a track, that meandered in the valley. Grape vines and orchards lay on either side of the road. A few buildings clustered in the distance, many against one of the fairy chimneys that appeared scattered in the canyon. It was a scene of jumbled possibilities for playing hide and seek or a great hike or run.

More slowly now, Barbie walked into the valley, the midday sun still shining fiercely. She stopped to look at a magnificent dovecote, a tall chimney with more than fifty tiny windows lined in white paint. It could have been a scene from a fantasy movie, it seemed so incongruous. The road quickly disintegrated into a dirt track, the dust swirling up from Barbie's feet.

While she walked, she thought about what she had discovered at the 'scene'. Why did she go there in the first place? She couldn't really answer that honestly without revealing that she was mettlesome, fascinated with sudden, violent death, or inordinately curious. That was part of it, but another part was the feeling that it wasn't finished business.

Surely, the police just hauled off the body without looking at where he was found. She hadn't seen anyone taking photos, or trying to collect evidence. They acted as if bundling up the body as quickly as possible was their only purpose. Perhaps they had decided how he had died and that was that. Perhaps they wanted to get back to their families and their holiday celebrations. The body could be looked at later, and if they decided that he had died because of a simple fall, then why bother with the rigmarole of 'investigation'? Besides, it was a foreigner, and that was always a difficult call. Contact the next of kin, get rid of the body and refuse to do anything more. After all, the problems that might arise would be taken care of by someone else, somewhere else.

"Ruoufff, ruouff," came a deep throated call to the wilderness and the dark forces it hid.

Barbie jumped and cursed out loud, "God Almighty, what is that?"

"Ruouff," came the answer. Deeper than any human voice could possibly sound, the rumble was so otherworldly that Barbie felt a chill travel from her back up to her head as she literally shivered.

Turning her head, Barbie could just make out a gigantic hairy hound behind a wooden slatted gate. No one else seemed to be around the modest shack beside the small pen where the monster stood. Black and sand colored fur stuck out on top of the ears, and even the paws seemed to sprout fur. The dog slowly extended his front feet up and peered over the gate top. It was some way off, but Barbie could see that it could easily jump out if it had wanted to. Another friendly "ruouff" showed off the animal's massive teeth and slobbering jaw.

"Nice puppy," whispered Barbie as she tore her eyes away from the true embodiment of Sherlock Holmes' "Hound of the Baskervilles" and walked on. Head down, she muttered soothing platitudes to herself, directed at the dog. "Good dog, nice doggy, hope you have a good day, why don't you go lie down, I'm sure someone will come and feed you soon, you are a sweet puppy…." Barbie said as she moved on feet that shuffled extraordinarily quickly away from the fragile looking dog pen.

A minute later, she turned around. The dog was out of sight and she no longer heard any noise. She wondered what it would sound like if it had been really angry and how easily it could have jumped the fence and chased after her if it had a mind to do such a thing. Barbie was okay with small dogs, little yappies that she could push aside. But big dogs frightened her. One day when she was a child, a large dog, a German shepherd from down the street, approached her. He had stood on his hind legs, barked in her face and licked her. Her screams of terror only made the dog more excited and he barked again, sending hot fetid breath against her face. She tried to raise her hands, push the dog away, all the while screaming hysterically. Her dad had rescued her, but the memory had stayed with her all her life, making her unusually anxious around strange dogs. And never having had a dog of her own, she carried the singular memory of the 'beast' with her. She could not shake or curtail the horror that lay within her psyche. When a dog came too close, or in this case, a dog's voice came into her field of consciousness, she reacted.

Still shaking, she put as much distance as she could in the next five minutes between her and the dog. Obviously one of Turkey's finest examples of a Kangal, the hound could have been one of the ones Kemal had warned them about. This one was behind a fence, or an approximation thereof, but what if someone let it run loose? She shivered again.

She stepped off the road and went up to a group of stunted tuff mounds and sat on one. She took a deep breath and started singing. She had always sung when she needed to calm herself. She had started as a young girl, and her mother, the old hippie, had encouraged her. She had heard music all her life, Bob Dylan; Peter, Paul and Mary; some of the later Beatles tunes were always in the air, in her home, in the VW van they traveled in. And when her mother had realized that Barbie possessed a very good ear, very good pitch and that amazing ability to throw her voice, she had encouraged Barbie in her musical endeavors. Now Barbie started quietly and gradually built the volume. She sang, 'Amazing Grace,' ending in a glorious crescendo, as the sound echoed off the canyon walls. She was pleased and satisfied with herself, as she had proved that she still possessed the power to push the sound out and up, or wherever she wanted it to go.

After the last of the echoes faded, Barbie stood, brushed off the dust from the seat of her jeans and went on. Smiling and happy now, she swung her arms and listened to the sounds. This valley was tucked down in between the town of Goreme and the road. Not really very isolated, but she could not see the roads or the buildings that stood on the edge of the valley that lined the curving road to Uchisar, Three Forts. Shops that sold souvenirs, carved stone, and drinks and snacks had gradually lined this road. Huge parking lots for the tourist buses welcomed the traffic. With their overlooks, the tourist outlets presented wonderful places to get a view of picturesque Pigeon Valley.

Occasionally the one fort left that topped the village of Uchisar could be seen in between the fairy chimneys and folded slopes that lined the route. As she left the fields behind, Barbie became lighter of heart. Forget the dog, forget the dead Ted Baxter, enjoy herself, she thought to herself. I'm on holiday in a beautiful place, with a big blue sky, warm air and no one to bother me.

But as she strolled, her mind twisted back into the topic of the dead Ted Baxter. She found she could not put it out of her mind. Once again, she brought up the image of the place, the road, the ditch, the rocks, the footprints and all that she had seen. Before long, she knew, without any doubt, that Ted Baxter had not died a natural death; that someone or ones, had helped him along. Drunk, probably, falling down, probably, but hitting his head and dying from that, NO.

One more time she left the trail, climbed a slight rise and sat on a convenient rock. Why did she think it was not natural, what was it that said this was a crime, not an accident? Careful, she told herself, just because you have been involved with violent death before, does not mean that this one is also violent.

Be careful how you analyze this. Don't be hasty, creating ideas for which there is no evidence. Go one point at a time.

"Penelope, where are you when I need you?" she shouted. Penelope, a friend of many years, had been teaching with her in Cairo and had collaborated with Barbie in adventures there. She was a superb listening post as well as being able to ask good questions. But Penelope was currently in the US, at her sister's house, trying to sort out a new job. They had left Cairo together, but Barbie had already lined up this job. Penelope went home to spend some quality time with her family. Skype, she thought, I can skype her tonight. Ask her what she thinks. But to do that, Barbie needed to be able to relate a straight-forward story, a coherent account of the incident.

What had happened at dinner last night? That seemed to have some relevance, didn't it? She tried to recall who had been there, what they had said, what might be relevant and what not. They had come together on the bus from Ankara, arriving late in the afternoon. The sky was clear and the sun began to set as they arrived at Aladdin's Cave. Kemal had met them, given them keys to their rooms and welcomed them with glasses of tea. They had gone to their rooms and didn't appear together until later when they walked to the restaurant. They had all sat at a long table and ordered their food rapidly. Recep his wife and their two children had sat at one end of the table. The Americans had ordered beer or wine, and Barbie had thought that Recep and his wife, who were more conservative, didn't want their children near any of the alcohol. Everyone was still dressed in the clothes they came in, although there had previously been some talk of 'dressing up'.

At some point, Faruk had joined them. Barbie had been sitting at the other end and had not spoken to him at all. It had only been today that she had real communication with him, and noticed him in that dramatic way. But last night, no one seemed surprised at his presence, maybe because many had taken him for a fellow American. When did he join them? What did he eat? He certainly drank wine and later beer. Geoff had conversed with him a lot, but later Faruk had moved his chair to sit nearer the 'eens'. He had flirted and talked about the quad bikes.

Geoff started off on his best behavior. Barbie knew he could have a temper. Once when Barbie had inadvertently gone into a classroom he had reserved for a special class project, Geoff had really blown his stack. And Recep had to intervene to gain the peace. Barbie thought about that evening, not one of her prettiest performances to date. She had shouted back at Geoff, upsetting the students and some of the other staff. Really, she hadn't known that the 'Hollywood Room' at the PAEA was reserved for movies and watching videos. She had thought it had been empty every time she had checked, so why not use it? She simply had to go back to the dirty, cramped, and drafty Boston Room. Recep had then changed her room to the more spacious London Room and that was that. Barbie had apologized and explained that she hadn't known about the Hollywood Room and so was unaware of its significance. She had tried to steer clear of Geoff for a few weeks after that, but had broken the ice just last week and they seemed to be on good footing again. Now Barbie began to wonder. What was Geoff's relationship with Ted Baxter? Barbie thought of herself as mild-mannered and easy going, and Ted Baxter was one of the more irritating persons she had ever encountered. If Geoff had become enraged about the classroom, how difficult could he be about something Ted Baxter had done? Geoff was not particularly annoying, was he? Barbie had to think some more about what else she knew about Geoff.

He was from New York City, she knew that. He was about three years older than she, which meant that he, too, was having trouble with relationships. If he was here, no partner in the picture, it was because he was in between spouses, girlfriends, or…? No, she was fairly sure he was not gay, given the lecherous way he had treated the 'eens' and some of the female students. Over six feet tall, brown hair, hint of a reddish beard, blue eyes, weak chinned. Barbie, she told herself, if he doesn't have a good strong chin, it's a genetic propensity, not an intellectual or psychological one. You cannot fault a man for being weak-chinned. But now Barbie found herself disliking him for his arrogance, his insinuation that he was an excellent teacher and that others were not. She knew that he had been fired from a job, at least once. He had called it 'being pushed out', but nonetheless, it was an unhappy parting of the ways. She knew that he had been in Turkey before he had taken the job at PAEA, but did not know the details. She also had no inkling how long he had been at PAEA, but longer than she. Oh, and she hated the way he stuffed food into his mouth when he was alone in the canteen. It was gross, like he was training for an 'all you can eat' hot dog contest. But did he have a quarrel with Ted Baxter?

Everyone had a quarrel with Ted Baxter. Recep was being super nice about Ted Baxter's death. Maybe he felt guilty because everyone seemed to be aware of Recep and Ted Baxter's dislike of one another. Barbie had personally found Recep to be very flexible and forgiving. He had been cooperative and accommodating when she first arrived, and showed her over the school (without, however, indicating the significance of the 'Hollywood Room'). He was such a pleasant, amiable person, and he didn't get along with Ted Baxter. But did Ted Baxter have a particular quarrel with Recep? Or did Recep have a particular quarrel with him?

The particular quarrel was with Georgia. Ted Baxter had made innumerable lascivious remarks about Georgia. She was so attractive with that brilliant flaming red hair, green eyes, and slender athletic body that any man looking at her would immediately think of going out with her, and more. Barbie thought jealously about how attractive Georgia was. Ah, but that was before anyone encountered her tongue. Sharp, acid-like, how many words could describe a woman who used words to deflate egos, put someone in their place or show off her own knowledge? Is was not that she was unkind, but just that she was brilliant, opinionated, and knowledgeable about many, many topics. If she had no opinion or didn't care about a topic, she was candid about that as well. But when the arrogant Geoff or Ted Baxter met the fiery Georgia, sparks flew.

She had been at PAEA for about a year, and had certainly had more than her share of run-ins with Ted Baxter. But it appeared that the really important one had been the comments about her sexuality. Even Barbie had heard them. They apparently had started long before Barbie had come to Ankara. The stories that Barbie had heard about the argument was that Ted Baxter had wanted to spend some intimate time with Georgia and when she repeatedly refused, he had said of course she was a lesbian. Instead of simply denying it and letting it drop, Georgia had become extremely agitated about it. Ted Baxter, perhaps not really believing that Georgia preferred women, made it a running 'joke'. She had heard Georgia one day, in the canteen, threatening Ted Baxter.

They had their breaks or ate at different times because their classes were spread out during the day. The small teacher's room wasn't conducive to eating, but the canteen, shared with students, was a pleasant place. It looked out over the Kocatepe mosque, which made a magnificent sight in the evenings, all lit with white and green lights. The man who ran the canteen kept it clean and tidy. He was friendly and helpful and so the teachers went there for their breaks and some meals. It happened there one day, just as Barbie had stepped into the room. The only ones there were Georgia and Ted Baxter. He must have been teasing her once again, because Georgia stood over him, her face contorted in rage, her voice in a strangled cry, "You had better watch your back, you wicked monster. Someday someone will put a bullet in your head or a dagger in your heart or poison in your drink. You deserve nothing less. And the sooner the better." Ted Baxter laughed in her face, "A promise, you laughing fool?!" Georgia turned and marched out. Barbie was not sure Georgia had even noticed her, and seemed so outraged that she was not in a mood to care who had heard her. Was it grandstanding? Georgia could be very flamboyant at times, but this had seemed genuine hate.

Motive, means, opportunity. There was Georgia's motive. Constant teasing however, didn't seem to be motive for murder. Bullying? Could constant teasing be seen in a different light? How many wives had killed their husband's for 'abuse'? Well, Georgia had some motive. Maybe there was more than just the teasing that everyone had heard. Just as Barbie had heard the threats, maybe there had been other words, or more, behind closed doors. The hallways of the PAEA could hide many secrets.

Means and opportunity seemed available to anybody. The second rock that Barbie had found could have been used as a weapon. Barbie picked it up easily, certainly Georgia could have picked it up, or anyone else who was reasonably healthy and strong. It was a light stone. And the death was in the middle of the night. Even one of the 'eens' could have sneaked out after the others had gone to sleep.

Stop, stop, Barbie told herself. The 'eens'??? Okay, so means and opportunity were available to just about everyone, so motive was the key. What motive did they have? And why not think of them as Maureen, Colleen and Charlene and not the 'eens'? Aren't they three separate people? Ah, don't go there.

'There', that might be a key question to ask. Why so far out of town? Why in that place? Barbie tried to think just how far it was. She had walked there in a few minutes. It was not far from the restaurant to the place. Not exactly 'on the road' between the restaurant and the pension, not 'on the way,' but not far off. How did Ted Baxter get there? What was he doing there? No one had asked that question yet, had they?

Barbie sat a while longer, pondering these questions. She felt a slight breeze and shivered. The sun was heading for the horizon and casting shadows on the hillsides. This was Barbie's favorite part of the day, the late afternoon. The sky had now gathered a few stringy clouds, soft tails of the sheerest white that crossed the sky. Suddenly she realized why the balloons went earlier in the day; the wind must be stronger now, and could blow the balloons off course, making it difficult to land. She hadn't particularly noticed this morning, but now she thought about bracing for the landing, and the gentle way they had dropped directly onto the truck. It made it more difficult to get out of the wicker basket, with no steps or ladders, only the narrow step on the back of the truck. Recep's wife had had difficulty getting out and in the end, they had pushed and pulled her so as to get away more quickly. Did these clouds predict bad weather? If so, Barbie would be bummed out to lose the brilliant blue sky.

Time to move on, thought Barbie as she stood, took a sip of water and looked around once more at the intriguing landscape. As she slithered down the tuff mound, miniscule sand pebbles made it a difficult descent. As she hit the bottom of the canyon, she stopped. Small sand rocks continued to fall behind her. She turned to look, but the sun struck her eyes, momentarily blinding her. But she thought she heard a different sound. Still the tiny sand rocks slithered across the rocks. Then she heard the sound change; change into a regular pattern of slither, plonk, slither, plonk.

She wheeled around, blinking her eyes, trying to see where the sound came from. It was not her sand, not her 'plonk' any longer. It was someone else's. Barbie thought quickly. Run? Confront? Hide? Stand her ground?

"Who's there?!" she shouted, turning to her left and continuing up the valley. "Who is following me?" she threw out the words behind her.

Stomping loudly, she continued walking, her insides turning to liquid. She swung her head from side to side, staring into the sun in front of her and into deep shadows to her right and left. She paused and listened again. There was no sound now, no presence at all. She heard once more the sound of cars on the road above her head, birds calling in the distance, but no more sand slithering. Standing up straight, she threw her shoulders back and walked on.

As she walked, she again heard the noises behind her, mixed in with the sound of her own footsteps and breathing. She stopped and turned again to listen. Just a second after she stopped, the noise stopped. But for just a moment, she had heard it. Someone was following her, someone who wanted to remain out of sight, who did not want to identify themselves.

Barbie ran, her feet sinking into the sand. Within one minute her breath came heavily and labored. Her pursuer now was not trying to hide the noise of footsteps. Barbie halted again, and glanced behind her. Still nothing to see, and nothing to hear after that short second of the noise of running feet, that stopped almost as soon as she did.

Hide, that's what she needed to do. The canyon at this point began to crowd in on itself. On both sides, fairy chimneys rose up, even closer than before. The road had deteriorated into a path between the tuff towers. Small paths led off both sides, heading for puny patches of grape vines, dovecotes or small pens for sheep or donkeys. Barbie dashed off towards one field that also had a little pen, and just as she approached, she noticed yet another pen behind a tuff tower. Struggling up the slight incline, she ran for it. She leapt over the fence and ducked into the hole that had been cut into the tower. The smell of donkey droppings and old straw hit her, but she ignored it, trying to find a corner in which to hide. A wall in front of her contained another opening in it, only a small one, but big enough for her to crawl into. She lay on her stomach, thrust her water bottle in front of her and squeezed into the second chamber. Scooting towards the back, she noticed yet another tiny hole, right at the level of the ground, giving her some light to see her way. A niche carved into the back wall was just her size and she squeezed into it sitting on her haunches. The light coming from the hole illuminated her white shoes and khaki pants, but Barbie didn't know how to conceal herself any better.

She sat quietly, listening for her pursuer. She heard the footsteps outside coming closer. The person was breathing heavily as well. He or she had seen her come this way, maybe even seen her crawl inside. Barbie forced herself to stop breathing, to wait and to listen. The small hole was dug at the very bottom of the wall, and was not big enough for an animal like a sheep or a donkey to get in. In fact, it seemed to have been an afterthought. What was it for?

The footsteps approached. Barbie had to breathe, but did so as quietly as possible. Her feet were beginning to cramp, but Barbie knew that she couldn't give her hiding place away. Whoever was chasing her was not a friend, not someone she wanted to meet alone. Someone had seen her go to the place where Ted Baxter had been found, and had followed her here.

Whoever it was had not let her know his or her identity. S/he was the enemy.

While Barbie was thinking this through, the steps came closer. She could hear the fence she had jumped being examined, moved. She sat still, trying to become part of the tuff tower. The steps went into the first room and then out again. She heard them circle the tuff tower, receding and coming back again. The footsteps came around the other side of the cliff, approaching the small hole. Barbie stared at the opening, wishing it to close up.

Then she saw the person's shoes. Jeans came down over the tops, to just the heel in the back, but the sides were clearly seen. Pink, yellow, green and blue, brightly colored and striped, the shoes stayed for a moment in the light, then kicked at the sand in front of the hole, sending some of it swirling into the cave where Barbie hid.

Chapter Six: Cocktails at Aladdin's Cave

Barbie awoke with a start. The small cave where she had hidden was now almost completely dark. She shook her head and listened. Bird chirps could still be heard, and the traffic on the road above was louder now than before. She peered at her watch, but could not see.

She stood up, gently stretching her limbs that had become cramped crouching in the alcove of the petite cave. Gingerly she crawled through the opening into the donkey's pen. Here the light was brighter and she was greeted with an amazing sight. On all the walls of the small space, hardly bigger than the dining room at her parents' home in Santa Cruz, were paintings. The colors had faded and dark stains from candles, fires or something that created soot, had obliterated some of the figures lower down on the walls. Pilgrims over the years had carved their names into the soot. Fascinated, Barbie recognized Greek names and something that could be Armenian. The paintings on the vaulted roof were still well enough preserved that Barbie recognized the figure of Jesus on a throne with Mary hovering on one side and what must be John the Baptist, wild haired and holy, on the other. A halo encircled their heads and the one on Jesus consisted of a gold cross, with bits of gold still clinging to the ceiling. A donkey paddock? Well, why not, make it into something useful rather than letting it be totally destroyed by the weather and (un)holy pilgrims. Sucking in great gulps of air, and then sneezing because of the dust she had inhaled, Barbie thought it best to retreat as quickly as possible.

How had she fallen asleep? She had been quite tired when she got here, hiking and running and full of anxiety and fright. But when had she nodded off? She remembered the shoes in the light of the small hole as she stepped out into the twilight. It was not as late as she had thought, but she hadn't brought her flashlight and the light was fading rapidly.

She headed down the road the way she had come, and fifteen minutes later arrived at the first of the street lights. She heaved a sigh of relief to see civilization, street lights, people and no dogs. Quickly she walked to Aladdin's Cave, just a few minutes up the hill. She felt light headed and disoriented. Light spilled out of the entrance and Barbie heard the noise of laughter and the tell-tale sounds of the beginnings of drunkenness. It was that amiable noise that seemed, when you are tipsy, to be amusing and friendly. But when that noise came from inebriated companions when you had not had a single drop, it seemed uncivilized, silly and a waste of time. However, it could also create vats of jealousy, because the sober one wanted to join the plastered ones. What could they be drinking?

Barbie edged into the entrance, aware of her rather dusty state and was met with a cozy scene of near debauchery. The 'eens' had draped scarves around themselves and were practicing their version of the 'Dance of the Seven Veils'. Geoff had also draped scarves over his head and it appeared that he was auditioning for a remake of Lawrence of Arabia. Georgia, her hair a new shade of red, dashed about with a camera. Kemal held a newly opened bottle of wine, blindly asking if anyone wanted another drink. Recep, his wife and children had brown liquid, probably coke, in their glasses, but they too had joined in the fun, laughing at the antics of the dancers. Faruk was present as well. His glossy locks had fallen into his eyes and his lips were parted in a smile that encompassed the whole party. Barbie stared, suddenly wanting to join them.

Faruk turned and looked at her, his smile broadening at her appearance. "Barbie, you have come! Now the true party can begin. We are having a wake for your friend Ted Baxter."

The rest turned and welcomed her. Shouts of abandon and giddiness greeted her. Happiness, Barbie thought, not likely. Just relief that they were alive and poor Ted Baxter was dead. Barbie tried to remember if he had ever been a good party-goer with the rest of them. She couldn't remember. He had begun to fade from her memory already, or was her memory in disrepair?

Barbie accepted a glass from Kemal who filled it generously. She knew that he didn't drink; he had quietly refused liquor the evening before when someone had produced a bottle. He said that he was a Muslim, but that his friends were welcome to drink, after all, he had said, Cappadocia had once been known for its wine. The homemade wine was not very good, Barbie thought, but it was a nice gesture.

After she had taken a few sips, she began surreptitiously looking for the shoes. Recep's family were all wearing normal shoes, no bright colors with jeans. As they got up to get more wine, move to a different seat or get something from their rooms, Barbie noticed that none of them were wearing the shoes she had seen in Pigeon Valley. So much for the thought that a fellow teacher had followed her.

She found an empty seat next to Kemal, away from the others. As casually as she could, Barbie whispered, "What is the latest word on our 'problem?'

"Ah, we have progress. Ted Baxter's wife is arriving tomorrow. They will let me know later exactly which time. And of course, she will come here. I am lucky, I have an extra room. The one next to Ted Baxter's room is free. No one rented it and I kept it because you had never said exactly how many rooms you needed. Now, I am very glad I have one room for the Mrs. Ted Baxter."

"And what will you tell her when she arrives, about her husband's death?"

"That he died. I do not know the details yet. The police, you know, are having their holiday and want to ignore this as long as possible. Because there was no need to bury immediately, no one is worried. And because he was a foreigner and he just died, the police don't care. So, I must care. But first she must come. And then we will see what happens."

"Kemal" Barbie said very quietly. "I think there is something wrong with Ted Baxter's death. I think that the police do not have all the information. I think I know more…"

Kemal laughed, "Oh, my lovely friend Barbie. You are so fond of creating excitement. I am sure there is more than the police tell, but what can you know? I know that no one is sad that he is gone. I think maybe even his wife is not really sad. But I think you need to wait some more time. I think the police will ask the wife some questions. Really, you are his work friends, not his family. What do you know? The police know, we do not know."

"But that is what I am saying, I think I do know something they do not know."

"Ah, police. You must understand that police in Turkey are different from police in other countries. They work in a different way. They love, con… conspi… What do I want to say?"

"Conspiracies. Yes, I know, it is a big game in Turkey. Who do we blame? But I think that in this case, that there may be a conspiracy. Well, not exactly a conspiracy, but something more." Barbie looked at Kemal, who laughed again.

"Now, you are making conspiracies. You will become a true Turk!" he laughed again and turned away.

Barbie thought that perhaps she had better keep this to herself. It was a mistake to talk with Kemal, who did not want any more trouble than he already had. He did not want to hear about her trip to the place of death, nor her fright in Pigeon Valley. She seemed to be on her own in this.

"Conspiracy? Did I hear you talking about a conspiracy?" Geoff asked, calling to her from the opposite side of the table. His eyes narrowed and a familiar sneer entered his voice.

"No, just a suggestion, but what we were talking about was Turkish ideas of conspiracy. If the press gets ahold of this, they might turn it into a conspiracy theory. So, maybe it is best to be very quiet." She smiled brightly and turned aside, away from Geoff's probing eyed and unctuous tones.

She inquired of the table, "What did you all do today???"

The 'eens' went first, revealing a mixed bag of shopping, napping, logging onto the internet, eating snacks and other innocuous activities. Georgia said she had taken the dolmus into Urgup and had a look around. She had arrived back not long before the cocktail party. Recep volunteered that his family had napped and then walked through the town, finding a small café for a long afternoon coffee and a courtyard for the children to play in.

Geoff arched his eyebrows at Barbie and declared, "None of your business." The set of his jaw warned all not to pursue the topic.

In a flurry to cover up potential unpleasantness, Kemal quickly offered more wine or coke. The 'eens' opted for more wine and making a fuss, Kemal disappeared to open another bottle.

Barbie took a deep breath and scrutinized as many faces as she could while she enunciated loudly and clearly, "I took a walk in Pigeon Valley." Most of the group looked politely at her, waiting for more. Barbie felt eyes watching her, but she could not penetrate behind them as to what they might withhold. She opted for discretion. "I saw a Kangal tied up, he barked a lot, and I found a little church. It was very interesting."

"But we will see the most beautiful ones tomorrow at the Open Air Museum, won't we?" Maureen asked.

"Yes, I suppose we will."

Faruk bent over to observe Barbie, "You didn't ask me what I did today," he said, smiling easily at her.

"I suppose you were working?" Barbie smiled back, feeling that warm stirring in her inside again. What did this man do to her? How did he do it? And it wasn't just when he was in front of her, but it was even better when he was.

"Oh yes, all afternoon I sat in my small office, waiting for my friends to come. But no one did. Maybe you can meet me tomorrow?"

"Ah, the Museum tomorrow." Barbie quite enjoyed flirting with Faruk. His voice was warm and his eyes twinkled when he spoke to her. He was one of those who looked at his companion in conversation and enjoyed every minute of the exchange. Maybe that was why she was willing to suspend her better judgment and act like a silly teenager. "Sorry, but I absolutely MUST see the wonderful painted churches."

"Well, everyone, I have called the Anatolian Kitchen and made a reservation. They expect you in about thirty or twenty minutes." Kemal offered more wine.

But everyone had jumped up when told of the dinner plans and began heading to their rooms.

"Dress up, dress up" Charlene announced loudly. "As per our plans!"

Barbie couldn't remember what plans had been made about dress up. Maybe it was something she had missed, and at this point, did not want to get involved. She ignored this command. Although she was quite willing to wear outrageous clothes, she only wanted to do it on her own terms, not by being coerced into it by the kids. They dispersed rapidly, heading for their rooms for quick showers and a change of clothes.

Faruk hung back and sat smiling at Barbie. "And what do you plan to wear to the dress up?"

Barbie hesitated, trying to shove thoughts away of skimpy underclothes and what his face would do if he saw her wearing them. "Oh, I expect I'll wear the usual jeans, tee shirt and sweater. What about you? Will you also dress up to join us? I assume you will join us?"

"Dress up, not exactly, but I will join you. I've been asked." Faruk's smiled widened.

"Oh, by whom?"

"So, I must go now and find my special clothes. See you soon." Faruk managed to slip out easily, slithering out of reach like an oily rope or a ripe mango slice.

Kemal waited until all but Barbie were gone, then looked at the mess of chip bags and dirty glasses. "Oh, where are my sons? Every time there is mess, they disappear. I want to train them to take over my hotel, but they don't want to. All they want to do is play computer games, or play with their friends or something not important. I want them to learn this business."

"Kemal, how old are these kids?" she asked.

"Oh, the young one is fourteen and the older one is sixteen. It is time they learned to do work, don't you think?"

"But my parents wouldn't agree with you. I worked starting at age twelve or thirteen, babysitting and so forth. My parents never wanted to work, they are like your sons. They had to do some work, but we never had much money. That's why if I wanted any money, I needed to work for myself. We were always living in strange places, once we lived in a 'carriage house', a small servants' house or guest house for a big house. My father was a musician, a poet and a gardener. They paid him for the gardening, but it was the music that he loved. But I have worked hard, always. Because I don't like being poor."

"Oh, so your parents were poor and had no steady jobs?"

"My parents were both well-educated and extremely capable, they were just hippies." Barbie sighed thinking of her childhood. It was privileged in so many ways, so disjointed in others. At least she was the only child as she felt that neither parent could have coped with any more. As it was, they could only cope by being together, one working while the other looked for work, or both working part time. But, the trade-off came in where she lived. She had grown up in Santa Cruz, California. The weather was almost always perfect, the sky blue or streaked with clouds, or cloudy on hot summer days. The people she had grown up with were as accomplished as her own parents, well-educated, energetic and they cared. They cared about the environment, about the poor and downtrodden, the famine and war ravaged peoples of Asia and Africa. They had only so much care to give, and it was often given to others, and not to her. They loved her, but they didn't know what to do with her. Was Kemal's way better? Was it too much for him to ask, having expectations when his sons were young, too young to make up their own minds about whether they wanted the same things or not? At least Kemal had something to pass on to his children, a nice well-run pension.

"I want them to learn English. Will you talk with them in English?" Kemal asked suddenly.

"Of course, I will speak English with them, but first I have to meet them!"

"Oh, where are my sons?"

"Kemal, is there anything I can do when Ted Baxter's wife gets here? Show her around, or help in any way?"

"Yes, there is one thing I think you can do."

"Yes, anything, I really want to help."

"Don't tell her anything. You know Turkish conspiracies. All the things I heard. Just do not say anything."

Chapter Seven: Dinner at the Anatolian Kitchen

Barbie looked up from her diary. She cocked her head, listening for noises of leaving, slamming doors and the like. She glanced at her watch. Wow, she was really late. Time to get going. How had this happened, she thought as she brushed her short blonde curls and swiped some lipstick over her dry lips.

Grabbing her bag, she scooted out the door, desperately trying to turn the old-fashioned lock. Frustrated, she was tempted to leave it unlocked, then thought better of it. No, after today, it was better for her to keep as many things secret as she could.

She had spent some time cleaning up, taking a shower, washing her hair, and even renewing her nail polish. But then, she really wanted to write in her diary. She had wanted to skype Penelope, but it was too early to do that. The ten-hour time difference meant that she needed to wait until later to find her friend logged on. So she had taken her small diary and wrote what she did today, carefully leaving out the scary events of hearing footsteps and the chase through Pigeon Valley. Maybe she shouldn't have put in those few sentences about going to the scene. But she didn't write about what she had found there, just that she had gone. The rest of the entry was just what had happened and all public knowledge. Everyone knew these things, so why not write?

Now, she rushed downstairs and found the lobby deserted. She poked her head into the office and found it empty except for a teenage boy at the computer. "Hello, Kemal's son," she called and dashed out the door.

The streetlights at this end of town made things seem very bright, but they still left shadows where vicious dogs could hide, murderers lurk, or figments of Barbie's imagination cower. She strode very quickly down the street. When she came to the main road, she slackened her pace slightly. Cars cruised past, small wild dogs, tails tucked between their legs, slunk across the road. She made a left turn and strolled on.

Two minutes later she came to the bus station, the center of Goreme. A wide parking lot could accommodate dozens of large intercity buses, and a row of shorter spaces indicated the dolmus section. Dolmuses were small vans, typically twelve to twenty seats that ran on a basis of 'when stuffed, go'. 'Dolmus' meant stuffed. They were a cheap and excellent way to go short distances. This was where Georgia would have caught her transport to Urgup, just seven or eight miles away. To the right, across the road, was the quad bike business. Barbie saw a tiny office with a low wattage bulb burning, but no one visible.

She crossed through the bus station and headed up the street. She was convinced she knew where she was going, but almost missed the restaurant in her hurry. It was atmospherically lit, restaurant-speak for very dim. She peered into the gloom, certainly less bright than the street lamps outside and saw the long table set for eleven. A single place was left in the middle on one side. Barbie tried to slip quietly into it, but failed. Everyone jumped up and tried to help her move the chair to sit down. As she eased in, she swung her knees around and banged them on a large table leg. No wonder the seat had been left empty. Two tables scrunched together never make a happy group. "Thanks for saving the seat, such a lovely comfortable seat," she said, trying to make her voice 'drip with sarcasm'.

The rest of the group laughed. "Just be thankful there wasn't a whoopee cushion or a cracker to go off when you sat down, just a table leg!" Colleen shouted. Even Recep's usually quiet wife giggled behind her hand. Barbie couldn't help a smile herself. It was something that she might have done, and stuck that thought away for another time. She wondered where she might find a whoopee cushion in Ankara. Maybe someone could bring her one from home.

Immediately, the waiter came to the table. He was dressed in a modified Ottoman style outfit, gold braid everywhere and a funny little hat. On a board that looked like the end of a pizza paddle rested a huge puffed up loaf of bread. He placed the bread ceremoniously on the table and added two tiny tubs of butter mixed with herbs. Recep sighed with delight and promptly took a sharpened knife to the top of the bread. Quickly the bread deflated like a balloon, the steam fleeing from the bread and tossing its fragrance about the table. The guests reached eagerly for a piece. Soon the bread disappeared and when the waiter returned to take Barbie's late order, he brought another one. Charlene punctured this one and it too disappeared, but in a more leisurely fashion.

Barbie ordered the chicken in a clay pot, and the waiter smiled as he took the outsized menu from her. "Excellent choice. You will not regret."

Barbie looked at the rest of the group and noticed that the 'eens' were plastered in makeup and even Recep's wife was wearing a multicolored scarf with colorful embroidery on the edges. Everyone had indeed turned out wearing gaudy, dress-up clothes. Recep had on a shirt made of ikat cloth, colored red and yellow with thin green stripes. It looked a little gaudy on him as he usually dressed very conservatively. Barbie gawped openly at him.

"Ah, I see you are admiring my shirt. It is made of cloth from my home town, Trabzon, really it is Rize. It is the special cloth of the region. I don't wear it very often, but tonight was supposed to be a special dress up night. We were all supposed to wear something special. Don't you remember?"

Barbie looked puzzled and shook her head. "Maybe I missed something. I don't remember…"

"It was really Ted Baxter's idea," said Maureen. "Maybe you weren't there the day we discussed it. We all felt we should go forward with it, even though he couldn't be here…"

"Look me, look me" called out Bunyamin, Recep's six-year old son. He stood up and showed off his shirt, a miniature of Recep's.

Recep leaned over and said quietly, "Look at me. It's 'look at me'."

Barbie chuckled at this parental correction and laughed even harder as Bunyamin did what students all over the world do when corrected; he completely ignored the correction.

"Look me, look me, look me!!!"

Barbie beamed broadly, "You look wonderful. Your shirt is very beautiful."

Bunyamin smiled back and peered at her intensely through his thick 'Harry Potter' glasses. Looking down to admire his shirt, Bunymain noticed that one side was tucked in more tightly than the other. Shaking his head vigorously, he pulled out his shirt and tucked in both sides again. Barbie grinned to herself. Here was a boy with his act together. When he pulled his shirt out to retuck it a third time, Barbie thought again, maybe he exhibited 'togetherness' compulsively.

Georgia glared at Barbie. Her voice had a heard edge to it as she proclaimed, "It was a long standing 'dress-up' night. Even before you got here, we decided that we would have one dress up for our holiday. It was Ted Baxter's idea, so, as Maureen said, we felt that we needed to go through with it. We are supposed to wear something that identifies where we are from." A look of sharp disapproval crossed her face as she said, "Didn't anyone mention it to you?"

Barbie shook her head. She squinched up her nose and tried to remember if someone had said anything and she had missed it. "So, what are you wearing Georgia?" She asked chirpily in an attempt to placate Georgia.

The innocent question seemed to raise hackles. Georgia faced Barbie and barked, "A raincoat, because I'm from Seattle!"

"A tartan cap because my ancestors are really Scottish, not English," Charlene volunteered in a Scottish accent. The others had similar quirky things that they wore.

The soups came and the table became hushed while they ate. Barbie's mind began to meander. With a jolt, she thought again of the shoes. If they had changed clothes, maybe someone had changed back into the 'multicolored shoes' that Barbie had seen in the small hole of light in the church/barn that afternoon. How was she going to find out? This afternoon, in the pension, people were seated, but it had been much more casual. Here, everyone had their feet underneath a heavy tablecloth and it was much darker. She needed to get underneath and check their shoes. How was she going to do that?

Taking her heavy soup spoon, Barbie daintily took a sip of soup, then banged it against the bowl, yelped and let it fall. It fell into her lap, but no one needed to know that. Quietly she bent over and stuck her head under the tablecloth, while clutching the spoon. She bumped her head on the table leg, but stifled a further noise. She nimbly slithered down into the space under the table.

It was black, an almost total darkness. She could see nothing. She blinked several times, trying to make her eyes adjust, but it remained far too dark to see anything clearly. In the meantime, someone must have seen Barbie's 'business' and called the waiter because she heard his voice over her head.

"Madam, madam, please. Clean soup spoon. Do not worry, no problem. I have new spoon for you," the waiter shouted at her.

Realizing what a foolish move she had made, Barbie tried to get out, back side first, slowly extricating herself from the tomb-like atmosphere under the table. Before she had managed to right herself, the whole table was in an uproar. Everyone called her name, suggested ways to get out, or sympathized with her plight. When her head popped up, a round of applause greeted her. The waiter bowed as he handed her a shiny clean soup spoon. Barbie smiled at all of them. "Yes, thank you," she said dropping the spoon discreetly and stretching her lips in a widening grimace.

Faruk was sitting beside her when she emerged. She remembered someone else was to her right, but there he was. He beamed at her, a small twist to his smile. Once more, he stared at her as if she were the only one in the world. Barbie began to feel the stirrings again, but this time the feelings were of interest about him, about the man. This was a sympathetic soul, someone who obviously thought enough of her to want to sit beside her. Was a sexual attraction hitting him as well?

'Well done," he whispered. "Did you find what you lost? You were so graceful in doing that!"

"Stop teasing me," Barbie countered. "You know it was not graceful. Far from it. But it is something I cannot help. Look at me, blonde hair, not always so graceful, ditzy in fact and to top it all off, my parents named me Barbie! What can I do??"

His arm slipped around her waist. "Just be yourself!"

How long had it been since someone said that to her? Barbie had been fighting feelings of sexual attraction, but now she decided to simply revel in the attention. She did, however, slip out of Faruk's slightly awkward embrace, not ready to trust herself to closer contact. She looked sideways at him and saw that he was not offended. On the contrary, he continued to smile warmly at her, as if he seemed pleased that she was not 'falling' as fast as she felt she wanted to fall. Maybe she was right to push away a little, not wear her heart, or her obsession, on her sleeve. She settled comfortably in her seat.

A different waiter appeared. He too was dressed in Ottoman style, with loose scarlet trousers, a tight-fitting white shirt, with a small vest, heavily embroidered with gold. His waist was wrapped in an ornate heavy cloth and stuck in the front was a long, curved knife. He hurried around the table, serving dishes with a flourish. Several of them had ordered the clay pot dishes and these were placed in front of them. They were about twelve inches tall, the sealed top thinner than the middle and the whole sat on a small pedestal. Barbie was confused as to how she was expected to eat whatever it was she had ordered. Where was the food? She had had clay pot dishes before, but they had come to the table in flat clay dishes. She thought this would be the same.

Suddenly, the wicked looking knife flashed up beside her ear with a menacing whoosh. Barbie screamed. The waiter chortled at her fear and swing it up higher over her head. Then it came down diagonally across her pot, with a loud 'crack.' The waiter then lifted off the whole top. He rapidly went to everyone else at the table, similarly breaking the tops off of their clay pots. When he finished, he bowed dramatically, gathered the tops and flung them into the garden just beyond the dining area. Barbie turned and saw the trash of a hundred clay pot meals. The tops were neatly stacked as borders along the street side and on the small garden that lay between the street and the restaurant. Their own clay tops lay on the grass, but undoubtedly someone would pick them up tomorrow and stack them along with the others.

Everyone had their meals now and began to munch. Barbie enjoyed her chicken, cooked with vegetables in the pot in a heavy broth. Turkish food was not as spicy as some cuisines that Barbie had tasted, but the flavors were important to Turks, and this was no exception. Good, filling country food; especially good when the weather turned to snow and ice in the winter.

The spoon dropping had gotten her nowhere, so how was she going to get a look at everyone's shoes? The old 'need to powder my nose' ruse seemed to hold some promise. She stood up, and looked around. She gingerly took her bag and surreptitiously looked down at the floor as she inched her way around her friends at the table. She could not see properly; it was dark and the heavy tablecloth blocked her view. She scooted sideways around Faruk, then Colleen, and then came to the end of the table. As she squeezed past Geoff, she looked at his long legs stretched out and crossed in front. On his feet were a pair of shoes, bright pink, yellow, green and blue.

Barbie inhaled sharply, but kept her head bowed. She moved past Geoff and turned her face away. Barbie knew that she had a bad habit of letting her face show all her emotions and she did not want anyone to see the panic that stirred in her head now. Geoff wore the shoes she had seen that afternoon.

The water in the toilet sink was cold and Barbie splashed it on her face, trying to wash off the surprise and shock she felt. Geoff had followed her to the place where Ted Baxter had died; Geoff had then followed her to Pigeon Valley and chased her, all the while keeping his identity secret. The only reason he would do this is if he knew something more. He must know that Ted Baxter was murdered. And he had probably murdered him. How could she go back to the table knowing what she did? How could she keep her face still and silent? How could she manage to get through the rest of the meal? Or did she need to? Maybe it was better that she leave now, tell Kemal to call the police and tell them what had happened?

Just as she thought this, another thought crowded it out. What did she know? She might speculate, but what did she really know? That someone who did not want to reveal themselves was in Pigeon Valley at the same time as she was? She was certain that Geoff was wearing the same shoes, wasn't she?

She pressed her eyes shut with her fingertips and tried to recall exactly what the shoes looked like. She tried to picture the stripes and diamonds and swoops and curlicues. Was Geoff really wearing the same pair of shoes? The shoes were so distinctive, and it appeared as though they were the ones she saw. Barbie took a deep breath, composed her features and vowed that she would be brave, say nothing and try to remain very, very calm. To try to find out what Geoff knew was not in her best interests at the moment. She needed more proof and the way to get that proof was to remain calm and not get confused.

Using a technique of positive self-talk, one of the ways that Barbie had used successfully in the past with her students who were particularly test adverse, she squared her shoulders and inhaled noisily. "You are prepared; you know what you are doing. You will succeed; you will conquer." She exited the toilet. "Sorry," she said insincerely to the two women who waited for her.

She slipped easily into her seat this time, knowing that the post lay in the path of her knees and tried to gauge the talk around her. The 'eens' were laughing loudly and Recep was urging them on. Music had started in the background and now, the volume suddenly spiked. The 'eens' began swaying together in their seats. Barbie thought that the three had such an incredible symbiotic relationship; it was as if they had been born triplets and had grown up this way, always being able to read each other's minds. She did not know whether to envy them this closeness or to pity them for always having to be in each other's faces and lives. Recep suddenly began to sing along with the song on the restaurant's music system. The three 'eens' got up almost as one, and securing their scarves around their necks, began to dance.

The rest of the group clapped and egged them on, as the 'eens' held each other's hands and swayed to the music. Barbie did not recognize the song, but knew the type of music, the ubiquitous Turkish dance music. The 'eens' laughed as they lost their footing and fell into each other. Barbie watched their feet as they flashed in the lights. Their shoes had streaks on them that were meant to catch the headlights of approaching cars, making the wearer more visible while walking or jogging at night. As Barbie looked more closely, she tried to focus on the shoes, as all three pairs appeared to be the same. But in the dark and with their feet flailing, she couldn't manage to see clearly.

Suddenly Recep urged all to get up, join the line and dance. Barbie felt herself pushed and pulled and reluctantly joined the line. She had always known that she was clumsy. Her father had often accused her of the 'two left feet' curse when she went hiking or as now, when someone wanted her to be graceful. Barbie did not know the dance, she did not know the steps and she abhorred doing something physical like this until she was ready. Practice had taught her that she did not possess two left feet, but dancing and being nimble did not come easily. If her parents had really wanted her to be a 'Barbie doll', she was ill prepared and must work at it. She joined, but resisted kicking up her feet, only shuffling along with the music. She at first kept her eyes forward, trying to concentrate on moving with everyone else.

Then she recognized the shoes, all the shoes, all alike. They were the shoes she had seen that afternoon. The same brilliant colors, the same pattern; and everyone was wearing a pair. She felt horrified, then puzzled, then gave a weak chuckle. No one seemed to notice her discomfort. They danced on and on, shouting while Recep sang. The other patrons of the restaurant arose to join them and the restaurant became noisier. Finally the song came to a glorious end, someone turned the music down and they took their seats again.

"Well, that was fun," Barbie ventured. "So much fun. All dressed up, dancing along with Turkish folk tunes. Who would have thought we could have so much fun?"

"Oh, you know it was Ted Baxter's idea. He thought the dress up and so forth would be good fun. And this is the first time you have been with us, so he did not tell you much." Recep informed her.

"Well, he told me nothing, nothing at all about this," Barbie replied.

"It has become a little tradition. I mean, none of us have been at PAEA very long, but little 'traditions' are good aren't they? So, tonight we all dressed up. And look, we all have new shoes!" Recep lifted his feet. The rest of the group did the same, everyone lifting their feet to show Barbie their shoes.

Bunyamin burst into an infectious giggling laugh and stuck his feet up in the air, rolling back on his seat to make them higher. "I have new shoes too, just the same as everyone's." He put his feet together in a precise manner, two shoes exactly side by side. "See, two shoes, two new shoes."

Barbie stared at the miniature version of the pink, yellow, green and blue shoes that she had seen on the feet of her pursuer. She forced a grin onto her mouth. She could not be angry or sullen with Bunyamin.

"You know that Ted Baxter brought a pair for you too? New ones. But we don't have them. I think they are in his room at Aladdin's Cave and we didn't want to go into his room. So maybe later, we can give you a pair of new shoes like this," Recep said.

Barbie smiled wider in return, but it pained her. How was she going to get out of this one? She knew that she could never wear a pair of shoes like that. "You know, I am sure they are the wrong size. I have such very, very strange feet, and I can never find shoes to fit me. So, thank you all very much, but I think maybe…later."

The group around the table applauded and laughed. Such a good joke. Such a good time they were all having, Barbie thought. But the shoes…

Chapter Eight: Shopping for Carpets

Small pieces of baklava appeared in front of each person. They were petite diamond-shaped pieces with thick sugar water dripped over them and a light sprinkling of green pistachios on top. Charlene picked up her fork, but Geoff stopped her.

Once again, in his unctuous teacher's voice, he pontificated, "You know that this is not the best place in Turkey to eat this dish, don't you? Pistachios in Turkish are literally 'antep nuts' and the best place to eat them is in Antep. You might know it as Gaziantep, that's its new name. But they grow the best pistachios in Turkey, maybe the world."

Charlene had put her fork down while Geoff declaimed, but now picked it up again. "But, you know," he began again. Charlene put her fork down. "The way to find out if it is truly fresh is to listen to it." He bent his ear to the delicate dessert. Bunyamin got up on a chair and looked anxiously at Geoff. "When you cut into it with your fork, if it is truly fresh, truly worthy to be called the best dessert in Turkey, you can hear the top crackle as the fork, or perhaps your teeth if you use your fingers, bites into the crust on top. If it is truly the best in Turkey, you can hear the crackle of the crust." He demonstrated by carefully listening as his fork bit into the delicate crust.

The group held their breaths as he strained to hear the desired 'crackle'. None was audible. "Ah well, I shall eat it anyway, I LOVE baklava!" The rest gave up on listening for their dessert to sing its praises and hastily finished the morsels. Bunyamin used his fork to cut his precisely in half, then in half again, separating each piece delicately on his plate.

The check once again caused confusion and hassle, but when all was settled, the teachers decided to stroll about town. Out in the street, they saw shops selling goods from all over Turkey. Cushion covers with fairy chimneys and camels on them were draped on displays. "Made in Bursa, no doubt," Geoff scoffed. Silk scarves were declared to be from anywhere but Cappadocia. "Ah, but Cappadocian carpets, made here, or at least in the surrounding areas, are real."

Just as they had left the restaurant, one of the 'eens' had spotted the large store just up the hill. Sitting near a large fairy chimney that was lit from the outside, as well as from the inside, the store boasted two floors of carpets hung from the balconies, the walls, the rooftops. They were of all types, but they were all Turkish carpets and kilims. The colors were mostly red, with the rest of the rainbow mixed in.

"The biggest carpet shop in the town, it is the oldest, the richest," Faruk declared, singing the praises of the shop.

"And the most experienced in fleecing tourists," Georgia added. "No thanks, Faruk, I'm staying out here and taking some nighttime photos of the local scenes. This fairy chimney right here is just fabulous. I'm sure I can get some really atmospheric shots. Geoff, are you carpet shopping? If not, lend me your shoulder as a substitute tripod."

Geoff agreed readily and the two stayed outside while the rest of the group entered. A young salesman bowed and scraped, and tea was ordered. As they were being seated, a large man, his belly overhanging his belt, waddled into the showroom. Barbie felt overwhelmed at the piles and piles and piles of carpets that surrounded her. The fat man introduced himself as the owner of the 'best carpet showroom in Goreme.' "I have the most carpets of anyone here in Goreme. My father has been collecting carpets and his father before him. We sell carpets all over the world. Now, how can I help you? What kind of carpet are you interested in? We have carpets and then we have kilims."

The 'eens' sat on a small rug covering up the stack of carpets underneath them. "What's a kilim?" asked Colleen. "I've heard people talk about them, but I don't really understand what they are. Aren't they just carpets?"

"Ah, madam, you have come to the right place, I will educate you and your friends. There are really two kinds of carpets, one is knotted, like this," and here he picked up a small square that conveniently lay at hand. It was similar to one of the small squares the girls were sitting on; it was red and had a simple geometric design. He turned it over and showed the girls the knots. "This is a hand knotted carpet, not made by machines. It is very tight, you see, you cannot pull out the knots, because they are pulled over and tied, one by one. This one, this is very cheap, the wool is thick and not so even. But this one", he picked up a larger square at his side, "See the knots, see how many there are? The quality of the carpet is in the number of the knots per square. This one is very fine, see," he rubbed the knots and then passed it over to Colleen's outstretched hand.

"But the kilim, you see, is woven, like cloth. There is the warp and the weft. But it is more than just the weaving like cloth, because you see," he picked up a modest-sized, but lovely, mostly blue carpet. "You see the small slits here, where one color ends and another begins, this is the mark of a very good kilim." He waved his arm and a small boy brought the tea into the shop. The tiny glasses sat on a hammered copper tray, carried by means of a round handle attached by three thin copper struts. The small boy pretended to put down the tray, but then backed up and swung it, along with the numerous glasses of tea, over his head in a giant circle. Charlene gasped and Recep laughed. The boy placed the tray neatly next to the owner. The fat man scowled, and then laughed. A good party trick, thought Barbie, but not really amazing if you knew how to work the centrifugal forces.

Bunyamin's eyes widened with intense interest, and with an air of enchantment with the party trick, attempted to follow the young waiter out the door. Recep neatly jumped up and grabbed him, hauling him back with a barrage of Turkish. "You see," he explained. "We have a tray exactly like this at home. I am afraid that there will be many, many broken tea glasses, I don't really want him to learn this trick. Not now, at least. You see, our Bunyamin is a kind of perfectionist. When he gets an idea into his head, there it stays. If he has an enthusiasm for anything, he will stick to it until he is an expert. Everything with him must be complete, orderly and by the rules. It's one of the reasons he is so good at chess."

"Maybe he can learn how to do it well from the little expert and then you will have fewer broken glasses," Faruk suggested.

"No, no, no swinging of tea trays!" Recep glared at Faruk for even suggesting that Bunyamin should learn how. The two glared at each other. One, Recep, so conservative and mindful of safety, Faruk, so carefree and devil may care. They each have a point, thought Barbie, I wonder which way I might lean on this one. She thought of her one child, a son, now grown up and not inclined to have much contact with his mother. She thought of what he might have wanted to do in this situation. Definitely he would want to learn how to swing a tea tray 360 degrees and astound his parents and friends. His father, wherever he might be now, would have shrugged and not cared one way or the other, never having taken much interest in his offspring. And Barbie, in reaction to her ex-husband's uncaring, selfish ways, might have been cautious, or totally encouraging. Barbie did that, swing from one attitude to another.

Recep grabbed Bunyamin and forced him down beside him to watch the carpet show. By now, the fat man was in full swing. He had his assistant bring out some carpets from a back room. Swift, low-voiced conversations sped between them. Barbie watched closely how the fat man read the group. Was it to be expensive first, cheap later? In order to make a sale with this group, he knew that he could not sell $2000 carpets. But he might sell $200, or even $500. He needed to be able to lure the buyers in with a bait and switch technique that kept them interested, but in their price range. Then there would come the bargaining. Barbie had witnessed this many times in the past, when she had bought and when she had not bought. One time, in Uzbekistan, she had fallen in love with a $2000 carpet, but she did not have the cash on her, she would have had to find an ATM. Finally, the shop owner had said, very diplomatically, that perhaps it was not to be. That this carpet was not for her. It was very large, and Barbie had admitted that her rooms were not big. She had also said that her floors were already covered in carpets, and that to find a place for this one, albeit a magnificent one, would pose many problems. The seller had sympathized, but folded up the carpet and then sold Barbie a different one. This was one she had loved above all others, maybe because it was small enough for her rooms and it had taken the place of the magnificent one. Now, Barbie watched to see if this seller was as crafty as the Uzbek one had been.

Faruk and Recep constantly chipped in with advice as the 'eens' were educated on carpets and kilims, old ones, new ones, and then, the patterns. Each part of Turkey had traditional patterns and it was possible for knowledgeable people to recognize immediately where a carpet had been made, how old it was and if one was in the market, for how much it would sell. Barbie noticed that the fat man first calculated the quality and quantity of the girls 'oohs' and 'ahhs', finding out which colors and styles they liked. Then he switched to expensive carpets, exhibiting first some that the 'eens' could never afford. Even Recep's wife had begun to gasp at the colors, the fine quality and simple yet enchanting designs. When one of the 'eens' found one she liked, the price would be asked. The fat man knew exactly how much each carpet could fetch, but waffled, staring meaningfully at the tag attached on the rear with red wax that gave it the possibility of being sold and shipped out of the country. He hesitated only in judging what effect his words would have on his erstwhile customers. Would they think he asked far too much and lose interest? Would they, although not within their range, fall in love in any case? Reject the carpet and the price and just walk? If he judged the price was going to appear to be exorbitant, he made comments such as how old, but well-preserved it was, or praised the color and design, saying it was one of the best examples of its region. If it was going to be cheap, he pointed out that it was not evenly woven, the colors had faded, how dirty and worn it was, or in the case of the horrible machine-made ones, telling the audience this with the utmost scorn.

Barbie inquired about a particular carpet, just to keep the show on track. The fat man became more and more animated and dozens of carpets were thrown at their feet. The assistants had grown from one to two and the stack of carpets had grown to over a foot high at their feet. The fat man ordered more tea and then he said, cooing like the ubiquitous pigeons, "And which ones do you like? I will put away the others and we can choose what we like best."

Barbie recognized the preliminary spiel before going in for the kill. She had seen nothing amazing tonight and would not buy, but maybe she could get a good deal for someone else by pretending and then the fat man would say, "And for two, we can give you a better price." Then one of the 'eens' might be able to afford a small carpet.

While they sipped their third cup of tea, Georgia and Geoff joined them. They indicated they had walked around town, poked their noses into souvenir shops and read the menus of the other restaurants in town. They had taken photos of some of the more spectacularly lit chimneys and had had enough for the evening. However, watching the carpet show was going to be worth sticking around.

The buyers, or ersatz buyers, chose their favorite two or three, then it was narrowed down to one favorite. They had all chosen ones that were an appropriate size, handmade and within the price range of an English teacher. Maureen offered half of what the fat man wanted for a small red kilim with a tree of life design. Colleen offered even less than that for her favorite, a very small silk knotted carpet that would be hung on the wall. Charlene liked a rather large, cheap kilim with a moon and sun design. She shook her head and declined to name a price, saying that she knew the carpet was cheap, but she liked it, and she could not afford the price asked. Barbie mumbled about two or three, but said that she would come back later in the daylight and look at them again, "The light isn't good enough. I can't see the colors and if they will go with my furniture or not." She grinned at the fat man.

"Then I will keep them aside," and he snapped at the assistants in Turkish, as one of them set the three carpets aside.

"Now, now ladies, what is your best price, your very best price?" the fat man pigeon cooed again.

Maureen and Colleen repeated their offers, and Charlene named one that was ludicrous.

"No, no these can't be, I must have a price that I can deal with. I will show you how it is done. I will lower my price, then you must make your price higher." He proceeded to drop 10% of the price.

The 'eens' gasped at this lowered price and immediately began upping their prices by even less. They tittered and giggled and made plans for their lovely purchases, all the while ignoring the fat man's urgings to raise their offers.

Recep's wife stepped in at a lull and asked about a particularly stunning carpet that she obviously coveted. Recep looked at her wonderingly and shook his head. Barbie strained to hear the whispered conversation, but she only heard one word, 'expensive' that she recognized.

Tired and exasperated, the fat man pleaded, "Ladies, my dear lovely ladies, please just give me your very, very last price, your very, very best price!!"

The 'eens' looked at him, and repeated their last offers and smiled sweetly. "We are just poor English teachers and we cannot afford your beautiful carpets."

"But you cannot find such wonderful carpets in Istanbul or Ankara, they are only found here, in this small shop. I buy them directly from the women who make these carpets or from the families who want to sell them. But these carpets are the real ones!" The fat man was becoming agitated and angry. It appeared that his customers were slipping away from him.

"But they are too expensive for us!" said Maureen. "If you asked less money, we would buy them!"

"These are fine carpets, you cannot just give me a few lira and expect me to be happy!" the fat man wailed, now appearing to be in agony induced by three innocent tourists.

Charlene entered the fray, honey dripping from her tongue. "But I really want this carpet, it is not so expensive." She then named a price slightly higher than her last offer, but still much less than the fat man hoped.

"Take it, take it, you rob me!" he stormed out of the room, muttering under his breath at his assistants.

Charlene flipped out a wad of TL, paid for her carpet and the group left quickly. Barbie thought that she would not return to look at the carpets she had chosen. She didn't really want any of them.

"Why was he so angry?" Maureen asked. "We did what he said. We gave him our best prices. He was asking way too much in any case, who does he think he is? He has a crappy little showroom in a town at the back of beyond, and he asks such outrageous prices! The tea was cold!"

"At least I got what I wanted," crowed Charlene.

"But he practically gave that to you," Georgia pointed out. "Half the asking price, that's unheard of!"

"Don't worry, he made money. People like that NEVER sell something under their cost. He might not have made as much money as he thought he was going to make, but he made more than enough to pay for our teas. And besides, did you see anyone else there? He had nothing to do anyway. Serves him right, greedy man!" Geoff added.

The 'eens' stuck together, glad that Charlene had acquired a carpet. They shared a flat in Ankara, and they would all enjoy the carpet.

Georgia sighed, "I'm glad that the tourists won this round, but do you want to leave Goreme with all of the shopkeepers hating us?"

"Oh, don't be sympathetic to them, be sympathetic to me," Faruk joined in. "My services are worth the money spent! You will come tomorrow, won't you?"

"Maybe I'll rent a bicycle," Georgia said. "But your motorized mini-monsters are certainly not on my list of preferred transportation."

"No, a quad bike," Faruk said, anger creeping into his voice. Then he changed his tactics as he wheedled, "You promised!"

"No, Faruk, perhaps it was Ted Baxter who promised we would rent the quad bikes." Geoff said in a scornful tone, to the suddenly very distraught Faruk.

Faruk's jaw went taut; then he smiled, "You are right, it no longer matters. My friend Ted Baxter is now deceased and unable to keep his promise, but it doesn't matter. You are still welcome if you want."

They had meandered together down the street, past the restaurant and now stood in front of Faruk's small stand, temporarily watched over by a colleague.

He stood beside the door, his now tranquil face masking his emotions. "Well, I will say good night to all of you. It has been a very interesting day. I hope tomorrow you have a good time."

"Yes, we're going to see the Open Air Museum tomorrow morning. Good night, Faruk," Charlene called out.

The rest said their good byes and strolled on. Barbie turned to look once more at Faruk. During the evening's entertainment, she had been able to hold it all in, but now, as she watched him stand alone, the old aching and yearning returned. She had watched him laughing, joking, being friendly with everyone, and then flirting with the other girls, much younger, much more available than she. She felt a twinge of jealousy. But then she remembered his warm arm around her, the stare of desire in his eyes. Was it his desire? Maybe just hers.

Barbie found herself beside Georgia and ventured a question, not completely at ease, but compelled nonetheless. "Georgia, how well did you know our friend Ted Baxter?"

"Well enough for me. You heard me once, didn't you? Screaming at the top of my lungs, making a fool of myself? He had just called me a lesbian once too often. And he tried to spread that around the school. You know how it is here in Turkey, or anywhere in the Middle East. You've been in Egypt. Calling someone a homosexual or even insinuating it, is not a good thing. People start avoiding you. They think you have less than appropriate morals and are not fit to teach them English, or that you will try to seduce them, or even worse, seduce their children. It's not a nice thing to do. It's a despicable thing to do. There was no love lost, I can tell you that. Even so, he's dead, isn't he? Don't want to speak ill of the dead, do we?"

"No, I guess not. But I do have a question, about last night. I mean, he was found way outside of town, why should he have been there? We are assuming that he had been drinking and that he went wandering, but why so far away? Have you thought about that?" Barbie looked at Georgia expectantly, trying to read her expression.

Georgia's face was half-hidden in the shadows and her voice now tightened. She seemed to choose her words very carefully. "No, I have no idea. He was strange, that one. I have no doubt that he didn't know either. He was always doing strange things, talking to strangers on the phone. More than once I caught him talking to someone on the phone, but when he hung up, he tried to lie about who it was. Once he said it was a student, but he was speaking very quickly and colloquially, like you would talk with another native speaker, not like you would talk with a student who is studying English. And another time, he said it was an international call from the US, but I really, really doubted that. It was just NOT the time of day to talk to someone in the US, it was in the middle of the night back home. No, he was a really strange one. I will not say I am sorry he is dead. But in public, I will be sufficiently humble and put on a long face."

"What do you know about his wife?" Barbie asked. "Kemal said she is coming tomorrow."

"Wow, that one blew me over. Never a word about a current wife, let alone an ex. Usually people say something. I knew the guy for months and had many conversations with him, but never a breath. I frankly thought that the reason why he was so insistent that I was gay was because he was! So, another bit of evidence for the dark horse of PAEA." Georgia shook her red hair and ran her fingers through it, as if she were 'washing that man right out of her hair'. "Well, off I go!" She immediately broke into a run and started in the direction of Aladdin's Cave. Barbie watched her feet, wearing the shoes, bright pink, yellow, green and blue. Her jeans came down over them just to the back of the heel. She jogged away quickly.

Barbie found herself alone then and hurried to catch up with someone. She saw the 'eens' ahead of her meandering slowly. The others had obviously gone on ahead. She strode quickly and easily caught up with them. They paused under a street light to rehash the evening's carpet buying and Charlene pulled the carpet out of the bag. The 'eens' and Barbie admired it once more, but also found a number of flaws, besides being greasy and dirty. "Paid way too much!" Charlene said.

"But it's pretty and we'll walk on it anyway," Colleen put in.

They all helped Charlene wrap it up again and stuff it into the recycled shopping bag.

They walked just a short ways and turned the corner of the street that led to Aladdin's Cave, off the main road to Uchisar. The lights were fewer and farther between this way and dark shadows lurked in the corners where two and three-story houses and pensions met the narrow cobblestone street. They came to a pile of trash that had been strewn across the street and tried to negotiate their way around it.

"Really, who does this kind of thing?" Charlene said. "I know that these people are villagers, not long off the farm, but this is just stupid." The garbage glistened in the dim light and the stench caused murmurs of disgust. She carefully moved towards a narrow strip of clean cobbled street, near the buildings on the south side of the street. They followed suit, going in a single file of four.

A dog barked, a big loud dog bark that reverberated off the walls of the narrow street. Barbie screamed as the memory of the Kangal came rushing over her. She instinctively turned her head to find the sound, swiveling her eyes upwards towards the roof just above her head.

She saw the underside of the pot as it fell towards her. Primal instincts took over and she jerked her head and shoulder to the side. She felt the whoosh of the heavy planter as it came within a half an inch of her arm. The leaves and branches of the plant scratched her arm as it came past her. The sound of the pot shattering at her feet caused her to scream again. And then her own scream was joined by dozens of others, culminating in wails of fright and anger. The dog continued to bark, joining in the chorus.

Chapter Nine: Skype with a Friend

Kemal had all of his guests gathered in the office or just outside, sipping tea. The sequence of events was very confusing as too many mouths had tried to tell the story. No one was hurt, so re-telling the tale was all that could be done. When the 'eens' and Barbie had started the cacophony, the rest of their group, scattered, but in or on their way home to Aladdin's Cave, had come to the rescue. The only 'rescue' needed was to the reddened area of Barbie's right arm. As she had been wearing long sleeves and a light jacket, damage was minimal.

"Well, if you girls are all accounted for, I shall go to bed. That is, unless, you need a body guard and then I shall suggest Kemal provide one of his sons to sleep outside your door." Geoff laughed and headed to bed.

"I just don't understand what exactly happened," Colleen declared. "One minute we were walking peacefully down the street and the next, kerbloom, and that damn dog started howling. Did the dog knock over the planter?"

"I thought the dog started barking first, and it was my impression that he certainly did knock over the planter. I mean, the door was hanging open and the staircase of that pension just went straight to the rooftop. Why anyone would want to leave a planter right on the edge is beyond me. You don't have any planter pots like that, do you Kemal?" Charlene was a little calmer than Colleen.

Kemal looked sheepish but shook his head. It was not obvious what he was trying to say, that he didn't understand why someone would put a planter pot so close to the edge or that he himself had no planters on the edge of a balcony. The tea cups were emptied or abandoned and guests drifted off to their beds. Recep's wife and children had already retired, and Recep, too, wanted to go.

Barbie stopped him with a question, "I don't understand about the 'arrangements' that Ted Baxter made. I mean I volunteered and I thought I had made all the arrangements. I contacted Kemal and made the plans for the balloon rides etc. But now everyone tells me that Ted Baxter had coordinated the shoes and the dress-up and all. I knew nothing about this. What was the deal?" Barbie tried not to sound querulous and complaining, but it was hard to keep the whine of betrayal out of her voice.

"Calm down, Barbie, you did make the arrangements. It's just that Ted Baxter had some sort of in with the seller of the shoes and we all gave him our shoe size and he bought them for us. It was supposed to be a 'team building' type of thing. I'm sorry he wasn't around to give you your pair. We were just having fun. I guess your shoes are in his room. I haven't been in there, I was waiting for Ted Baxter's wife to arrive. And now, the police, well, they are having a holiday and I guess it really doesn't matter, it is not a matter for the police, but a medical matter to be taken care of."

"Recep," Barbie lowered her voice, "I have some reason to believe that it was not an accident."

"Barbie," Recep's voice became hard and uncompromising. "What makes you think that?" Sweat had broken out on his forehead and he became very agitated.

Barbie read the cues and began to rethink her statement and questions for Recep. She looked down at his feet, shoes pink, yellow, green and blue, with jeans that came down to the heel in the back.

"Conspiracies, always conspiracies. Turks are crazy about thinking that everything is underhanded and done by someone else and now? Now foreigners believe all of this as well. Be careful Barbie, be careful of what you say!" Recep's voice remained steady.

Barbie began again. "I guess maybe it is just because of where he was found. You were there. Why was he out there on that road, it's so far from town? What was he doing there? It just seems so suspicious. That's all…" Barbie trailed off after looking at Recep's eyes.

"You be careful Barbie, you be very, very careful. You can find yourself on the wrong side of the police. That is not a good idea in Turkey. You need to think very carefully before you accuse anyone of something."

"Oh," Barbie squeaked. "I'm not saying anything about anyone. I have no ideas, just some little thoughts and I have, had some questions. But I would never question the police."

"Now," Recep said. "What makes you think it was not an accident?" He peered at Barbie's face in a more receptive mood.

Scared now, Barbie tried to find something else to say, to deflect any more questions. Why, oh why, had she said anything to Recep? Why was he all of a sudden in this mood? What had she said that had provoked this? Careful, she told herself, don't reveal anything to Recep. He was Turkish, he understood the police and then again, maybe he knew more than he was saying. "It's just that I am concerned. Concerned about our trip, concerned about what we should do. He was our colleague and we are, all of us, concerned and we don't understand." That was it, Barbie thought, pull the 'we are foreigners and don't understand the customs' card. "You know, we are foreigners. And we do not understand everything. The way of doing things, the culture, you see is so different. We are just stupid yabanci. We are curious, but we cannot do anything. And we don't know what to do."

"Now, now, Barbie, I will take care of everything. Don't worry. You and the others just go about your business. I am in contact with the authorities. I will deal with everything. Please do not listen to any more conspiracy theories. This is a very bad habit of Turks. I understand because I have lived in America. I mean Americans are a little weird about President Kennedy's assassination and the 9/11 attack, but these are so minor when it comes to Turkish affairs. You 'yabanci' need to just be patient and let the things that will happen, happen." Recep smiled at Barbie in an attempt to pacify her, reassert his authority and quash any more talk.

"You are right, Recep, sorry. I am just too nervous. I will try to be calmer. You are right, it is not my business and the others may be made more frightened. I will not spread any conspiracy theories."

"Good, then I will say good night. It has been a very long day. I know that we are all tired." He turned and mounted the stairs. Barbie heard a small child wail overhead and Recep quickened his step.

Kemal had evicted his son from the computer and now sat in front of it, checking the email that he hoped would come in and earn him more guests. His son sat in a corner, morosely playing a video game on a small, cheap pad. Kemal looked up as Barbie came in. "More tea?"

"Kemal, if I have one more cup of tea I shall not be able to sleep all night. As it is, I am not sure how much shut-eye I can get." She slumped onto the couch. "Dead bodies, planters falling on me, dogs, being chased in the valley. What more can I take???"

"Would you like a little more wine?" Kemal asked. "It can help you to sleep." He quickly found the bottle and a glass. Barbie sipped the homemade wine. Confirming her previous opinion, it was not terribly good, but it was something to do. "Oh well, I guess I can log on and check my emails. Can I get wifi in my room?"

"Sometimes. People tell me that in the cave rooms, it is more difficult to get the wifi. But others say that upstairs, it is good. And you know the balcony? Some say that is the best place."

"A little cold right now. But I will remember that. Thanks for the wine. Good night." She turned to Kemal's son. "And good night to you too."

He mumbled a reply that Barbie took to be a greeting and let him resume his game.

Upstairs, she heard some noises from the two rooms occupied by Recep's family, and Geoff was obviously in residence as she heard the water running. Otherwise, the sounds of the night were distant and faint. Some cars and trucks, dogs barking, all the noises were those heard in small towns all over the world. Would there be roosters crowing two hours before dawn? She thought there might be. She tried to recall if there had been any this morning as they stumbled out to the balloon ride. She couldn't remember.

She locked the door and put a chair in front of it. She hadn't done that in a while. Even in Cairo during the revolution she hadn't thought it necessary to barricade herself in. But after today, she felt it prudent to do so.

She grabbed her computer and sat on the bed. She flipped it open and immediately she was connected. Wow, she thought, this is good stuff. Turkey was way ahead of her hometown in terms of wifi. The computer had remembered the password for Aladdin's Cave automatically. She clicked on Skype. She saw Penelope's name lit up. Great, she thought, someone who is truly innocent. Someone she could talk to about all the events of the past day. Penelope would not call her naïve, a believer in conspiracy theories, or anything else. She was someone who would take Barbie seriously. In return, Barbie could describe what was happening here and did not have to exaggerate or speculate, just tell it like it was.

The 'bing bing bing' of Skype thrilled her. Five years ago, this was not possible. But nowadays, wow, she thought. She could talk to her mother whenever she wanted and old friends had become even better friends, all because of this marvelous program.

"Hey girlie, how are you doing?" Penelope's voice came over the airwaves. Her wild curly hair and sideways slipping smile greeted Barbie.

"Oh Penelope! Things are really, really weird here. You will never believe what has happened!"

"Don't tell me, let me guess. Someone has died under circumstances that are not entirely clear?"

"How did you know?"

"You mean really, someone has died? Barbie, how awful, how absolutely awful!"

"Okay, this is the story." Barbie started with the balloon ride and the finding of the body. But as she began to tell Penelope about the visit to the site of the dead body and the afternoon chase in Pigeon Valley, Penelope stopped her.

"Whoa, whoa girlie. How about starting at the beginning. I remember that you have said some things about this Ted Baxter guy. You didn't particularly like him either, if I recall, but that doesn't mean you had anything to do with his death. So, can you start from the beginning?"

Barbie stopped and blinked. "Beginning? I don't know the beginning. I can only tell you about what I know. I've only been here for a couple of months, and I am not so sure that I know very much at all. Where is the beginning? When I came? Or when he came? Or when things started going wrong? Have things gone wrong? I guess they have, haven't they? But that was before I got here. I don't know, Penelope, I just haven't got many clues about what happened. But I do know one thing, I am sure now that it was murder, not an accident."

"Okay, no accident, but why do you say that. Number one is…?"

"Number one is the place where he was found. I think he was killed there with a rock. I think maybe someone lured him there and then hit him on the head with a rock and then made the body look like it happened there."

"Whoa, slow down, explain please."

"Well, first of all, Ted Baxter was out of town. It wasn't far, less than a ten-minute walk, even less by car or motorcycle. But it was not on his way home. And though he may have been drunk, you would have to be awfully drunk to go so far out of your way. And if he was that drunk, I think maybe he wouldn't have been able to walk at all. So that is the first point. The second thing is the body. There was a rock, a decent sized rock, lying on the ground, right next to his head. The theory that everyone is going on now, is that he tripped and fell and hit his head on the rock. That seems really far-fetched. The police and the medical crew just took his body. We were there. We stayed the whole time. They did nothing about 'securing the scene' or photographing anything. They treated it as if it were just an accident. They scuffed up the place so that even if there were any footprints or hidden or dropped things, they could never have found them. I mean even Sherlock Holmes, and he is fiction for heaven's sake, looked for things like that."

Penelope butted in, "But what about the scene made you think, and when did you think, that it was suspicious?"

"Well, at the time, you can imagine what it was like. We KNEW him Penelope. We knew the guy, he was one of our fellow teachers, he wasn't a stranger or anything like that. We were so upset, no one really said or thought anything. It was obvious that he had been drunk, and Georgia mentioned vomit, so I guess maybe we thought that he had fallen when drunk. And there was blood, on his head and the rock. So maybe we assumed too much. But we were all so upset and shocked. So that is the second thing."

"There's more?"

"You bet there is more. My God, when I think back on today! Okay, so when I went back to the site this afternoon, I took a look around, and I found the other rock. Now this other rock wasn't near where the body was found, it was a little ways away, but it could have had blood on it. And yes, there was another place that was bloody as well. My idea is that someone lured him there and hit him with a rock. Then he bashed him again with the little rock, and then moved the body a little. The blood was covered over with dirt, I think deliberately to disguise it. I don't know if the murderer thought that he, or it could have been a she, would get away with it, but it looks like they fooled the police. Come to think of it, maybe it was a woman. That's why the body wasn't moved further away. If she couldn't drag the body very far, certainly not pick it up, then she would have just moved it a little ways and covered up the blood and put the rock farther away."

"This rock, the one you think killed him, was it a small rock or a big rock?"

"I could pick it up, I tried and in fact, I found some stains on the side that was face down in the dirt. But I dropped it when I head the noise."

"Barbie, what noise?"

"The noise of the killer come back to spy on me!"

"Explanation, Barbie, explanation needed here."

Barbie told Penelope about the noise on the hillside and how Barbie had left a little more suddenly than she wanted to because she was frightened. She related her climb up the hill and then into Pigeon Valley. She gave details of her scare with the dog, then the chase and hiding in the church/pen. She described the shoes. "I fell asleep, if you can imagine. Sitting up, crouched in a corner. I guess that being scared and the whole day, getting up early and so forth, made me tired. And then when I felt as though I ought not move, I just fell asleep. Weird. But there it is. And then dinner and the flowerpot."

"What happened at dinner? Did anyone say anything? You know if you want to find out who could have hit him on the head, you need to pay attention to what people say. It's not as if you can go around asking questions, so you need to get people to talk."

"Well, I tried. But all through dinner, I was on the lookout for that pair of shoes, the ones that followed me. And when I saw Geoff wearing them, I freaked out. But that was only for about fifteen minutes, until I realized that everyone was wearing them. Then I didn't know what to think. I guess it might have been anyone who had access to a pair of those shoes. I wonder if you can buy them here in Goreme or in Urgup or something. That might explain the number of people who it could have been."

"But Barbie, you know that it was only one person. And that person more than likely knew Ted Baxter. What are the motives, the opportunities and means? You need to be more organized about this. Wait a minute, you already mentioned number one and number two, but what are your other points??"

"First was the body, where it was out of town. The second was the rock that 'killed him', it was probably another one and was deliberate, not an accident. The third is the person or persons who was watching me at the site and who followed me to Pigeon Valley. I did call out, I did ask someone to identify him or herself. So that is the third point. The fourth point is the shoes. That person who was wearing jeans and the very distinctive shoes was the one who followed me and I have no doubt at all that that person is either the killer and knows a lot more about it. Maybe there is more than one person involved. So, the fifth is the flower pot. I want to say that it was just an accident, but it is sooooo coincidental that I am very sure that the same person who followed me also pushed that pot off the roof. It would have been very easy to do. And I was with the 'eens', so that leaves them out, but I can't really see it being them in any case. But it could have been anyone else. And it could also have been a woman's crime. Although I can't really see Recep's wife doing something like this. I mean, Ted Baxter could have insulted her, I guess, like I heard him do to someone else like that. But the 'eens' were, all three, with me, so they would have had to have an accomplice."

"Tell me in detail about the flowerpot incident. Where were you standing and why and how could it have hit you?"

"Someone must have gone to the street garbage pile, taken a bag or two of garbage and strewn it across the street so that we would have to walk around it, have to walk near the wall of the pension. Then there was the dog barking. I don't know whether that was by design or accident. Maybe a lucky accident? Anyway, the dog caused me to look up and see the pot as it started down. I saw it just in time to turn my body away just enough not to be hit by it. This is the sort of thing that I would have called an accident or coincidental if I hadn't had enough other scares today. I think someone was targeting me. Someone thinks I know something. Which I do not. Can I tell that person? Can I tell whoever it is that I don't know who they are?? I don't know exactly what they did or how they did it and certainly not why."

"No motive?" Penelope asked. "You must have some ideas about motive. You have told me enough horror stories about Ted Baxter in the last few months, that I might actually suspect you of hitting him over the head. Lord knows that you have gotten ticked off at him enough times."

"Yeah, angry, ticked off, but not violently enough to kill someone. Murder is really, really angry. That or stupid, or wanting money, love, revenge. Death is the final frontier. No one has ever come back from the dead, Jesus and a few others perhaps, but not the rest of us non-gods. Murder is the end, and the one who murders, well, I don't have a lot of sympathy for them. Not deliberate murder. Maybe this one was just more of an accident. But after the things that have happened to me today, I don't think it was. And the murderer knows that I think this way." Barbie's voice had dropped to almost a whisper as she said this. This was a dangerous admission on her part. Not that anyone but Penelope could hear her, but saying it out loud had created a real fear this time. "Penelope, I'm scared."

"As well you might be. What happened at dinner last night? It seems to me that there must have been something said or hinted at or <u>something</u>. He was killed after dinner, so what went on at dinner? That might help narrow it down."

"Ted Baxter managed to say something mean or nasty about everyone at the table. I said that I couldn't see Recep's meek and mild wife doing anything. But what Ted Baxter said to her last night might just have tipped her over the edge. It was a mild Ted Baxter comment, but it was NOT nice. Let me see if I can recreate the dinner, quote all the things that Ted Baxter said.

"First of all, we got to the restaurant and we sat at a long table. The 'eens' were together along one side, I sat opposite them, with Geoff on my right and Georgia on my left. Ted was at the end with Faruk sitting next to him, next to one of the 'eens'."

"Barbie, wait a minute," broke in Penelope. "Who is Faruk? Someone else who went with you guys? You haven't mentioned him before."

"Oh," Barbie hesitated. She was uncertain if she wanted to confide the most secret thoughts she had about Faruk to Penelope. Perhaps not just yet. She could play it cool for now. If and when this mess resolved itself, then she might do something, put herself out to see if Faruk was really interested in her or just in all women. She quickly thought of what she should say now. "Well, it's just that he is this guy who runs a small outfit here, renting out quad bikes. He really wants us to rent them, so he has been hanging out with us. He has been making eyes at the 'eens' for two days, he has even gotten desperate enough to flirt with me."

"But who is he? Where does he come from? And why you guys from PAEA?"

"That is really a good question. I think maybe he is American, and Kemal is definite he is Turkish, but Penelope, this guy's English is native-speaker like. He must have spent enough years in the US to become Americanized, so whether he has a Turkish passport, an American passport, or both, I don't know. But he also has the mannerisms of a native English speaker as well. The gestures, the 'understandings.' So if he is Turkish, he is very, very Americanized. But he does also speak fluent Turkish and Kemal says he is from Malatya. Georgia says that Ted Baxter and Faruk knew each other before we got here, but I haven't really thought too much about it. He has wormed his way into our group and he wants us to go quad biking. That's all I know. He is following us to get our business. And maybe he met Ted Baxter on some other trip to Goreme.

"Where was I? Ok, seating. Recep, wife and kids were at the end of the table opposite Geoff and Ted Baxter. And during dinner, Ted Baxter drank quite a bit. He had wine, a whole bottle at least. Others had one beer or maybe two, but not much. We had different things to eat. The regular, kebabs, chicken, salad, tea. The kids had ice cream. I'm watching my weight, no dessert for me. People left one by one, and the three 'eens' went together, and Recep and family left together. I left after the 'eens' and Recep's family, but before the others. So I can't tell you who else left when and where they went. I went back to Aladdin's Cave and went to bed.

"What was said? Okay, Ted Baxter said that Recep's wife obviously had no life because she was only a housewife, she spoiled her kids and they were bound to grow up to be 'momma's child' kind of people who had no minds of their own and that would never contribute anything worthwhile to the world. They instead would perpetuate seventh century ideas. That is an unkind jibe at conservative Muslims who want to turn back the clocks to the time of the Prophet. So, insulted her big time. She just sat there looking at him. She sometimes pretends that her English is limited, but that can't be true. She spent years in the US and she speaks, or at least understands, much better than she lets on. If 'looks could kill', she would have killed him. But I really don't see her doing that. Her husband, however, was just as insulted as she and he may have been more likely to try to get revenge on Ted Baxter for insulting his wife, his children and his religion. Men have died for less. But Ted Baxter didn't leave Recep out of it. He prefaced his remarks with a disclaimer, saying that he wasn't trying to tell Recep his job, but… You know the thing that is done by nasty two-faced people. So then he starts to tell Recep that he should be meaner with the students and meaner with the new teachers. He shouldn't be nice to new teachers, he should do this and do that. It was as if he was planning to fire Recep and he was telling him all the things Recep had done wrong. I didn't really understand it. He also alluded to the boss in Istanbul, a Mr. Aydin, or rather, Dr. Aydin, and that he, Ted Baxter, would make an excellent director of an outlet of PAEA. It was a very snotty, poor job. He was praising himself at the same time as putting Recep down. It was embarrassing. Recep is so sweet, he just didn't say anything except that old saw, 'thank you for sharing'."

"I had no idea Ted Baxter was sooooo bad. I'm glad I wasn't there. How did you feel about it? Did you feel like punching him out? I know you said murder wasn't in the mix, but doing something? Like reporting him to this Mr. Aydin?"

"No," Barbie admitted. "I was a real wuss. I did not do what I should have done, which is to stand up to the jerk. But he attacked me as well. Geoff and I were kind of lumped together as second-rate teachers who couldn't get jobs anywhere else and so took jobs at a third-rate private school in Ankara. The implication is that if we were any good, we would have been able to do Istanbul at least. What he meant was that the real jobs are in places like Rome, or Budapest, or Vienna or Barcelona. And that Ankara only hires the left overs. Now, you can say that he is here as well, so what is the criticism about? He said that teaching was not the only reason he was in Turkey, that he was a true businessman and that teaching at PAEA was just a hobby. Whereas Geoff and me, we were pretending to be real teachers. Well, I didn't say much about that. I'm new and my students are not always happy with me, so I am keeping my head down. But Geoff has been around for a while and although I have never seen him teach, I guess he's okay. And it was mean, nasty. I don't think what he said was really worthy of death, but nasty.

"And the 'eens' were attacked for being lightweight, non-professional clowns in the classroom and just not suited at all for being proper teachers. Colleen gave as good as she got. She called him a dinosaur, out of touch with today's students, unpopular with the kids, disliked by colleagues and lazy. The last was because she caught Ted Baxter stealing one of her worksheets to use in class. Colleen had done a lot of work on it and she was quite happy to share, all anyone had to do was ask and she would give them the worksheet. But instead of asking, Ted Baxter took it out of the trashcan in the classroom and then used it. The kids loved it and I guess he took the credit, because one of the students told Colleen that they had done this new activity and wasn't Ted Baxter clever. Colleen was really angry about that. I mean, we are teachers. Teachers are generous, aren't we? Well, if you want my worksheet or game or whatever, just ask. But to sneak it like that and then take credit for it. Cheap shot, cheap shot."

"What did Ted Baxter say to that? Was he angry back?"

"No, he just laughed. By the time that conversation rolled around, he was pretty drunk and the 'eens' just ignored him. Actually, we broke up not long after that. He made a dig at Faruk as well. He insinuated that Faruk was a loser as a businessman, that he couldn't make a go of his quad bike business. Maybe he should think of becoming an English teacher in Ankara. Or was that today, one of the 'eens'? Oh, I can't remember the order of things. But then, Ted Baxter gave Georgia his usual dig. You know, that Georgia likes girls and how disappointed in life she must be because the Turkish girls wouldn't do anything with her, even if she asked. And that the men were put off, so Georgia must be very frustrated. Not enough to accuse her of being lesbian, again, but to say that she is undesirable is just mean.

"So, you can see, he just made enemies all round. But they were rude, mean-spirited remarks, not enough to kill anyone for, surely. But as we left, no one was interested in even wishing him good night. And then, this morning, when we noticed that he wasn't with us, there was no stampede to knock on his door to make sure he joined us. But knock him over the head with a rock in the middle of the might? So, what do you think?"

"Incredible," Penelope said. "What a nightmare. Barbie, what do you think you are going to do? Listen, I think it is none of your business. I think you should do nothing. I mean, other than going to the site this afternoon, you haven't really done anything. But I think that was a big mistake. I mean, do you really care about this Ted Baxter? Do you want more flowerpots on your head? And strange people chasing you every time you go out for a walk? It's not your business."

"Wow, that's what Recep said. And Geoff. And Kemal." Barbie shook her head. "When you put it that way, I guess it really makes sense to just let go. I mean, I have a certain sense of justice, but it has started to become personal. I need to take care of myself, and now, I've become tangled up in the death of Ted Baxter. This was not what I set out to do. But something thrust it on me. Penelope, I need to figure out what it is all about. It is no longer just Ted Baxter's death. And you are right, I don't really care about that any more. I care more now about keeping myself and the others safe. Maybe it is one of us and that person is targeting the others in the group. That I will not stand for. And especially if that person is targeting ME. But Recep, the 'eens', Georgia, Geoff? Really? I can't see any of them as murderers and attackers of innocents."

"How well do you know them, Barbie? How long have you been there? I know that we often stick together with the other English teachers, but sometimes we are not the best judges of character. You need to watch not just your back, but your head and where you put your next step!"

"Oh Penelope, my good friend, how I wish you were here. I feel like you are the only person I can trust. Hey, can you fly in tomorrow?"

Penelope guffawed. "Just like that, you want me to drop everything and fly out to your rescue?? You must be thinking of Cairo. I'm here in California with things to do in the next couple of weeks, if not months. Call me tomorrow night if you want, tell me the latest. And Barbie, take care of yourself!!"

Just as Barbie was about to sign off, she heard a great 'bump' in the hallway. Barbie jumped up, pulled away the chair and jiggled the lock, finally getting the door open. No one was there. The night had descended into a state of darkness and quiet. The dogs had even stopped. By the time she returned to the computer, Penelope had signed off. Barbie felt lucky to have had the good connection for as long as she had. She left the door ajar and quickly sent a chat to Penelope telling her good bye and promising to watch out for herself.

She played with Skype for a few minutes and found no one else to online. She shut down her computer and picked up her diary. She started writing the events of the evening and felt herself become calmer and sleepy. Before closing and locking the door for the night, Barbie stuck her head out and looked again. The lights were off in the rooms across the hall, Recep and his family, and next door, Geoff.

As she curled up in bed with the quilt pulled up and over her chin, Barbie thought that she would not be able to sleep. Too much excitement during the day often made it harder to drop off. If she had too much material to process, she lay awake, angry, fearful, or depressed. She thought of clever ripostes to critiques or not-so-genuine compliments. She thought of what she would do in her next assignment.

Now she drifted off rather easily, then began to dream. The shoes appeared on every person she met and she began to run from them. Then the children of Goreme started to chase her as well, all wearing the shoes. She glanced over her shoulder and then barged into someone. She peered into a face, the face of Ted Baxter, with a smirk on it. She dropped her gaze and saw the shoes. The pink and yellow and green and blue shoes, with jeans that came down just to the heels in the back.

Chapter Ten: The Sounds of Midnight

The sound woke her. The room was black. The phrase 'black as night' was inadequate to describe this inky darkness. No light came from the window or under the door. The rear of the room was carved out of the cave, so no light came from that direction. Barbie struggled to find her flashlight on the bedside table. Her hand patted various objects and then she heard something small and lightweight fall on the floor.

She heard the noise again, louder, more distinct this time, but the direction of the noise was indeterminate. Well, she thought, it must come from outside the room, so just find the light. She found the lamp and turned the switch. Nothing. She slipped out of bed and began to search on the floor. A minute later, just as another 'creeeek' sounded from outside, Barbie found the small flashlight. She turned it on and in the faint light that it threw, she grabbed her jacket and slipped it over her pajamas.

Taking the chair away from the door, Barbie tried to unlock the door stealthily. She heard no more sounds as she eased the door open. More light came in from outside, but it was obvious that the reason why her bedside lamp failed was because the electricity was out, all over the town. Faint moonlight and some starlight gave a glow to the atmosphere.

Retreating inside, Barbie put shoes on and grabbed her phone from her bag. Using the now swiftly fading light from the flashlight, she emerged onto the landing. She immediately headed towards the breakfast balcony, trying to allow her eyes to adjust to the darkness by not looking at her flashlight beam.

'Creeeek!' the noise smacked into her, immediately in front. Barbie screeched in fear, "Eeeek!" Pressing her free hand to her mouth, Barbie hoped she hadn't woken anyone else. But a rustle from behind Geoff's door told her she had. 'Creeeek' came the noise again as a storm window attached to the outside of the pension swung in the night breeze.

Geoff stuck his head out. "Barbie, is that you? What's the matter? Seen a ghost? Someone attacking you? A mysterious man bent on murder?"

A creeping chill rose up her spine and she croaked out, "Nothing, nothing, just the window, flapping in the breeze. Scared me. Nothing's wrong, go back to bed." Barbie reached around the corner of the balcony and caught at the flapping window cover. As she touched it, it detached and smashed with a 'crash' to the street below.

More noise erupted now from Recep's family's suite and soon Barbie and Geoff were joined by Recep. They peered into the street where the window cover lay. The dog across the alley began a low throated howl, which was immediately taken up by other dogs along the street and into the town center.

Recep demanded angrily, "What is going on? What has happened?"

Geoff smirked and pointed at Barbie, now standing near the balcony railing, examining the street. "Nothing," she said again. "The window cover came loose and when I tried to grab it, it broke and fell. End of story, nothing else, go back to bed everyone."

Recep swung around and entered his room, murmuring to his wife about what the noise was about. Geoff stood beside Barbie and pondered the piece of wood lying in the street. "What next, I wonder. It's as if this street has suddenly become haunted with flower pots falling, window screens coming loose, not to mention our late, sadly lamented Ted Baxter being found dead. Not the delightful vacation of your dreams, huh?"

"I wasn't looking for a vacation of my dreams, just a little getaway. I had always dreamed of coming here, it is such an incredibly interesting place. But it has been less than relaxing," Barbie admitted reluctantly.

"Kemal will fix that in the morning, never mind it now, go back to the nice warm bed. See you in the morning." Geoff pulled his lightweight jacket around himself and Barbie noticed that he was wearing jeans. She thought to herself that sleeping in ones' clothes was a bit odd. But maybe he had had time to slip on his jeans before coming out. She wondered what he was wearing under his jacket, his daytime shirt, or something to sleep in. Maybe he was one of those 25% of American males who slept in the nude, and, so as to be decent, had to put on all of his clothes. His shoes were not the ones she had seen at dinner, but an old battered pair of leather ones, probably old work shoes that no longer looked decent enough to wear to the Academy.

Barbie lingered a while, letting the soft glow of the night illuminate the fairy chimneys in a ghostly town devoid of electric light. Barbie was used to the power outages in Ankara, and she guessed they would be the same here. But here, it seemed so much more natural. Who needed electric light? Arise with the sun and go to bed when it is gone. Use more primitive light sources early in the evening and go to bed early. The simple healthy life. Maybe she could get a job here in Goreme, live in a less stressful environment. Sounds so good, doesn't it Barbie; do you really want to do that? You like your TV, skyping with friends, well-lit restaurants and your washing machine, refrigerator and all the mod cons. Admit it, Barbie, modern life is much preferable to the primitive.

She returned to her room and tried the lights once again, just to make sure they were truly off. After locking the door and setting the chair, she crawled back into bed. Not having enough battery power to read, she snuggled down and prepared to sleep. The dogs outside still howled, although their yelps and barks were beginning to lessen. The pension was serene. Because so much of it was made of wood, Barbie noticed that it was difficult to wander about the place without making noise.

She found a soft place that was warm and comforting and closed her eyes. Thoughts, dreams, plans, all of these came to her at night. She was never sure if she thought of class activities or what to do with a problem student in her nighttime dreams or in her ruminations at bedtime, or as now, at midnight. She had outlined a series of concerns or questions that needed to be answered for Penelope, but which of those were important? Which ones needed some thought, or 'sleeping on'? Barbie had never tried this before, think of a problem to be solved, set out the question or questions and then allow the night-time brain to sort it out. Could she try doing that? Which problem should she choose? Which problem could be solved using the knowledge she already had?

Barbie fell asleep trying to decide. She had not been asleep for long, when she woke, suddenly. She bolted upright in bed. She tried the bedside light, just on the off chance the electricity had come back on. It had not. She fumbled for her flashlight. She listened for any noise that could have caused her to wake. It seemed peaceful with no repeat of the earlier type of noise. Just a disturbance. Barbie repeated the chair removal and unlocked the door. She felt more at home in the extreme darkness now. Her flashlight was now so dim, that it was no better than a match, so she moved more by feel. She peeked out. The night was very dark, as there was still no electricity in the town. She thought she heard a faint 'swish, swish' sound.

She once again grabbed her coat and shoes. Slowly she edged out onto the balcony. The whisper-like sound kept up as she crept to the edge, keeping her head down. She knew that her blonde hair could capture the ambient light, especially if she stuck it up too high. When she reached the edge, she carefully and slowly raised her head and peeped over. The sound came from the street. She could barely make out a figure in the street, just where the flowerpot had fallen from the balcony of the pension. There was slight movement and a muted sound. A person was cleaning the street, sweeping up the garbage that had been thrown onto the street. Barbie understood now that the garbage had been a diversion, a means to make her walk closer to the edge of the street where the flowerpot had been. And now someone was sweeping the trash up. Who? And why? Barbie leapt to the conclusion that the person out there was the one who had done it. Done all of it. She needed to catch him at it, stop him from doing away with the evidence.

She slowly moved towards the stairs and, as silently as she could, began a halting descent. The wooden staircase was covered with old carpets, but the steps underneath were not as solid as they appeared. One squeaked emphatically. The screech was like that of a mouse that had been stepped on. Barbie stopped and held her breath. No reaction came from the rooms upstairs. She proceeded down, hitting another 'mouse step' and ended in the lower courtyard. Here the darkness was thicker than it had been upstairs. She stumbled against a chair. Barbie clutched the back and then realized that all the noise she made could be heard in the street. In fact, the sweeping noise had ceased. She lurched to the door and tried to open it. Locked.

Shuffling sounds of footsteps came from below. A ghostly figure emerged from the stairs that led to the downstairs dining room/lounge. Kemal's sleepy voice echoed in the darkness. "Who's there? What do you want?"

Barbie felt immensely foolish. What was she going to say? I saw someone in the street and I wanted to go out and see who it was? I heard someone sweeping up the garbage in the street? She had to answer something. "Hi, Kemal. Couldn't sleep, thought I could use a coke. Do you have any? Tea keeps me awake."

"Barbie, why are you here? It is very late. Yes, we have coke. It is downstairs."

Now Barbie felt stuck and her brain whirled. She shone the meager light of her flashlight beyond the wagon wheel against the wall, the sturdy old-fashioned glass-fronted cabinet full of carpets and the chair that had been placed in the middle of the lobby. Kemal flicked the switch and a light came on, enabling Barbie to see the stairs. Yeah, just like the lights to come on now, just when Barbie appeared her most foolish with a burned-out flashlight and no good reason for going out.

They carefully made their way down the stairs to the large room below. It contained a long table and chairs, some serving tables, a minimal kitchen and a big space in the middle of the floor. Dancing, Barbie thought. She turned to admire the mural painted on the wall behind the long table. It was a fanciful copy of one of the paintings from the cave churches. It depicted the Last Supper. A frankly twentieth century looking Jesus sat in the middle of a series of modern-day hippies, bikers and druggies. Their hair was long and wild and the expressions on their faces, meant perhaps to be awestruck, looked more like they were spaced out on drugs. Barbie could not bring herself to offer any critique on the painting. 'If you have nothing good to say, say nothing at all.' The old quote inserted itself into her brain.

"Kemal, do you always lock the front door at night?"

"No, and I don't usually sleep here. I have a home. And a wife and four children. This is not what I usually do, but today is special and I feel that I must stay here and watch. And then I hear you."

Upstairs they heard other noises, as if Barbie had awakened the whole pension. The pitter-patter of feet told them that at least one child was awake. And giggles that heralded the 'eens' were heard.

Barbie inhaled deeply, she really, really needed to confide in someone. It couldn't have been Kemal in the street, he had just come up from below, so it was not he out sweeping the street. "Kemal, I need to tell you this. I woke up because someone was outside in the street, sweeping up the garbage that he threw there. It was put there deliberately so that we would have to go near the wall, and whoever put it there was out there cleaning it up. Just now. That's why I wanted to go out to see who it was. But I suppose that all this noise scared him away. Kemal, someone is out there trying to scare me or kill me."

Kemal laughed. "Scare you maybe. It is perhaps normal here that boys and young men scare the pretty ladies. I know that I locked the front door, but that doesn't keep outsiders out. There is a very easy way to get to the house from the hillside. You know the top floor, where we dry the laundry? The wall is low and next the cliff. Anyone can jump over. You can jump over. So, locking the front door does not stop anyone. But the front door, it makes people feel better. And also, I want you all to be happy."

Barbie tried to take in the information about the proximity of the hillside and the ease with which an outsider could get in. It made sense; these small pensions were not attractions for the rich and famous, so why would someone need to secure them too well? Locking the front door should be enough. But how often did Kemal do that? This night maybe. Last night? Barbie rather frankly doubted it. And if he didn't lock the door, then anyone from here could have 'come home' and then left again.

All at once, the room downstairs was filled with guests, including the two small children in footed pajamas. Everyone seemed to want something to drink or a midnight snack. The banging of the window screen and the squeaking on the stairs must have caused everyone to be restless. And when Kemal invited Barbie for tea, then it seemed to spread through the pension like an out of control wave. Feeling guilty for waking everyone, Barbie bounded to her feet to help Kemal.

The 'eens' appeared rested and ready for a new day, Georgia and Geoff looked like they had been dragged out of a sound sleep. Recep had put his clothes on over pajamas and his wife had thrown on a loosely-tied headscarf, rather than the wrapping, tightening and fussing that she usually did. She looked unhappy, but Barbie assumed that she had come because the rest of the family had and she had no intention of leaving any of them behind. She was an attentive mother and wife.

Charlene looked around over the top of her mug of apple tea. "Faruk's not here. Where's the ever-attentive man? Ah well, maybe Kemal can stand in for him."

"What a funny thing to say." Georgia put in. "Faruk is not one of us. We don't know him at all, do we? I find him a bit of a nuisance, frankly. I will take Kemal over him any day." She smiled and flicked her eyelashes at Kemal, who gave her a look that could be read as lascivious or strongly amused. It was a curled mouth, with a heightened red in his cheeks.

Geoff leaned back and for once said nothing. He pushed away from the table and sat in the corner, closely watching all the guests. Barbie surreptitiously watched him watching and wondered what he was thinking. Was he a murderer? Was he wondering what everyone knew? Whoever had been targeting Barbie should have been watching her, but she was sure he paid more attention to the rest of the group than her. He knew where she was; his room was next to hers. He could hear her, maybe even skyping with Penelope. Could he understand what she said? Probably not, unless he pressed his ear to the door. Was it he out in the street sweeping up the garbage strewn there? He could easily have climbed the hill, leaped over the low wall, come down the stairs and appeared with the rest in the room downstairs. He looked as though he had had time to get dressed. Maybe he had already been dressed. But why would he murder? What was his motive? Being dissed by a jerk is not a real motive, is it?

Barbie suddenly felt very tired and as if she might be able to sleep. Her eyelids drooped. She stood and tried to take her glass to the sink. Kemal reached for the glass and told her to not worry. He watched carefully as she climbed the stairs.

In her room, she wriggled into bed. Realizing that she still had her outdoor clothes on, she painfully pushed her way to a sitting position. Glancing at the door, she realized that she had not yet propped her chair against the doorknob. She dragged the chair noisily into place, threw off her jacket onto the floor and stumbled slowly to the bed. As she closed her eyes and felt her entire body relax into a state of torpidity, she briefly wondered if someone had put something into her drink. What could it have been and when did anyone have the opportunity to do that? She relaxed and floated into the Land of Nod. The idea slipped away as she sunk into the bed covers.

Chapter Eleven: Breakfast at Aladdin's Cave

Barbie woke to darkness, but a cacophony outside her door. Because her room was at the top of the stairs and on the same floor as the balcony where breakfast was served, she was not surprised that it was the happy sounds of coffee cups being filled and cereal bowls and spoons rattling that woke her. She felt as though her limbs had had a double dose of sleep, they were stiff and difficult to move, as if they had lain still all night. She pushed back the blankets. However sluggish her arms and legs felt, her mind was sharp and clear. It had been a refreshing sleep and she was anxious to go.

Ten minutes later, after a hot shower, she joined those breakfasting on the balcony. The scene that met her eyes was magical. It was early and some balloons still floated over the town. She slipped to the edge of the balcony and gazed upwards. She reached her hand up and murmured softly at the floating, silent balls. The colors of the balloons were intense in the morning sun and she swiveled her head, trying to see how many different colors she could count. Most were multi-colored, but a few were brilliant solid colors with logos. They floated gently with the early morning breeze, slowly drifting across the airspace of the town of Goreme. It was at once surreal, technology meets raw geography, and at the same time fantastical, as if drawn by the hand of a Disney imagist. To the right up the street, there were none, but to the left, down towards the Open Air Museum and the start of Rose Valley, they scattered, big and small going at various speeds and heights towards their landing spots to the north.

As she leaned there, Kemal brought a cup of coffee for her. "This is just fantastic! Every day like this? How lucky you are to live in this beautiful place!"

"I live here, and it is beautiful, that is true. But if you see something beautiful every day, then it is not special any more. I am glad that you know it is beautiful. Do you want some eggs, scrambled eggs or fried eggs?"

"Oh, scrambled eggs would be nice. Yesterday, I don't remember breakfast at all. But today, I will enjoy it. Good morning everyone!" Barbie called out to the group, most of whom had made it to the breakfast area in good humor.

"Good morning," came the response.

Barbie, not wanting to break the magic that appeared around her too soon, stayed near the balcony edge. She casually glanced over and down into the street. The place where the flowerpot from the pension had fallen was still blackened with the dirt from the pot and a few green leaves. No one had made any attempt to erase the scene of the accident. But all across the street, where the garbage had been strewn about, was clean. Nothing was left to see. She was certain that if a proper detective took his magnifying glass and swept things up, he might find evidence. But as it was, the street was fairly dirty. She vowed that she would go down later and see for herself. But she was also certain that the figure she had seen the night before had cleaned up well.

Barbie settled at a small table and Kemal brought her eggs. "Did everyone sleep well??" she asked with a hint of sarcasm.

The 'eens' giggled, but admitted that the excitement of the day before had left them exhausted. Barbie wondered if someone had put something in their drinks. She gave Kemal a sideways look. Although she had helped him with the drinks the night before, it was Kemal who had actually taken them around and served each person. Maybe a little drop of some magic liquid?? She was certain he would never admit it.

The balloons now had all gone from town, although if someone leaned over the balcony and peered to the left, they could still see a few laggards. Georgia was the last to join the group and she immediately went to the edge of the balcony to see the disappearing balloons. In her hurry, she leaned too far and nudged a potted plant. She caught it before it tumbled over, but Barbie then noticed a number of other equally precariously placed terracotta pots around the balcony. It occurred to her that this was probably normal in Goreme. She thought about one story of Singapore; that people were fined for having pots on balconies where they might fall on passers-by below.

Barbie got up to fetch another cup of coffee and more bread and honey. The honey was in a wooden frame that held the comb intact. The honey dripped and spread in the pan below and small black things floated in the dark amber goo. Baby bees or bee poop? Never mind, she thought as she gouged out a hunk of comb and honey and put it on her plate. It had a few flecks of the black matter. If the locals could eat it, so could she. Fresh apples sat in a dish; small, some discolored, but picked very, very recently. The smell they gave off was as strong as the honey. Three dishes of different kinds of cheese lay neatly stacked. A smaller plate of halva also sat near plates of dried fruit. Barbie chuckled, halva for breakfast? Well, why not? She took a piece. Miniature pouches of Nutella were lined up in another bowl. Barbie thought she could stay here and eat all day.

Then she remembered. "Are we all ready for the Open Air Museum?" Barbie asked eyeing everyone. "We still have lots of time yet. Kemal says that we should wait a bit after the opening. Too many tour buses come there first and then it's too crowded. If we wait,, we have more space to see the churches. Well, if anyone wants to look at my guide book, they can. I'll lend it to you. Anyone??"

She was answered with silence as everyone focused on their breakfasts.

Geoff and Georgia sat together and Barbie began to feel some tension as they asked for the salt or the jam. Barbie knew they were not the best of friends, but this unpleasantness seemed out of character and out of place. Maybe it was because of last night's disturbances and not getting a good nights' sleep.

Barbie was going to move a little closer and inject some pleasant joke or something when Georgia leaned over and said softly and slowly. "Well, Geoff, are you feeling just the slightest bit guilty?"

"Guilty? Guilty of what?"

Georgia looked at him, "Not paying your just debts."

"Debts? What debts? My debts to society for allowing me to live? My debts to my mother for giving me life? My debts to my father for pushing me where he had failed? My debts to my teachers and my friends who thought I would never to be able to find a job? My debts to stupid school administrators who never understood what genius they refused to allow loose? So many debts I owe to society, to everyone. And how can I repay these debts?" He sneered at Georgia as though she were the representative of all those whom he felt no need to repay.

Georgia lowered her voice and hissed at him, "I meant the money you borrowed from Ted Baxter? Will you pay her when she gets here?"

Geoff looked down his nose at Georgia, his eyes looking cagey and perhaps the slightest bit scared. "And what will I pay her? And for what? And who is 'she'?"

"Ted Baxter's wife. The money you owed him. The money you did not want to repay," Georgia replied with a catty sneer.

Just as cattily, Geoff came back, "And how did you know that I didn't want to repay it? After all, it's not much."

"Because I heard you say so. I also heard you threaten to ignore it and never repay him."

Geoff looked startled and then said slowly and carefully, "Well, if you heard that, then you didn't hear the whole conversation. I did not like his attitude, at all. Did you ever like it? And when he said he would see to it that I was fired or at least was reprimanded, just because of a small loan, I just blew up. It was unprofessional of me, I admit, but I can and planned to repay that minor, small loan."

Georgia looked at him out of the corner of her eyes, a sneer on her lips. "So you 'planned' to repay him. But now he is no longer here, will you repay the wife?"

"Will you tell her and thus force my hand?"

"So you were planning on ignoring it?" Georgia chuckled conspiratorially.

"And your loans from the master loan shark? Will you repay those?"

"They, I am very sure, are much smaller than yours. And if asked, I will do so. But seeing as how they were never written down, I never signed an IOU and there was no expectation for when or in what form, then I was feeling free. But if you say you will pay back your loans, then I will pay mine." She arched her eyebrows at Geoff.

"As I said, they are quite paltry, just pocket change. So if it is important to his wife and she brings it up, then of course, I will do the gentlemanly thing and give her the filthy lucre."

"Do you think he went forward with his plan to 'tattle' on you, accuse you of unprofessional conduct?"

"If he told Recep, then I am assuming that Recep would simply ignore him. Ted Baxter raved about everything, too often, and this is so minor."

"So minor, you say, then how much? How much did you owe him?"

"A few lira, no more."

"How much?" Georgia demanded in a whisper.

Barbie had been pretending not to hear, but of course they both knew she could hear them, even with the whispering. She had been silently eating and looking at the magnificent scenery in the opposite direction.

Geoff turned to Barbie, "Did you owe him anything? Did you ever 'borrow' from Ted Baxter, or more likely, did he lend so easily and so generously to you?"

Barbie faced him and innocently answered, "No, I never took anything from him, but he certainly offered a number of times." Barbie hedged, "But it was usually only for something in the canteen, not really anything big. And I never took him up on it. But once it seemed so tempting. That time in the rooftop bar. All those cakes and cocktails…"

"Sucked us all in, did he? As I said, it was small, not really enough to worry about, and certainly not worth the threats he threw at me." Geoff stared straight ahead.

"Glad to know that's all cleared up. So, we won't be talking with the widow then?" Georgia smiled at the two of them. "Or I can offer to repay my miniscule amount and then direct her to the others who also need to repay their debts?"

Georgia grinned again, with more menace this time. The she raised her voice, "Hey, did anyone else owe Ted Baxter money? We were going to collect it all up and give it to his widow. Anyone else have anything to contribute to the fund?"

The 'eens' eyes swiveled as one to Georgia, then towards each other. Turning back, they grinned meaningfully, "We already paid it back, didn't we girls?" Maureen said very loudly. The other two 'eens' nodded vigorously.

"It was just a lunch at the canteen." Charlene offered.

Geoff hid his mouth and made a stage aside to Barbie, "They're lying. But they are entitled to the money. They had to accept it from Ted Baxter, but they can wash their hands of him and his money now. Just deny it ever happened or that it was paid back."

"Anyone else?" Georgia probed in a honeyed voice backed with steel. "Recep, owe the deceased any money? Just a few lira?"

Recep jumped slightly, then looked frightened and turned red. His wife pivoted slowly towards him and noted his guilty look.

Barbie thought that Mrs. Ayse did know English quite well and had followed Georgia's conversation with the 'eens'.

Perhaps the 'eens' did owe Ted Baxter money. This was a revelation for which Barbie had not been prepared. She encountered Ted Baxter in the canteen shortly after she had arrived. He had tried very hard to pay for her coffee, but Barbie would simply not let him. She felt, even then, unease with Ted Baxter and didn't want to owe him anything, even if it was the price of a cup of coffee. If she had accepted, she would have felt under some sort of obligation to this creepy person. She had become independent and fiercely so, since divorcing the ne'er-do-well she married too young. She kept quiet as Recep and his wife publicly struggled with their private consciences.

"This is very private, and has nothing to do with anyone here. I will speak to Mrs. Ted Baxter." Recep pulled himself as tall as he could, with as much solemnity and dignity he could muster. His manner indicated that he would answer no questions about money owed. But surely, this indicated that he, too, had been in debt to the deceased Ted Baxter.

Geoff chuckled to himself and whispered in an aside to Georgia. "He is truly an 'aslan' lion. That is his family name, you know? And it appears that he did borrow money from Ted Baxter. I wonder how much. And I also wonder who else borrowed money from him. Once he told me that he wanted to invest in Turkey. So maybe he started with Recep. Hmmmm."

"I've got my guidebook here, so if anyone would like to learn more about our journey today or anything else we have to see, just let me know. I can read out loud!" Barbie enthusiastically attempted to deflect the conversation, and the 'eens' joined in to rescue the atmosphere.

"Tell us about hiking places nearby," Colleen called out to Barbie.

Barbie happily pulled out the map she had been given by Kemal and looked to see what else was available. She already knew about Pigeon Valley and because it was the closet hiking spot nearby, she would have to mention it, but would decline to say much, only repeat what little she had said the evening before. "Well, if you are willing to go hiking immediately after the Open Air Museum, you could go to Rose Valley. The entrance is just directly across the road. And there are lots of churches."

"Quad bikes there." Kemal interjected.

"Well, there is Zemi Valley, just on the way back from the Open Air Museum. Looks like a nice hiking area. Kemal, what do you think?" Barbie deferred to Kemal.

"Better than Rose Valley, but Pigeon Valley is nice. Dogs there, but really very nice. Good hiking, and when you get tired, it's easy to walk up to the road.

"I thought my guidebook talked about a place where they did ceramics. Here in Goreme??" asked Colleen.

"Avanos," Kemal answered. "Your balloon trip ended near there. If you want, you can take the dolmus, just from the bus station. It is only nine kilometers. There are many places where you can go and try to make your own. Very fun. I can find the names of ones that you can visit."

"We can't walk there?"

"It is far, but even if you take the dolmus, you need to walk a little. Let me show you on the map." Kemal went downstairs to get the maps.

"Tomorrow we can rent a vehicle to take all of us, or we can sign up for a trip on a bus tour and go to the underground cities, Derikuyu and Kaymakli, Mustafapasa, Ilhara and other places." Barbie offered.

Kemal came bustling back with a handful of maps. "Here, here is the map that shows you Avanos. There is a river there and a famous bridge. The Romans made pottery here and this skill passes down from father to son. Even now, the young men are making pottery like their fathers did." Kemal lectured. "Unlike my sons who have no wish to be the master of a true cave house pension." He mumbled. "And they also make wine. You know the wine we had yesterday? This was homemade Avanos wine. There are famous wineries there too. The best wine in Turkey is made here in Cappadocia. You can try some if you like. Avanos is a very nice place. And if you want to play by the river, they have boats. Very funny boats, from Italy. They are for the tourists."

"You mean gondolas?" asked Maureen.

"Whoa, whoa, before you start dreaming, dearie, I think you need to look into it a bit more. But it sounds nice, very worthwhile for an afternoon. And it will be cheap, because we can take the dolmus and do everything ourselves. So let's wait until tomorrow to spend all of our money. So, anyone else for hiking this afternoon?" Charlene was one of those very practical people who weighed her time vs money and planned for a combination of fun, interest and expense.

"We will all go to the Open Air Museum together?" asked Recep.

Everyone nodded enthusiastically.

"Then we can walk easily. I will find a taxi for my wife and daughter and Bunyamin and I will walk too." Recep looked down at his son, who grinned happily, proud not to be the baby.

Kemal said, "I can take anyone in the car who doesn't want to walk, no problem. Just let me know when you want to go. Shall I arrange a trip for tomorrow? Do you want to hire a van or do you want to go on a tour bus?"

"Can we tell you after lunch? I think we might want to think about it. How much does it cost?" Barbie took over her job as a tour leader again.

"Quad bikes? They are very cheap!" Faruk said.

No one had seen him come, he just appeared amongst them. Charlene giggled. "Good morning Faruk. What would a day without Faruk be like? Lonely, boring, not worth living."

"Last night, where were you when we were having all the excitement?" Maureen asked.

"Excitement, here at Aladdin's Cave?" Faruk smiled easily. "This is a joke, surely? You had excitement, but didn't invite me?"

"Your absence was noticed," Barbie put in. This morning she was not so sure that Faruk was the same man she had fallen so hard for the day before. That smile was there, the earnestness, the energy, the sheer animal magnetism, but the intensity of her feelings had been lost in the disturbed sleep from the night before.

"What happened?" Faruk looked around at the group gathered on the balcony.

"It was nothing really, just a pot fell from the balcony of one of the pensions and almost hit me. But I escaped, with only a scratch to show how close it came. I have survived." She smiled at Faruk. He smiled back, that warm 'eyes-only-for-you' smile that charismatic men use to lure their victims. Barbie tried very hard to resist this morning. She had never liked really handsome men and now she noticed the imperfections in Faruk's face. She felt that handsome men had never learned to be genuine, they were always too busy using their good looks to get what they wanted rather than trying to be kind, helpful, genuine, loyal and all the other things demanded of modern men. Barbie tried hard to see Faruk in this light now.

"This is terrible, but you are okay, not hurt at all?" Faruk looked quizzically at Barbie. "Tsk, tsk, tsk. These hotel owners should be more careful with their potted plants. He went to the edge of the balcony and picked up a potted plant that sat too close to the edge. "These things can be very dangerous. I suggest that you be more careful. Tsk, tsk, tsk."

Chapter Twelve: A visit to the Open Air Museum

The road to the museum was close to Aladdin's Cave. The group had no trouble finding it and they ambled along, careful that Bunyamin didn't get tired. He was excited and refused to even hold his father's hand, except when Recep insisted as they crossed the streets. The short walk to the bus station took them past the scene of last night's 'accident'. Barbie looked carefully, but there was no sign of any trash tossed in the road. She was right, whoever had scattered it had cleaned it up in the middle of the night.

They walked through the bus station; the 'eens' anxious to find out what times the dolmus went to Avanos. "All the time, anytime," was the answer. They decided that fifteen minutes one way or the other was inconsequential and that they would just 'go with the flow' and hop a dolmus when they felt like it. Barbie was interested in going with them, but did not want to commit herself now. Time enough for that later. At the end of the bus station, a bridge led to the row of shops where the Blue Moon Café was situated. Was it only yesterday, Barbie thought. So much had happened between then and now.

At the end of the block of shops, the road narrowed and two large chimneys flanked either side of the road. Geoff whipped out his camera and started photographing. The back side of the one closest to the small town of Goreme had something dug into the chimney from a courtyard.   The chimney on the other side of the road hid a restaurant, which also housed the starting point for balloon rides. Barbie remembered yesterday morning. Was it here that they had been taken in the early hours of the morning, to get their meager breakfast and to be loaded into the little van? She couldn't see well, but she thought not. They all looked alike in the dark. Thinking again, Barbie thought they probably all looked alike in the day time as well.

Barbie found herself trailing the group and she looked again at what they wore. Every single one of them, including Recep, wore jeans. Blue jeans, stone-washed blue jeans. Was this a universal costume for post-modern men – and women? No one wore the 'shoes' today. They did however, all carry or wear a long-sleeved shirt or jacket. The weather for this autumn was nice, but it tended to get chilly in the shade, or as the sun went down. Georgia probably wore the shirt to keep her delicate skin from getting sunburned. They were of various colors, but tended to be dark. Barbie looked at her own attire. Was she criticizing what the others teachers wore on their days off? She was wearing the same thing. She noted that the lightweight blue jacket she wore resembled the maroon one worn by Maureen. She had gotten hers cheaply in Kizilay, the central shopping area in Ankara, which was home to many shops selling cheap Chinese-made clothes. Maybe Maureen had bought hers there as well. Their shirts distinguished them apart. T-shirts with logos, bright colors and stripes or swirls. We all wear the same pants, but different shirts. Why not wear the same shirts?

Past the chimneys by the road, Barbie saw the Open Air Museum perched on the hillside straight ahead of them. A cute little restaurant, rustic and locally run, was nestled into the hillside to their right. An intriguing sign sat next to a trail that went straight up the side of the hill, cutting between chimneys and outcroppings of corrugated hillside. The sign pointed to a church. Barbie wanted to go there. No, she chided herself, keep to the schedule. There are reasons why the Open Air Museum is on the World Heritage Sites list. They are the good churches, this one is probably just a little hole in the wall. She recalled the small church she had hid in yesterday. No sign, not terribly good paintings and it smelled of donkey droppings.

An upscale hotel appeared off to their right, and just beyond that, another road with a road sign. This one led to Zemi Valley and two more churches. The sign was new and, in English, described the two trails that led from here. One of the destinations was to the 'Church with No Name'. Another possibility for a hike, thought Barbie.

The road boasted only intermittent sidewalks and so they had spread out for the walk from Goreme. Now sidewalks again appeared and below them on the right, they could see the parking lot. It was a massive one that could hold at least a hundred buses and/or innumerable cars and small vans. There were fewer than twenty in the lot now, something that cheered Barbie because she had listened to Kemal's advice about times to come. The holiday had filled the town with Turkish tourists, but they had either seen the place, were sleeping in, or were not bothering with this specific tourist attraction.

A camel honk split the air. After having done many camel treks in Egypt, Barbie knew that sound, an excited, angry camel. Shouts accompanied another angry honk and Barbie sidled close to the edge of the sidewalk's barrier and looked over. Under a tree were two camels. One was very young and had no saddle, but the other, presumably the mother, wore an elaborate saddle with red pompoms. Tourists waited and the camel's owner tried to convince her to kneel so the tourists could mount. She protested, or maybe it was a blasting announcement that she was now ready to work. Another 'honk' and she lurched down and settled. Barbie wanted desperately to see the tourists climb on and have her stand up. Barbie was experienced, but others who were not, or who were unclear on camel anatomy, were always good for a laugh. A man and a young child climbed aboard.

Georgia sidled up to Barbie as she watched. "What are you doing? Tourist gawking?"

"Watch this," Barbie answered. "Inexperienced tourists. Good for at least one good chuckle."

The camel bellowed again as the owner kicked her in the hind legs. She let out a long groan that ended in a honk and lifted her hind legs. The passengers were thrown forward, almost going over the pommel. The child shrieked and the father swore. Then the camel jerkily raised her front legs up to full height, throwing the man and child backwards. Another shriek and more curses.

By this time, Barbie was laughing and the other PAEA teachers sauntered over to watch the final jerk to total upright position. The man laughed, the child cried and demanded to be let down. The camel owner beamed proudly now that his customers were ten feet off the ground and could not get down until their camel decided that she would consent to reversing the process. The owner kicked the camel again and she began a strolling lurch around the parking lot. The young camel followed. Barbie applauded and was joined by the others.

Charlene smiled, "Camel ride, wouldn't that be fun?" The other 'eens' agreed and started making plans to come down after seeing the Museum. Across the street was the entrance to yet another church, part of the Open Air Museum complex. As they climbed nearer the main entrance, Barbie began to see the tourists. They were scattered out over the hillside, so it didn't seem like too many. But she was aware of what Kemal had said about time limits to see the churches. So many tourists, so many beautiful paintings to see.

At the entrance to the Museum, there was a scramble to find 'Muzekarts,' the cheap cards that gave free entrance to most of the national museums in Turkey for residents. Barbie remembered that it was Ted Baxter that had told her about the cards and had helped her find her foreign number so she could purchase one. It had already paid for itself with two visits to the Anatolia Civilizations Museum in Ankara and a trip to Istanbul with the expensive museums there. All the others produced theirs. The only ones who did not have their cards were Recep and family, Turkish citizens. Barbie chided Recep. "You know it is very cheap and a good contribution to the museums in Turkey. You really should buy some for you and your family."

Recep nodded. "I know you are right, but, all I can say is that I am lazy."

A line of souvenir shops greeted guests and everyone slowed to peruse the various souvenirs from Goreme. One attractive thing Barbie noticed was a deck of cards. One deck had been opened and as Barbie flipped through, she saw that every card had a color photo of a famous tourist attraction in Turkey. She salivated at the thought of visiting these historic and scenic places. She asked the price and she cringed at the answer. She was willing to bargain, but not buy it at that price. No bargaining was forthcoming, so she turned away.

Tiny balloons made of felt with a real balloon inside were declared 'cute' and collected oohs from the 'eens'. There were also hand knitted slippers and gloves. The gloves had colorful designs, with each finger a different color. Barbie looked for some of the scarves that had crochet and tatting on the edges, but she didn't find any. She thought maybe they were too 'country' for these vendors.

There were rows of dolls, hand made by ladies from 'Soganli' Valley. "Recep", Barbie called out, "What is "Sooogan, sooann Valley??"

"The 'g' is soft and almost not pronounced, so it is 'Sooanli' Valley. It means onion. It's not far from here. The dolls are very sweet, my wife says."

The individually crafted dolls were made from bits of old cloth, with faces drawn on with black, red and blue pen strokes. Barbie felt compelled to buy one that carried a tiny clay pot, made from red local clay that had the name of the place it was made. She told Maureen that she would give it away to her friend's niece, but she knew that she wouldn't. She would keep it for herself, a little bit of childhood to be with her in Turkey. She petted the velveteen skirt, covered with tiny metal sparkles and then lifted it. The doll wore pantaloons, in colors totally unlike her skirt and blouse. Her feet were made from old toweling and ended in tiny stubs. The sign said "10TL".

"Barbie," Colleen called out, "hurry up, we'll leave you".

Barbie slapped 10 TL on the counter, grabbed the doll and hurried after the group, now rapidly disappearing up the path.

"We can skip the unnamed chapel right now, and go on to the Apple Church" Recep said, taking over the role of tour guide.

In a stroke of luck, they found a window of opportunity in between tour groups and entered the church through a narrow tunnel into a courtyard where they waited. Another tour group also waited and the PAEA group eavesdropped as the guide filled in specifics.

"Most of the churches here were started about the eleventh or twelfth century, but the churches themselves were destroyed, changed etc., so that now each church seems to have only one style of painting and so we can date the churches from the style of their paintings. The Apple church is different in that you can see two distinct styles in one church. Underneath is the geometric style from the Iconoclastic Period. This was a time when the church was against any figures of persons. So, the church was decorated with crosses, birds and geometric borders, mostly done in red onto the bare stone or perhaps some plaster. Later, figures were allowed and so these were painted over the earlier simple designs. St Barbara's Church, which we can see immediately after the Apple Church, has many of these earlier, simple Iconoclastic designs. But now, into the Apple church, probably called this because an apple tree stood in the courtyard immediately outside."

A uniformed man standing in the courtyard nodded to them that they could now enter the first church. A sign stated that only three minutes were allowed inside, and NO photos. Maureen sighed in frustration. "Came all the way here and can't even have time to enjoy it!? And then, can't take photos so I can look at leisure later. Damn."

As the group entered the church, Barbie heard sighs of surprise and pleasure. It was old, so old. And very human sized. The church was carved out of the stone itself; the floor was uneven and made of bare earth. There were columns, solid rock left standing as the builders scooped out the church around them. And they were covered, completely covered, with paintings. The lower levels had been defaced with initials and names. Some had whole passages carved through the paint.

Barbie saw Greek, Armenian and Arabic. A few modern Turkish initials also caught her eye. But above the level that a human could easily reach, the paintings were rich in color and showed whole figures and scenes. The columns held male figures, elongated and curved at the tops, wearing ecclesiastical clothes and carrying staffs, crosses, books or other signs of office. The domes, also carved into the ceilings, contained more paintings of Jesus, Mary, saints standing, on horses, and angels with gigantic wings spread wide, as if ready for flight. Soft yellow nimbuses surrounded all the figures. Soon, the guard appeared and attempted to move them on, explaining that more tourists wanted to come in. Reluctantly, the group left, but immediately encountered another church. Again, they were hurried away before they had a decent chance to see it all.

"The next church is the Yilanli, or snake church. St. George and his dragon give it the name," read Charlene from a modest guidebook she had bought at the souvenir stand at the entrance. The group walked up the hill along a smooth cement path. Trash receptacles lined the walkway, which was wide enough for dozens of tourist groups.

"I know that we came during a short down period in the tourist buses, but I don't really feel the 'crush' of tourists that I felt in Istanbul or Ephesus," commented Maureen as she spread her arms and spun around. "Much nicer place than Hagia Sophia at a holiday!"

Murmured assents came from the group. Recep and wife shepherded their children, who were remarkably well behaved at this point. Barbie thought they might get bored later. Three churches down and umpteen more to go.

The next site was the refectory, with only a small painting on one end, and no one to say they couldn't take photos. A long table in the middle and two long benches on either side were carved out of the tuff itself. At one end sat a large seat for the head monk or the daily reader, and over it, a faded painting, perhaps the Last Supper? The 'eens' quickly started taking goofy selfies, then gathered everyone on either side of the table and asked a wandering tourist to take the group's photo. Barbie thought that this was the first group photo that had been taken and they were missing one of the group. She could not force the smile that she knew everyone deserved. But, really, Barbie, she thought, are you missing his presence?

"The best is next!" Georgia proclaimed. "The Dark Church. And okay, everyone, fork over MORE money."

"No way", wailed Maureen. "We've already paid!"

"Yeah, like you contributed nothing, you have a Muzekart." Colleen answered. "We need to contribute so that no one gets more than three minutes to look at something, don't be greedy. And to pay the guards so that no one, but no one, takes any photos, even with no flash. I really don't understand what the big deal is? If I have don't have my very own photo, I have to buy a book? I can just get it from the Internet, copy something that some other photographer took. Does the Turkish government really believe that by not allowing me to take photos that it will somehow or other 'preserve' this for someone else? Misguided, selfish and ultimately, unenforceable rules. But hey, I'm here to do my bit for international tourism and the economy of Turkey."

"What brought that on?" Barbie muttered under her breath.

Hearing her, Georgia answered in a confidential whisper, "Spent too much money on souvenirs last weekend, no money left for this trip. She's just a bit whiney today. Forgive her, Barbie," She continued sarcastically, "After all, we are in a holy place."

Barbie chuckled, Colleen's rant was the least of their worries.

They climbed slowly up the hill to the courtyard below the entrance to the Dark Church. They paid and entered together. A long staircase took them to the upper part of the church. Below they could see a previous church, and ahead, the beautifully restored twelfth and thirteenth century paintings done by using mirrors as the church was always 'dark'. Maureen and Charlene took turns reading the guidebook, so the other could tip back her head and admire the paintings. Even though the group did not know all the saints, scenes and significance, they could imagine the painters on scaffolds, twisting their bodies to daub on the paint in the dim light. The paintings were of a primitive type, but vibrated with color and amazing eyes that followed the spectators. A huge fish sitting on the table of the Last Supper threatened to tip off and fall on the floor; lack of perspective gave it a childlike feeling. The scene of Jesus on the Cross was extraordinary. A thin suggestion of a white cloth covered Jesus' loins and his eyes closed in agony, even as his torso spoke of well-muscled strength. Blood spurted from a neat black hole in his side as a fully equipped Roman soldier stood in the background, waiting for Jesus' death to snatch the cloak.

Barbie stood open-mouthed as scene after scene appeared before her. Primitive, yes, but full of details and the paint was fresh and undamaged! Restored, she reminded herself. Fresh paint, so no wonder it looks good.

All too soon, they were thrust out of the church by the authority of the guards, who probably cared little for the job, nor the paintings, and certainly not argumentative tourists. The group left satisfied and full of images. Colleen started in on her Catholic childhood and how she recognized the various stories from the Bible. Judas figured in her story-telling in a big way. Maureen hushed her with the wish not to hear garbled versions of favorite bedtime stories. The two then began to compare their upbringings, one very old-fashioned and conservative, the other a more modern, 'new Catholic'. When they began on their admiration or not of recent Popes, Barbie wandered away. There were a few more churches to see, but she really wanted some time to just take in the beauty of the place.

Georgia called out a 'goodbye' to everyone and indicated she would take a hike further up the hill and get a view of the whole of the region. Geoff mumbled a desire to take some photos and he too, headed off towards the exit. The 'eens' slowly meandered towards the coffee shop. Recep's wife led the children off towards the toilets, while Recep, first checking with his wife that they each had mobile phones, expressed a desire to see how far south the park went and how high he might be able to climb in that direction. Barbie decided that she would just wander. She felt safe here, in the park, surrounded by hundreds of people. The fairy chimneys and dove cotes further down the hill called out to her.

A breeze blew up and shivering, Barbie took out her jacket, the cheap one she had bought in Kizilay. She knew that it was a common type, but it served the purpose well; it was rainproof and kept the wind out. She slipped it on as she said good-bye to everyone.

Following the cement path down the hill, she came to a wide overlook, where guests were held back from falling by a low fence. A magnificent view lay at her feet; a gorge, full of rough gray-green low-growing shrubs, the water invisible, if there was any. Directly across the canyon from her were hundreds of dovecotes. Carved into the hillside in neat rows and columns, they resembled book shelves or tiny storage units. Which they were, in a sense, a storage space for doves, their eggs and their guano. Accessible from the inside, many were elaborately constructed with a coating on the inside that made them slippery to discourage wild predators from climbing into the nests. No one knew how old they were, but hundreds of years old surely. The warm yellow soil here was not the red of other parts of Cappadocia. But even then, the white painted rings around the openings could be clearly seen. The story was that this was an attraction to the doves. Geometric designs appeared on the outside as well.

Barbie hung over the railing and studied the dovecotes, taking many photos. Then she looked further up into the clear blue sky. The skyline was flat on top, but deep grooves led to the valley below. As she watched, the shadows changed almost imperceptibly. Only by checking her camera could she tell that the shadows had moved. She found herself alone for a few minutes and she savored the silence and solitude.

Then she decided to try out her voice. She was alone, she would disturb no one, only a bit of lighthearted play. She studied the hillside opposite and cupped her hands around her mouth. "Romeo, Romeo." The soft sound that came from her mouth traveled through the air and bounced back from the cliff, louder and clear. "Romeo, Romeo, Romeo, Romeo." When the sound died away, Barbie whispered the next line, "Wherefore art thou Romeo?" There was just a heartbeat until the phrase came back, sharp, clear and far from its mysterious origin.

She turned and saw a few tourists coming her way and nonchalantly leaned on the railing. It was a party trick she did not want to share with strangers.

Again returning to commune with nature, she mused on the situation. She liked most of her colleagues, but this trip had been difficult. Ted Baxter dying hadn't made life easier for them and the niggling feeling that all was certainly not right with his death would not leave her for long.

Barbie heard a distant noise. A cry? A scream? A shout of exuberance? She turned around and realized everyone had deserted her on the lowest level platform overlooking the gorge. The entire Open Air Museum and its tourists were above her. She could see figures almost at the skyline on the hills that overlooked the Museum and other ant-sized figures here and there. She then heard the noise again. Definitely NOT a happy noise. She saw figures running to the right, towards the farthest end of the Museum away from the road.

She slowly headed in that direction, drawn by the excitement, whether it be good or bad, a universal human reaction to something out of the ordinary. She heard more cries or screams and then a loud, deep voice yell, "Help."

Barbie ran. She quickly got out of breath as she headed up the hill, the steep steps and inclines slowing her down. Getting old, she thought, or maybe too much running the past two days. She saw a group of people at the last and highest overlook, many being agitated, some crying, others calling for help and a doctor. As she neared the group, she found her way blocked by people, but they stepped aside to let her pass easily when they saw her. She was surprised at this, but did not think anything more of it. She had not identified herself as a person who could help, but the crowd stepped back nonetheless.

She found a crush of bodies near the cause of the commotion, but when they too looked up, they scooted backwards and let Barbie proceed. At last she could see someone lying on the ground and others stooping over the prone figure. As she came nearer, someone stopped her briefly,

"I'm sorry, do you… Are you..?" Quizzically Barbie looked at the man who asked this bizarre non-question.

"Am I what?' Barbie shot back. Then she looked at the fallen tourist at her feet. Her breath sucked in involuntarily as she stared at the woman lying on the ground in front of her. The same blue jacket that she wore, the cheap blue windbreaker she had bought in Kizilay, was wrapped around the woman. But when she looked at the back of her head and hair, it was as if she looked into a mirror. The woman could have been her sister or her daughter. Her hair, the same pale blond color, cut the exact same length and curled exactly like Barbie's, appeared in a fogged vision. Her face was obviously not Barbie's and anyone who knew Barbie would never have mistaken one for the other. But the other characteristics were uncannily similar.

What caused Barbie to choke and stifle a scream was that bright red blood oozed out of the younger woman's head, the blonde hair matted with the viscous liquid. Not far away lay a rock, small, sharp and partially covered with blood. The woman stirred and open her eyes briefly. She appeared to be only moderately injured, not dying and certainly not dead. Barbie breathed a sigh of relief. She would live, and hopefully not be so injured as to lose her whole vacation and hate the idea of Painted Churches and Fairy Chimneys for the rest of her life.

Barbie turned to leave; she could do nothing more. But she whispered under her breath, "Someone thought it was me."

Chapter Thirteen: Invitation to a Quad Bike Tour

Barbie slunk away. She felt eyes staring at her back as she made her way down to the entrance. Perhaps many had seen the resemblance and had also mistaken her for a relative, or a friend wearing the same jacket. She could do nothing; she wasn't a nurse or a doctor. It was not until she approached the entrance and ran into the 'eens' that she thought maybe she should have tried to find where the rock had been thrown from. The incident had shaken her too much to concentrate on finding the culprit. But she also knew that she was the intended object of the attack and that when the perpetrator found out, she would again be the target. She shivered.

Charlene spotted Barbie first, "Hey, Barbie, want to walk back with us?"

"What's the fuss about, I heard people talking about a rock fall or something," Maureen said, looking closely at Barbie's face.

Barbie tried hard to do her 'inscrutable' face. "Yeah, I was up there. A woman got hit. Blood. That sort of thing. I didn't stay long, there were lots of people to help."

"What happened?" demanded Coleen.

"Don't really know. A rock, a cut, blood. There were a lot of people crowding around. Hard to see. Lots of different languages. Nature is not always kind. It's full of wild animals, unstable earth and water, bad weather."

"So, it was just a rock fall or something like that?" Colleen said, backing off slightly because of Barbie's tone.

"As I said, don't know. Are you guys heading towards coffee, or lunch or something?" Barbie tried to deflect the conversation smoothly, trying not to alert the 'eens'. They had been with her when the potted plant fell, so they might have become suspicious if a 'from behind lookalike Barbie' was targeted.

"There's another church on our way down, our ticket is good for that as well," Maureen added. "And of course, the camel ride. Wanna go anyone? Charlene?"

"Naah. It's funnier watching someone else squeal, but I have already done it. I'll save my money for something that lasts longer," Charlene answered.

"Not even a photo that you can put on your Facebook page or your screensaver?" Maureen kidded her.

They had reached the end of the parking lot where they had spotted the camels earlier. The camels were gone, as were the thermoses and bags that had been piled under a tree.

Barbie stopped and looked around. The disappearance of the camels seemed ominous to her. Who were they, she wondered. Why had they left, just when the tour buses were due to be filling up? Had they gone higher on the mountain? Were they the ones who had thrown the rock? Maybe she was reading too much into this incident. Perhaps it had nothing to do with Ted Baxter. Barbie's imagination getting the better of her again? Or was it? These camel people were probably not from here; probably Kurds from the mountains in the south and east of the country. Strangers, tolerated, but maybe not well liked. Barbie chided herself for thinking that just because they were outsiders they would be responsible for something like this. No, coincidence. But maybe they knew something, saw something??

"Hey, Barbie. We're over here, looking at this church, the Buckle Church!" Charlene called to her.

They went into the church, newly renovated and closely guarded against photo takers. The entrance contained information about the renovation, when and how. The frescoes had been restored, many in the rather garish colors of hundreds of years ago. Colleen was lecturing, or was it pointing out, the scenes on the walls. The story of the annunciation, the birth, the Wise Men's visit, the flight to Egypt, and then the ministry of Christ, walking on water, loaves and fishes, raising Lazarus from the dead. And the last few days of Jesus' life, the donkey ride into Jerusalem, the road to Golgotha, the crucifixion, the empty tomb. It was all there. The gospels brought to life. And there were also saints with their halos, bishops with their miters and rich robes, the colors shimmering in the dim light. For a few minutes Barbie felt transported back into a lost time, before electricity, machines and the internet gave them too much complexity. Here was an example of a simple faith, a simple life.

Yeah, she thought to herself with a sneer of cynicism. They still had murder, complex relationships and liars. What had happened in Goreme yesterday was not at all different. The same kind of elemental hatred, fear, taking an opportunity for revenge. Murder was, for very good reason, against all religious tenets, in all religions. If killing was done, it was done for reasons: to appease the gods, in war, retaliation, punishment. But this killing, who had done it and why? She shivered in the coolness of the church and realized that she had lost her group. Another noisy group, Germans it sounded like, had come into the church and were being lectured by a tour guide. Time to leave.

In the bright sun outside, Barbie was momentarily blinded. The earth gave back a smell of dust, animals, and car exhaust. What had this place become? Tainted by modernization or saved from neglect and destruction by tourism? Stop with the philosophy, Barbie told herself. Try to enjoy what you can, keep your eyes open and work on figuring out what had been happening the last two days.

"So, Barbie, are you coming with us to the pottery shop?" Maureen called out to the distracted Barbie.

"Not before I have a glass of pomegranate juice," she replied, pointing to a stand across the street. The four English teachers crossed the street. Barbie felt herself salivating as the stand owner took a large, not very clean looking knife, and whacked open a dozen pomegranates. The red juice ran over the wooden board and dripped onto the ground. As she stood mesmerized by the dripping red liquid, her thoughts turned again to her questions earlier. Who and why?

A glass of blood red liquid was shoved into her hand and one of the 'eens' said to her, "I've got it, cheap enough!" Barbie sniffed and tried to block out the thought of the metallic smell of blood and to enjoy the deep, fruity aroma of the juice. She drank and the sharp astringent flavor of pomegranates filled her mouth, washing away the thoughts of the red body fluid.

"Oouh," Maureen wailed. "Look what I did!" She stared down at a long red slash of deep red on the front of her pale shirt. She bent forward and it began to drip onto the ground. "I've been stabbed!" She laughed.

"How'd that happen?" Colleen asked.

"Malfunctioning cup, look," Charlene pointed to Maureen's cup which leaked juice.

The stand owner quickly tucked up a new cup under the leaky one.

Barbie observed the group laughing and trying to wipe the juice off Maureen's shirt. She looked at her own two-thirds drunk cup of juice and threw it in the trash can. She watched as it splashed up and over the small can, throwing drops of blood red liquid onto the earth. Too much spilled blood, Barbie thought. Too much laughter. She looked at the 'eens' as Maureen scurried behind a nearby bush, and quickly took off her shirt, exchanging it for a long-sleeved jacket. It was too warm, but clean.

Laughing, they preceded Barbie down the hill. The parking lot, the juice stand, the churches receded behind them and they entered the narrow part of the road. The verges were miniscule, so they walked in a file. Towering above them were a large number of chimneys. The smooth sandy sides were here uncut and unpainted beside the road, but the back sides were used as other chimneys were in Goreme. The traffic was quiet and they proceeded through the chute without much noise or bother, emerging on the far side to a view of Goreme that stretched down into the river valley towards Avanos.

"Here it is, pottery," Colleen announced. "Now, let me tell you about this! Most of the pottery here is actually made in Avanos, just up that road. The river is named 'Red River', Kizilirmak, because the soil is red there. They make pottery from the red river bed clay. The Hittites started making pottery from this red clay and it is still being done to this day. And they paint it like the Hittites did! Very interesting patterns, with goats and ducks and deer. If you go to the museum in Ankara, you can see this pottery with the same patterns. They also sell things in the tradition of other pottery, like the Iznik tiles, painted in blues. This showroom is the premier pottery place of Goreme."

Barbie lost herself in the explanations of the pottery. There were rooms above rooms, off of still more rooms. Some contained cheap pottery: small teapots, small saucers, large saucers, trivets, wall decorations. Some had massive displays of Hittite inspired pottery, including a pitcher which consisted of a cylindrical tube. Colleen almost dropped it trying to show how the ancient Hittites stuck their arms through the round part and then used a gesture like a Japanese bow to pour the wine into a wine cup. Barbie laughed along with the rest. They trooped down the wide staircase to the 'expensive' room as Barbie thought of it. Huge platters, hand painted with tulips, pomegranates, fish, trees of life, awaited buyers with a deeper purse than any of them had. One large tray caught Barbie's eye and when she asked about it, received the explanation that it had been copied from one in a museum in Istanbul. It showed a scene of battleships, their sails spread wide; the sailors and soldiers manned the guns and swarmed over the decks. The detail could only have been done with the tiniest of brushes and the steadiest of hands. Barbie sighed, and never asked the price.

They continued into town, looking for the others. Maureen used her phone to call Georgia and Geoff, to see if they wanted to join the four of them. 'Well, call Recep as well, while you are calling." Charlene laughed lightly.

As they wandered through the tourist shops, Barbie noticed that they had been 'found' by Georgia, Geoff and Recep's family. It was only then that she noticed what they were wearing for the first time today. Two of the 'eens' were wearing the 'shoes', the pink, yellow, green and blue ones that had been worn by Barbie's stalker. All of them, with the exception of Recep's wife and daughter, were wearing blue jeans, the ubiquitous garb of the twenty-first century. Maureen wore her light jacket in lieu of the shirt that had been covered in pomegranate juice and Recep's wife was covered, with a scarf, long sleeves and a long skirt.

"Look," squealed Charlene, "Balloon rides.

"But," Recep looked puzzled. "We did that yesterday."

"Yeah, but I want to know how much they charge."

Geoff snorted, "If you find out they charge more, will you be happy that we had a cheaper trip, or maybe you will feel as though this one would have been a better balloon, or a better breakfast, or a more experienced captain, or a stronger basket? If you find out it is less expensive, then will you be angry with Kemal for lining his pocket, or will you admit that ours was the better trip? What difference does a few TL make? Comparison shopping is more disappointing than informative. Pay your money, take your trip, get your souvenir, stop looking, enjoy yourself," Geoff declared and then abruptly stopped his lecture. Charlene took one last look at the poster, a picture of a balloon of pristine, vibrant colors, floating through the most magnificent valley of Fairy Chimneys. "Photoshopped, Charlene! Not real, never get that angle, that scene."

Charlene put her nose in the air, offered nothing in rebuttal and marched down the street. They passed the bus station and come to Faruk's quad bike park. He came out of the small kiosk office and greeted them with a huge smile on his face. He took the 'eens' hands in his, one by one, and greeted them warmly, smiling into their faces. He slapped Geoff's hand, bowed deeply to Georgia, and greeted Recep and family in mellifluous Turkish. Finally, he came to Barbie. He took her hand, pressed it warmly and brought it to his lips. "And how is the beautiful princess this beautiful day?" Barbie could not help but laugh. Here she was trying desperately not to like Faruk, trying to forget the overwhelming effect he had on her and then he comes onto her like this. But she also felt a slight repulsion at the moist saliva on the back of her hand and then she felt a shiver of unease at the wolfish smile on Faruk's face. She enjoyed the attention but at the same time she wanted to reject the ridiculous greeting. Inappropriate was a word that came to mind. Well, never mind, he was harmless, she told herself. I will not succumb to ridiculous approaches like this. She looked deeply into his eyes, but today, the smile seemed more predatory and so did his eyes. Maybe Barbie was supposed to like this? She suddenly found herself drawn to the animal nature of his smile and the promise of closer contact. What did the scientists say about hormones and smells? Were they sending subliminal messages to each other? Barbie resisted the desire to lift her moist hand to her nose and smell what Faruk had left there. Stop it, stop it, she told herself. Be respectable.

Receps' wife took the opportunity to sit on a little bench outside the office. The two children joined her. Faruk asked what they would have to drink and used his mobile phone to ask the shop just across the street to dig up some cold cokes and the restaurant next door to the shop to bring tea. Faruk even produced a few small stools and invited the rest to sit. Barbie felt herself warming to this traditional Turkish hospitality and feelings of sympathy towards the displaced Turkish-American. She stepped into the small kiosk and said hello to the assistant who sat there manning the phone. Barbie perused the maps stuck up on the walls. They were detailed topographic maps of the Goreme region, printed from Google Maps. She was amazed to see the myriad fields around Goreme, tucked in among the fairy chimneys, hills and valleys. Small roads and paths could be seen running in among the churches, caves and chimneys. Rose Valley seemed to have the most meandering trails and paths. There was a veritable tangle of tortured turns in among the fields and natural landscape.

"Wow, look at all these trails!" Barbie said. She glanced at the assistant to see how much English he understood. Enough apparently, as he grinned broadly at her. He wore the ubiquitous uniform of T-shirt and jeans, and a meager potbelly hung over his thick leather belt. He also sported a neatly-trimmed beard. The beard was not that worn by very religious Turkish men, but rather a cross-over between tradition and modernity. It might be taken as a sign of solidarity by anyone of either persuasion. His teeth were in need of care, however. How could she tell Faruk to tell his assistant to get to a dentist, at least make friends with a toothbrush?

"Hello, my name is Hakan," he said slowly. "It is 'king' name."

"Hello, Hakan. These are wonderful maps. So many places to go! Where do you think is the best place?"

"Oh, Rose Valley is most popular. There are many trails and they are easy ride." Hakan replied.

Barbie discerned well-practiced stock phrases. But Hakan was understandable and personable, never mind if his English wasn't perfect. "And tell me, are there places where you cannot go?"

"Cannot go. Yes, Zelve Valley cannot go. It is a muze too. And Pigeon Valley has many dogs, they follow the bikes, so it is not good."

"What about Love Valley?" asked Barbie. She had heard Faruk talk about this, but had no idea how easy or difficult it would be. From outside she heard Faruk trying to rope the 'eens' into going there.

"So-so. Rose Valley is best, but very popular. Sometimes it is noisy and there dust everywhere. But the trails are good and easy."

Barbie could hear Colleen outside talking about the incident this morning. She recounted the story much as Barbie told it to her, but Barbie detected a few embellishments. Curious, Barbie looked out the door. She watched Geoff's face as he listened to the recount.

"And it really appeared as if she had been hit by falling rocks. I don't know how she could have gotten so close. Or rather, how the museum could allow people to go to a place that was so dangerous?!" Colleen declared.

Geoff looked disinterested in the story. Barbie peeked out the door further and found Recep and the 'eens' absorbed in the retelling. Georgia sat with her back to Barbie, but she too, seemed to listen but not be keenly interested. What did they think? Another mishap among the fairy chimneys? Did Barbie expect anyone to connect the incident with herself? She wanted to know if anyone showed any surprise or interest. None of this group had been there but Barbie; none of them knew that the woman injured had been a dead lookalike for Barbie, at least from the rear. What could Barbie learn from looking at their faces in any case? She turned her attention again to Hakan, but kept one ear tuned to the conversation outside, just in case more information emerged.

"So Hakan, how is business these days?" Barbie gave him a winning smile.

"Oh, madam, not so good. I am lucky to have this job, I really, really lucky. But this is not a good business now. Last year was good, and so, we have many new bikes. Faruk thinks that this year, this holiday season, quad bikes will be top. But, what can I say? This is not true. This is the year of bicycles and walking and tour buses and no one coming. I am man with wife and children. I must rent quad bikes. I must sell these ideas of beautiful places to go. But I am not sure quad bikes are best. Maybe going by bicycle is better. It is quiet, it is easy to stop. Or walking. The nature maybe should not have these trails for quad bikes. Maybe foots are better for the nature. But this is my job. I must try hard to make people believe quad bikes are beautiful, good, best way to go." He gave Barbie a crooked smile of stained teeth. Barbie thought that maybe telling Faruk to make the assistant go to the dentist was not going to be possible, given the climate of the business.

"But we have an angel. Someone has helped with the money, so that we do not have to send the bikes back. So, we do okay." Hakan said.

Barbie looked at Hakan curiously. "You have an angel? Where did this angel come from? What did he or she do for you? The angel gave Faruk money?"

Hakan turned rosy colored and lowered his head and voice. "Oh, it is what Faruk said. He says angel helped us out of poor house. We should be happy and kind to this angel. Before that, maybe I lose my job. But now…" Hakan said softly.

Barbie leaned forward and quietly but firmly asked, "Who is this angel?"

"Madam, I am sorry, I talk too much. This is not your business. I am sorry," Hakan hung his head even lower.

Faruk stood at the doorway. "What's this? Hakan, are you selling quad bike rides?"

Barbie, startled at Faruk's sudden appearance, stood tall. "Hakan, sweet man, was telling me about all the places to go quad biking. He suggested Rose Valley was the most popular, but that other places could be good too. Like Love Valley."

"Ah, Love Valley. Do you know why they call it Love Valley? No? Then you must come." Faruk smiled but Barbie felt as though this smile was not as warm as previously.

Faruk walked out of the office, leaving Barbie and Hakan alone again.

"Madame, madame. I am so sorry. Please, I talk too much. Please to forget. We are good now, there are no problems. We are happy now. Please forget the things I said to you. I will be happy to rent you quad bike?" Hakan looked a little green around the gills, as if he might be in trouble for telling about money woes and angels.

"Thank you Hakan. You are very kind. And not now." Barbie turned to leave. She was confronted by a photo of a group of large chimneys. Massive phalluses thrusting up into the sky. Oversized, masculine symbols of strength, power and dominance. "Love Valley?" Barbie asked Hakan.

He nodded.

Chapter Fourteen: In Search of the Perfect Lunch Spot

The group made preparations for moving onto the next venue. Barbie thought to herself that they were being a bit 'sticky' on this trip. Normally a group this large would divide up into smaller groups most of the time. This morning was an example. But for their meals, they seemed to want to be together. She wondered if it was because of the tragedy of yesterday.

They looked up the street directly across from the quad bike shop. There was a line of ATMs, very convenient for Faruk's business. He could insist on cash and point out that anyone with a card, domestic or foreign, could get their money and were then 'good to go'. No hassles about bad credit cards or a 'pay-you-later' plea. Just beyond that were more tourist shops, restaurants, hotels and pensions. After two hundred yards, the street gently climbed upwards and ended in a tangle of tiny streets with houses dotted along them. Just over the top of the hill was Pigeon Valley.

But the wandering group took another direction, to the south, heading upwards towards a cleared area on the top of the cliffs called Sunset Point. On the way were houses where people lived, a few tourist shops, a number of small cafes and of course, pensions and modest hotels. The road twisted and turned, carrying the group higher and higher into the village. The houses were mostly dun colored and had gates into courtyards. The 'eens' giggled as they went past, trying to imagine how many people lived there, the sexes and occupations by the clothes on clotheslines, vehicles in the yards and pets tied up and barking. Georgia questioned them, "What does a big barking dog prove? What does a small quiet dog show? What can that tell you about these people?"

Charlene laid out the rationale based on some outmoded version of conservative vs liberal and male vs female concepts of animal keeping. "Conservative equals dogs, liberal equals cats. Male of course, dogs; females keep cats. And the more animals, the fewer people who live there. Animals are substitutes for people as companions. And the clothes on the lines, of course. But seeing as how this is a holiday, there aren't many clothes on lines, so we have to go with the pet idea. And the vehicles and occupations are also really simple. Big cars belong to businessmen; smaller, more expensive cars, are tourist industry people. No cars, but tractors equal farmers. More theories?"

"Theories is right," Geoff scoffed. "What are we looking for, besides conservatives and liberals? A place to eat? Does the owner's sex have anything to do with the quality of the food? You can get ripped off by someone who loves dogs and hates cats just as well as you can by someone who belongs to a particular political party. I want a beer, that's all."

"Cats, look for signs of cats." Charlene answered.

Maureen sidled up to Barbie and tried once more to pry about the incident of the morning. "You did say that you saw the woman get hit, didn't you?"

"No, Maureen, I didn't see her get hit, I was way down at the bottom taking photos. I just heard a commotion and went up there. I did see her though. You didn't? You didn't hear anything? See anything? Where did you guys get to?" Barbie tried to deflect the questions away from her own situation and onto the 'eens'.

"We were all in the café/gift shop place. We overheard a few people talking as they came in the door. It was just overheard stuff until you showed up. I mean, it didn't seem our business. It was a foreigner, so that meant it wasn't Receps' wife and Georgia had gone up the hill. It was a woman, and we were altogether. At first, we wondered if it was someone we knew. They said a blue jacket and I remembered that you had a blue jacket. But it couldn't have been you, you were there, telling us about it. So, we didn't really panic, but it was a bit scary. Like last night, it was an accident; that pot falling was. But it felt eerie, hearing about another accident. But I guess if you listen enough, there are accidents every day."

Barbie let Charlene rattle on, hoping she wouldn't get any more questions about the woman hit with the rock and especially about the blue jacket. Barbie knew that the 'eens' had nothing to do with this and so was interested in their silence. She had seen Georgia's and Geoff's face and she was really certain that Recep hadn't murdered Ted Baxter. Had he? At this point, Barbie told herself she had to be careful. Whoever it was knew that she knew something more than the police and were trying to silence her. There, she had admitted it to herself. As she followed the group up the hill, Barbie began to get more nervous. Being alone was not what she wanted, but eating lunch with a killer was not her idea of a good time either. But, she thought, what about the others? Did she have any obligation to anyone else to protect them? Maybe she should try to warn the 'eens' about talking about the attack. Then again, if they are left in ignorance, then perhaps that would be better. But maybe they needed to shut up about it. She wished she could talk with Penelope. What time would it be when she got back after lunch? Maybe she could Skype with her then? No, ten hours time difference; Penelope would be asleep, not a good idea to wake her up.

"And then it was just love and I couldn't stay away," a young Australian woman was telling the group. In her twenties, with that Aussie look, tanned skin, blonde hair, dressed to show off a perfect figure, she sat on a wall and talked to the group. Barbie inched closer and listened to her story. "And my boyfriend had this lovely family who thought I was wonderful.

We plan to get married maybe next year. I'm here helping his family run their guest house."

"You don't happen to serve lunch, with beer, do you?" Geoff cut in.

She tossed her blonde mane, "No, sorry mate. Just bed and breakfast. But if you are looking for lunch, I can give you some ideas."

"Do the chimneys ever fall down? I know they look pretty stable and they've been there for years, still…" Georgia asked.

"Yes, they do fall. You see that street, down to the left? Well, last year, just a few days before Christmas, it was. We were driving down into town and the road was blocked. Apparently, it had rained and snowed and there was too much water. It had sort of melted and the top tipped over. It was blocking the road. It stayed there for a good week. But of course, it looks bad for tourism, a fallen fairy chimney in the middle of Goreme, so they cleared the street and didn't talk about it. But that was less than a year ago. No one was hurt, thank God. All is still well in the land of fairy chimneys, caves and underground cities."

"Will you stay here?" Colleen asked. "I know you said you were helping your boyfriend's family, but is this your job for life?"

"Could you direct us to a place for lunch?" Geoff persisted.

"Sure, there are a number of places just up the road here. My favorite is the Kismet House. They have a lovely terrace, covered, so it is not so hot in the summer, but the view is magnificent. Actually, I think the view is as good as Sunset Point. And the menu, well, the menu is pretty much the same as the other places in town. But they do a very good Nevsehir mantisi, you know, the small ravioli. The sauce is particularly good. And the Kismet Cave has pasterma borek. Pasterma is a local specialty of Kayseri, just a few kilometers from here and the lady of the house makes borek with it. Pasterma is a kind of dried beef…"

"Like pastrami," interjected Georgia. "Very tasty."

"And borek is a little like lasagna, only very soft dough. She layers the pasterma with dough and then boils it and then fries it briefly for a crusty edge to it. Great stuff!" The Australian woman grinned at them, knowing that she had made them salivate with anticipation.

"Bye, bye, thanks for the recommendations." The 'eens' started off in the direction of the Kismet House without much more coaxing.

Barbie found herself walking beside Geoff and she casually asked if he got his photos.

"Yes, I did. I actually went up to Rose Valley to get some good shots. I saw some camels up there, just grazing. I took some photos, but the young girl with them warned me off with some choice language and gestures. As if I would somehow or other make some profit off of her camels without giving her a cut, or that they were sacred beasts or something. I made it a point not to take any photos of her. Cow!"

"So, you didn't see anything connected with this falling rock incident?" Barbie looked sideways at him to see his reaction.

"No, not a clue. Sounds terrible. These 'accidents' are getting a little annoying frankly. As if the landscape is attacking us. Ah, lunch!"

They entered the small gate into a green courtyard. The gate was made of twisted grape vines and Geoff had to bend his head slightly to enter. A hand painted sign over the gate announced 'Kismet's House.' The courtyard was long and narrow, with a lawn and chairs scattered about. Over their heads, the group could see the guest house, built directly into the perpendicular cliff that rose from Goreme to Sunset Point. The front part of the three-story structure boasted a glassed-in room, with a terrace extending beyond that.

Noisily they climbed upstairs, the children leading the way in the dark staircase. When they burst out onto the terrace, they were met with a 270-degree view of Goreme. At their feet lay the town, a warren of twisting streets. The architecture, without fail, was dun-colored and traditional. Flat rooftops sported left-over junk which no one could see from the ground or from roofs that were not used. The guest houses had terraces, balconies and favorable viewpoints for their guests. They were much cleaner and well-kept than most of the locals'.

The owner of the restaurant bustled out and with the help of a youngster, pushed the tables together to make a cozy seating area for the group. Menus circulated and the ritual began. Pasterma borek was not on the menu this day, but other heavy meat dishes were. Lamb, beef, chicken, all were available. Barbie chose chicken kebabs. Always tasty. She stood up and wandered to the edge to admire the view. She swore she could see all the way to Avanos.

"This must be a good viewpoint for watching the balloons in the mornings!" Barbie said to the young man who was helping.

"Yes, it is the best. Because the balloon companies fill the balloons up there," he pointed to the left, to a flat hillside just on the edge of Pigeon Valley. "And also there," he pointed to the north and slightly to the right. "We see them fly to the air so beautiful. Sometimes the photographers come here to get a view."

"Do you have any rooms with this view?" Barbie asked.

The young man smiled, "The best, and the best price."

Barbie laughed and thought she had better not even think of it. She didn't particularly like to get up early in any case and balloons went up very early.

Food preparation noises and smells came from a kitchen just below them.

Barbie's phone rang. She dived into her daypack and managed to snag it quickly. "Hello!"

Kemal's voice came through, but indistinctly. Barbie tried to listen, but found herself repeating Kemal's words just to make sure she got his message.

"You are going to the airport, yes." "And you are picking up Ted Baxter's wife." "What can you say to her?" "Chicken kebabs, yes me." "No, not chicken kebabs for her. They are my lunch, for me." "What can you tell her?" "Kemal, it was an accident. You can tell her that." "Drinking? Well maybe not tell her he was drunk, but maybe she knows anyway. She was married to him, after all."

Faruk stood suddenly and pulled his phone out. Barbie watched him talking into the phone, waving his arms. He walked to the very edge of the terrace and cupped a hand over his mouth.

Puzzled, Barbie watched him and then realized that Kemal was shouting into the phone. She too stood and moved into the enclosed dining room, still watching Faruk's antics outside. "Yes, Kemal, what is it?" "You want to tell her something?" "What?" "Well, wait until she asks you. Don't say anything until you have to."

Faruk rushed distractedly out of the restaurant and down the stairs. Barbie thought to herself that maybe Faruk was trying to get out of paying again. But he hadn't eaten his food yet, surely?

"Yes, Kemal, I'm still here." "Call the police?" "Yes, I think you need to tell the police that she is here, although I don't know what they can do." "Tell the police what?" "No, you don't need to say anything more to the police, he was just your guest." "Responsible?" "No, Kemal, you are not responsible." "No, you don't have to say anything, if you don't want to." "Tell her what happened?" "What do you want to tell her?" "What do the police know? Did they tell you?" "They didn't tell you anything?" "Well, you can tell her that, that's a good idea." "You think the police should be there when she arrives? Well, that might be a good idea. I didn't know that you could tell the police to do anything!" "Oh, the police said that you should tell them when she comes? Then I think you should tell them that she is coming."

Through the windows of the inside restaurant, Barbie watched the 'eens' telling the waiter to make a packet of Faruk's food, since he missed his lunch. Barbie snorted in disgust. He ran out without paying and now the girls were helping to have his food packaged to go for him. What suckers! But then again, was it because she had wanted to do that? Was she just miffed because someone had thought of it and acted on it before she did? She tried to act nonchalant.

Barbie tried to listen to Kemal as he fretted away at the arrival of Ted Baxter's wife and the police presence or absence, and what he should or should not say. "Whatever you do, don't say that he was murdered?" "Why? Well because I think he was, but we can't prove anything." "Just don't say anything. We will come. We will be there, some of us will be there." "Goodbye, good luck!"

Barbie cut the connection and headed for her rapidly cooling food. As she settled into her seat, she leaned across the table and said softly to Charlene who had wrapped Faruk's food. "Suckered you again, did he? Paid up and all?"

Charlene looked at Barbie scornfully, "Yes, he paid!" She held up a 10 TL bill.

"And we promised to rent quad bikes after lunch!" Colleen remarked.

"So, he did sucker you!" Barbie laughed.

Chapter Fifteen: What to do about Ted Baxter II

"News, folks, Ted Baxter's wife is arriving momentarily. I told Kemal that at least some of us will be there to greet her at Aladdin's Cave. I guess we need to practice our collegiality!" Barbie announced the contents of the phone call.

"I guess we can meet and greet the lady and then do our tour," Maureen said. "After all, I do think Ted Baxter would want us to 'carry on'. He was one for doing what we said we would do!"

"What exactly does that mean?" Georgia asked. "It sounded nice, but the tone, Maureen, I'm shocked at you! I guess you never substituted for him and then had him bite you in the behind?"

"Well, it was nice of him to organize this trip, wasn't it?" Geoff asked them.

Murmurs of assent were heard from around the table, but Barbie was still puzzled and beginning to get really pissed off at this. She had organized this trip! The research on the web, the guidebook trolling, all the phone calls to Kemal at Aladdin's Cave that she had made were not 'organization'? She opened her mouth to speak when Recep weighed in.

"Ted Baxter was with us for almost two years, which is a long time for a teacher to stay in one place here. So, I think we need to honor that about him. As a manager, I think this is really important. And his students appreciated his concern and care for them. Many of them came back and re-enrolled again and again."

Under her breath Maureen said, "Yeah, didn't learn anything in his classes, so had to take them again and again."

"And he seldom called in sick at the last minute. I appreciated that very much, and you must too. It is such a nice thing to do, not to miss classes so suddenly like that. And he was supportive of the other teachers, too" Recep concluded.

"Debatable," Geoff contributed.

"Well, he had some 'quirks'," Recep said, laughing under his breath. "Don't we all, but he was a good man to have at the Perfect American English Academy."

"Well done, Recep," Barbie interjected before any more snide comments could be made. "We all appreciate a good colleague." She glared at the others, defying them to make any more derogatory comments.

They dug into their food and ate for a solid five minutes.

"He did one thing that I, for one, admired very much." Colleen began. "He used to have his classes start with a really interesting warm-up idea. He put a topic on the board and all the students had to spend at least three or four minutes at the beginning of class talking about that to a partner. And he organized the partners by who came in first and second, then third and fourth, then fifth and sixth. So there was very little down time, everyone got to talk and they learned a lot about making small talk. He chose topics like 'the weather' and 'what I did on the weekend' to start with and then later he would chose more difficult topics like 'the next election' and 'solutions for traffic jams'. He was very dedicated that way."

"Yeah, Colleen, he didn't make that one up, you know. That was taken straight from one of the books I have on warm-up activities." Georgia sneered.

"Humph, his students did it well," countered Colleen.

"And he spent less time on actual teaching!" Georgia retorted with an edge to her voice.

"Well, I think he did work hard on some of his activities. I would often find pieces of paper that he had prepared left over in the classroom. He would type out scenarios for his students to practice. I thought that was dedicated and clever of him." Charlene added.

"I too, have found those pieces of paper." Georgia intervened again. "And I am not so sure they were good teaching efforts. I once found some with rather suggestive bits for the students to practice on. Remember that many of our students are religiously conservative and talking so openly about sexual things is just not appropriate. I may personally think that Turkish students need to loosen up a bit, but the fact of the matter is, we need to look at who our students are."

"What kinds of things were on those pieces of paper? Why didn't you say anything?" Barbie asked, slightly alarmed. "I mean, it reflects on all of us if one of the teachers is acting inappropriately."

"Well, they weren't all that explicit, just suggestive. It had to do with boyfriends and girlfriends and how far you would go on a first date. Maybe he was teaching American slang. Don't recall the details, just the impression," Charlene replied. "As a matter of fact, I didn't really want my students reading these things, so I went around and picked up if I was teaching after him."

"Well, let us not speak ill of the dead," Recep intervened again.

"Yeah, you are right," Barbie chimed in. "By the way, Kemal wanted to know what to tell Ted Baxter's wife? About, you know, the circumstances."

"The truth?" Colleen ventured.

"What's the truth?" Georgia asked. "I don't think we know that. But how about fobbing it off on the police. It is their jurisdiction, after all. I mean, we 'found' the body, but really, it had nothing to do with us."

Barbie looked at Georgia sharply. Georgia was obviously declaring openly that she had nothing to do with the whole situation. Was this a bluff on her part? Barbie thought that she still may have had more to do with it that she was stating. Was this a way to deflect a closer look at her involvement?

They applied themselves to finishing their kebabs as they watched the kids eat some sticky sweet dessert, then asked for the bill.

Georgia, who had been fussing with her smart phone for the last few minutes finally cried, "Eureka!" causing her hair to fly into the air like a red bullet. "Wifi!" She had asked about the possibility, and had been given the password, but had not seemed to connect until just now.

"Jealous woman," said Geoff.

Barbie whipped around in her seat to stare at Geoff. "Who? Who are you talking about?"

"Mrs. Ted Baxter. She's a jealous woman."

"How do you know that?"

"Ted Baxter told me. He said that he left behind a jealous woman. I thought it was a girlfriend, not a wife. I didn't know he was married. But he did tell me that he had escaped a difficult situation. So that's why I said she was a jealous wife."

"But why are you saying this now, what brought this up?" Barbie asked confused.

"Well, you wanted to know what to say to her. Well, if she is a jealous woman, then you need to know that and not talk about any other women."

"What other women for heavens' sake? Us? All of us? Well, don't count me as one of Ted Baxter's women. Were you Georgia?" Barbie marveled.

"What?" Georgia's head came up distractedly.

"Were you involved with Ted Baxter? Would his wife have any reason to be jealous of you? And you, all you 'eens'? Were any of you stepping out with the deceased?" Barbie asked as if it were a rhetorical question, not one that she expected any answers to.

Georgia rolled her eyes at Barbie and did not answer. She went back to her texting. The 'eens' groaned collectively. Barbie looked at Geoff with a sneer. "Jealous, of us? Gimme a break? What about you, did she have reason to be jealous about you?"

"I will not answer that. I merely stated that Ted Baxter told me that he had left behind a jealous woman. I thought that it might be important to tell Kemal that." Geoff said huffily. He stood and left the table, heading out the door.

"Okay, point taken. I'm going back to Aladdin's Cave and wait for Mrs. I'll tell Kemal to be careful what he says about the females around and to be forewarned that she might be a wild cat." Barbie stood and dug in her bag for the money for lunch. Once more she felt as if she had eaten too much. Turkish food was going rapidly to her hips and she began to think about cutting back on the bread, the greasy mezzes and the borek.

"Uh, are we really going to do a quad bike tour?" Colleen asked her fellow 'eens.' "I mean, we told Faruk that we were going to, but do we really want to?"

Maureen hung her head. "You know, we said we would. I feel sorry for him. He's been pestering us for the last few days and it is obvious by the number of parked bikes that he needs the money. We can always do just one hour."

"Number of parked bikes? Do you think there are too many, I mean, how many are too many?" Barbie stopped rifling in her purse. "Do you think he has too many, bought too many, invested in so many that he can't pay for them?"

Maureen ignored Barbie's questions. "He has a lot. But when a group comes through, well, he needs a lot. So, I think, ladies, that we should at least make an attempt, don't you?" The other two nodded their consent and the three of them got up as one and made their way out of the restaurant.

Recep and family had already left by the time Barbie and Georgia found their way out and on the way to Aladdin's Cave. As they strolled downhill, Barbie asked offhandedly, "Hear anything more about the incident at the Museum this morning?"

"Nope, nothing. I guess it was just an accident. Carry on." Georgia was distracted by a display of scarves hanging along the sides and the eaves of the overhanging roof in front of a shop. The multicolored scarves wafted in the breeze, caressing the faces and arms of hapless pedestrians and enticing them into the shop. "Do I need another one? Hey, look at this one." She continued as she fingered a purple scarf, long, very long, and with a contrasting section of some other material. "How does it look?"

Barbie checked it out. "You know, with your hair that color, I think it doesn't suit as well as if your hair was more yellow."

Georgia laughed, "Could be that color again next week. Wonder how much it costs?" She stepped inside the shop as Barbie waited outside. She watched as the 'eens' rounded the corner and went out of sight.

"Naw, too much," Georgia said as she came out of the shop.

They walked side by side, each lost in her own thoughts. Barbie looked at Georgia surreptitiously. Could she be a murderer, Barbie thought. Barbie liked her, although there was something aloof, alone, secretive even, about Georgia. It was trust, Barbie thought. I'm not sure I trust her.

As they passed the quad bike shop, Barbie noticed that no one seemed to be there. It appeared as though even Hakan had gone home for a nap.

At Aladdin's Cave, Barbie looked around. Obviously, Kemal had not yet returned from the airport, so she climbed the stairs to her room. It seemed extremely quiet, maybe this was a good time of day for a nap. Or maybe she could check her emails.

On the computer, she noticed that Penelope's green dot was on, meaning she had forgotten to turn off her computer overnight, or that she was up very early. When she tried to call, however, the connection wasn't good. She unplugged it, went outside and climbed the stairs to the roof.

There she found the 'eens' in sunbathing mode. Barbie didn't want to talk with Penelope if the 'eens' could hear, so she fussed with her emails instead.

At a commotion from Charlene, Barbie looked up. "Aren't you guys going for a quad bike tour?"

"Sort of, I guess. Oh, Barbie, you will never believe this. Finally, a real pass from Faruk. You know those eyes of his, chocolate brown with little yellow flecks in them? Well, he had them trained on mine and then he did the 'octopus' thing. Arm around the waist, heat radiating from those sexy hands of his over the nether regions. I was wondering if he was going to try anything on anybody. He had been so nice up until then. Anyway, he got another phone call and off and away again. He was so sexy and such a come-on. And then, bam, cold as ice."

"When was this?" Barbie asked, trying not to sound jealous, distracted or in any way not in control. Be cool, she told herself, just don't let any of that get to you. Jealousy is not attractive. Don't blush, don't let that lip tremble, don't pay any attention.

"When we brought him his lunch, so that's why we are not so sure about this tour," Colleen replied.

Maureen interrupted. "Well, Colleen is miffed because the pass wasn't made at her. We should check again if he is there."

"I guess you could always talk to Hakan, the assistant," Barbie said. She amazed herself at her coolness.

"Ah, the idea was to go with Faruk, as a guide."

Charlene slipped her shorts off and sat in her panties on a low chair, legs stretched out in front of her. Barbie chuckled at Charlene's display of leg and said, "You know, there is more than one way onto this rooftop. Look at that," she pointed to a low wall that kept the hillside from coming down onto the patio. "You can just climb up the back side of the hill, step over the wall and take a good look at your frilly panties! And not just that, I think they can see you from over there," Barbie pointed to the flat roof of the guest house across the street. No one was there at the moment, but it was obvious that someone standing there could see directly onto this balcony. "Beware!" Barbie tried hard to keep her nose down and not up in the air as she felt it wanted to go. Young hussies, she thought to herself. They will find out soon enough about men, especially men in this part of the world and their visions of women.

Charlene quickly put her shorts back on and looked around. A set of sheets and towels flapped in the rising wind on one side of the rooftop, the hillside loomed on another, and the other two sides faced the town and down the road towards the Open Air Museum. Colleen looked at the sheets and said, "I think they are Ted Baxter's." She got up and went down stairs. Soon the other two followed her and Barbie wondered if they would ever get their tour. She tried to stifle a twinge of jealousy. Did she really want to go on a quad bike tour with them? With Faruk? The thought of him set her off again and she put her head down.

Barbie looked again at her computer. Penelope was online. She called. Penelope answered immediately with a cheery hello, not even a scolding for calling so early.

"Why are you up, though?" Barbie asked.

Penelope's excited voice could be heard very clearly. "I just had a job interview from Istanbul!"

"But it's a holiday! Who interviews on a holiday?"

"The owner of the school said he knew it was a holiday, but he also knew that I didn't have a holiday, so he sent me an email last night, and I got up early! I'm really excited about this. I think I may be offered the job because he asked if I could start next week!! Imagine, starting next week! He said he could arrange a room in a hostel to begin with, then help me find accommodations. He also mentioned that the visa may take a while, so I'd have to be patient and have all my documents ready etc. Anyway, I've got those, and I'm ready to go. My sister has had enough of me and I, her. My niece will be sad to see me go, but my brother-in-law, who, bless his heart, has been very patient, said that he'd miss my chocolate chip cookies! And I can probably find a place with some other women teachers and there were opportunities for advancement and there were others coming about the same time as well. So, I'm sooooo glad. This is a bit unexpected, but I'm really excited."

Barbie let her babble on for a few more minutes, then cut her off. "Penelope, be quiet, listen. There is more trouble here." She retold the story of the girl at the museum being hit with a rock. She was unsparingly honest about the fear that the poor woman had been mistaken for herself.

Penelope squeaked, "Barbie, you have got to be more careful! Don't go out by yourself. Take someone with you!"

"A murderer, you mean? I am being careful, I'm alone up here on the roof, but they are all here below. And yes, the reason I told you is that I am afraid. I am being careful. I just didn't want to tell anyone here, but I <u>had</u> to tell someone. Actually, they don't know that the woman was dressed like me. None of the others saw the incident, or so they said, and so they don't know what the woman was wearing. I've been telling them that I arrived only after it was all over and that I know nothing. But someone does know something. I wish you were here. I know that you could help calm me down, even help me find out who is doing all this. At the moment I have no real evidence. I might have had some evidence from the scene, the rock I saw. But I am afraid to go back, afraid that whoever did it knows that I know something. This is not the first time and I feel targeted. But the more I know, the more vulnerable I become."

"You have that one right," Penelope answered. "Oh Barbie, I wish I could be there to help. Maybe next week? No, that sounds silly. You will either be dead by next week or this will have resolved itself."

"It's not as if I have a great passion to find out who killed the jerk. I mean, I really didn't know him very well. And the part I knew, I wasn't impressed with. So, why I am involved in all this?"

"Barbie, don't blame yourself. I mean, if you look at it all dispassionately, you are on the outside! Other than the fact that you went looking at the scene and saw a bloody rock, you know nothing. You can't pinpoint anyone. You are just caught up in this thing. You can get out of it. Who do you think you are, Superwoman, defending the meek of the earth? You can just leave, get out."

"Penelope, I can't just walk away now. Ted Baxter's wife is coming. She is arriving momentarily. Kemal went to the airport to pick her up. Even though he was just a colleague, someone I didn't know very well, and didn't particularly like, he was an expat in a foreign country. If for no other reason than that, I need to help as much as I can. You understand that, don't you? Besides, I really feel sorry for his wife. Most of us didn't even know that he had a wife. Here she comes and I have no idea what she thinks. But her husband has been killed in a foreign country and she has had to inconvenience herself and maybe she even loved him, and now he's dead."

There was silence on the other side as Barbie finished her long explanation. She watched the sheets blowing in the rising wind and thought about the loneliness and fear that Ted Baxter's wife might be feeling. The blue afternoon sky was like an underbelly of an intense blue balloon. What a beautiful place, Barbie thought. The events had been so shocking and sad, and yet nature refused to reflect that. But, this afternoon there was a wind rising, a portent, nature giving warning?

"Barbie, are you still there?" Penelope voice came through thin and crackly.

"Yeah, still here, breaking up though." Barbie replied.

Just then a commotion erupted downstairs. Barbie leapt up and ran to the edge of the roof. She could not quite see into the street, as the second-floor breakfast balcony came out farther than the rooftop. But there were arrival noises.

"Sorry, Penelope, talk with you later." Barbie stared at the screen which had gone still. "I'll talk with you later…" Barbie tried to drag the mouse to the little red phone icon, but it was stuck as well. She folded the computer up, prayed it would resurrect later and took it downstairs. From the second-floor landing, she could hear the commotion below. Quickly she unlocked her room, threw the computer on the side table and went out, relocking the door behind her.

In the lobby she found Kemal, Recep, his wife, Kemal's son and Ted Baxter's wife. Barbie was taken aback. The woman looked like Ted Baxter. She could have been his sister, not his wife. Barbie remembered the old saw about husbands and wives coming to look like each other as they grew older. But this was too much. She was about the same height, almost six feet tall, with the same mousey-brown-blondish hair that lay on her head with wisps flying around. She had the same light brown eyes with reddish rims. She had the same washed out features as Ted Baxter, sallow colored skin, blotches of brown spots. She was stout where Ted Baxter had been fattish and run to seed. But surely???

Barbie approached the newcomer and in a low voice offered her condolences. Ted Baxter's wife looked at her with mild interest and a vague expression. Barbie thought of jet lag and perhaps surprise or shock.

The police arrived at that moment and immediately consulted with Kemal, who quietly spoke to Mrs. Ted Baxter. Recep hovered nearby in order to help with translations and formal things. Recep was, after all, Ted Baxter's employer of sorts.

Recep murmured in a subdued voice to Mrs. Ted Baxter, "They want you to identify the body."

"You mean, they don't know who it is? You mean they have the wrong body? You mean that it might not be Ted Baxter?" she said incredulously.

"No, no, I'm sure it is just a formality," Recep tried to explain.

"Well, why can't you identity him? I really, really do not want to do this! I came all the way here and now you tell me it might not be him after all!" Mrs. Ted Baxter's voice rose as she spoke, and ended with a shout.

"I'm sure, it is okay, just a formality…" Recep's voice failed him as he looked at the fierce, horrified face of Mrs. Ted Baxter.

"What," she asked, "are we going to do about Ted Baxter?"

Chapter Sixteen: Kidnapped

"Tea, we will have tea." Kemal ordered his son to bring tea for everyone. The young man disappeared downstairs and Recep's wife followed him to help. The 'eens' appeared and then disappeared into their room, mumbling about going on their quad bike tour. Geoff meandered in and rolled his eyes at this statement and went upstairs. Georgia appeared at the commotion and raised her eyebrows inquisitively at Barbie. Barbie shrugged as if to say that she didn't know more than anyone else.

Georgia sidled over and whispered into Barbie's ear, "What's up?"

"Mrs. has arrived," and she inclined her head in Mrs. Ted Baxter's direction, who was now sitting on the only comfortable chair in the lobby area. "The Police have arrived and it seems as though they want her to identify the body. She is a bit reluctant and thinks that it should have been done already. I'm sure it has, but she is the wife and all. The 'eens' seemed to have gone on their long-awaited bike tour. And young Kemal, the son, has gone downstairs to make tea. End of summary."

"Not needed here, I see, but I will extend my condolences. Bad form not to, wouldn't it be?" Georgia approached the seated Mrs. and spoke quietly. Barbie was impressed with the tact that Georgia summoned on the occasion. Then it occurred to her that she should show solidarity and went to stand briefly beside Georgia.

"…and if you need anything, please let us know. We know how difficult this must be for you and after all, Ted Baxter was our colleague." Georgia gave a sugary smile to Mrs. Ted Baxter and also to Barbie. Once again, Barbie thought that Georgia wasn't sincere and that there was something odd about her 'sweetness.' She wondered if Mrs. Baxter noticed, or if the woman was too exhausted by her journey and nervous and upset about the reason for it. Barbie mumbled something that perhaps didn't quite make sense, about 'again so sorry for your loss' and 'good colleague'. As she did this, she peered at Mrs. Ted Baxter, who didn't seem to care much.

Luggage was carried into the lobby by Recep and yet another son of Kemal's. Kemal directed them to a room in the corner just beyond the one that had been occupied by Ted Baxter. At least she doesn't have to sleep in the same bed as the deceased, thought Barbie. It was an unpleasant thought, even if it had been her husband who had died.

More police appeared at the front door and did not wait to be invited in. Barbie recognized at least two of them from the day before.

Geoff came from his room and joined the crowd. The tea arrived just at the time that Mrs. Ted Baxter excused herself to freshen up. Geoff helped pass the tea around. Soon, the lobby became crowded and noisy, like a yard full of fussing, out-of-sort chickens. Two languages floated around the room, with translations being tossed about, corrected, amended and repeated. The Police happily tossed sugar cubes into their tiny tulip glasses and then slurped at their tea, making as much noise as possible.

Mrs. Ted Baxter returned and a seat was found for her. A glass of hot tea was shoved into her hand and she promptly dropped it, sending scalding tea and shards of glass skittering across the floor in front of her. "It's so hot, I'm terribly sorry about that." A new glass, as hot as the first, was shoved at her with an apology. Barbie quickly reached forward and grabbed the delicate glass with her outstretched fingers, gently balancing it between her thumb and finger on the rim of the glass. Only a few months had taught her the proper way to hold a Turkish tea glass. That, and a hardening of the skin on her fingers, had made it possible to function in Turkish society.

She turned and looked at the offending son of Kemal. She gestured with her left hand for a plate or saucer. She glared at him for good measure. She turned to Mrs. Ted Baxter, "Here, I'll hold this for a bit until it cools. We'll get a saucer for you. Do you want any sugar, it's awfully strong."

"No, thanks, this is fine. But why so hot?" she asked.

"Custom, and it is also customary to have it with lots of sugar. Never mind, you can have it however you want. Oh, thanks," she turned to the young boy who handed Barbie a small saucer for the glass of tea.

"Perhaps my lady would like apple tea. All foreigners like apple tea," said the senior police officer, smiling indulgently and slurping his second glass of scalding tea.

"Perhaps not," Barbie said smiling. She turned to Mrs. Ted Baxter and whispered. "Artificial apple flavor and lots of sugar. I don't recommend it." Barbie turned to the police officer who suggested the apple tea. "Thanks, but I'm sure she would prefer this now."

The 'eens' made their condolences to Mrs. Ted Baxter and squirmed impatiently, anxious to leave.

Recep, however, stood and hesitantly attempted to make an announcement. He looked at the 'eens' and shook his head and indicated they should sit down. He then launched into a, blissfully short, speech about the loss of their colleague and extended condolences. "Yes, our dear colleague was the one who organized this trip on this holiday. And so we are doubly sad and wish to say to Mrs. Ted Baxter how sorry we are for this, this very sad time." He bent down and spoke quietly to her as she sat stoically beside him.

Once more, Barbie felt very puzzled at this mention of the organizer of the holiday as she was sure that she was the one who had done the work for this trip. She reminded herself to ask Kemal, as the one she contacted, if Ted Baxter had indeed organized anything. He had stolen all the glory, and left all the grunt work to Barbie. Once again, she felt unsure about her role in all this.

A sudden silence fell. The wind outside began to whistle and moan through the building, causing strange noises in the ill-fitting windows, the uneven staircases and the bushes on the balcony above. The 'eens' sipped their tea, increasingly anxious to leave and not afraid of showing it. Barbie thought her usefulness here was at an end and she felt the siren call of her emails. Emails from home, while almost always boring, were also soothing in the sense of futile uneventfulness and Barbie felt in need of that just now.

The police did not seem in a hurry and soon small cookies were handed around. Barbie thought that as the police were here, she might get some sort of information out of them about the woman hurt this morning. She appealed to Kemal to translate for her.

"I was wondering if there is any news about the young woman hurt this morning at the museum." Barbie inquired. Kemal translated.

The officer turned to Barbie, "Why do you want to know?" His flawless English caused Barbie to roll her eyes and shake her head at Kemal. No need for a translator.

"Well, I was there, just after it happened and I wanted to know if she is all right. Not badly hurt, is she?" Barbie managed to open her eyes wide, bat her eye lashes just a tad and give the man one of her brilliant 'just wanted to know, no reason' smiles. This was yet another one of her hidden talents. Having discovered this at an early age, Barbie had perfected it over the years, ask a stupid (but not really a stupid) question, then pretend that you don't know why you did ask the question. Most people, particularly men, were lulled into thinking Barbie was an airhead and then would answer the question.

"No, she is okay, she is not hurt very bad. She is in the hospital, but soon she can go home." The police officer looked at Barbie whose face expressed the essence of care and concern for a fellow tourist.

"And you know why the rock fell on her?" Barbie smiled perkily.

"No, it was an accident! These rocks are not fixed, they are always falling down." He gave Barbie a stern glare.

"I am so sorry to hear that. Yes, accidents happen. We hope there are no more!" Barbie maintained an innocent look and her smooth words were neutral. The police officer could find no fault in her questions. Barbie realized that she no longer wished to know anything more about this. One more in a string of incidents that maybe should stay that way. She glanced over at Geoff and Georgia who sat quietly chatting to one another. Either neither had heard her question, or they were stoically ignoring her. In any case, neither looked discomforted, ill at ease or guilty.

While Barbie had been questioning the police, the 'eens' had quietly slipped out on their mission of mercy for local commerce. Recep kept up a banter of small talk with Mrs. Ted Baxter, Kemal and sons made sure tea glasses were filled and more snacks appeared. The police seemed disinclined to leave as long as tea was being served and they indicated that they would wait for Mrs. Ted Baxter until she felt up to identifying the body. Recep was not inclined to let them whisk the wife away so soon after she had arrived from such a long flight.

Barbie sat, listened to the wind and the low hum of voices until she was interrupted by the door bursting open. Mrs. Ted Baxter jumped in her seat and stared at the 'eens' as they filed into the open-air lobby. They stood in the entryway and stared at everyone gathered. Silence.

"Is he here?" demanded Colleen.

"Who are you looking for?" Recep asked.

"Faruk, where is he?" Maureen chimed in. "We went to his stupid office and he wasn't there. Gone. Finally, we agreed to this stupid tour, and went all the way there, but he had gone. Skipped out."

"Was Hakan, the assistant there? What did he say?" Barbie tried to quietly diffuse the anger. However, the 'eens' were right to be angry. They had been hounded for the last two days about this stupid tour, and now, when they were ready, Faruk had vanished.

Geoff laughed at them. "The old 'maybe', or 'later' or 'some other time' or 'tomorrow'. Did it ever occur to you that he just got tired of waiting for the capitulation?"

"Geoff, it was hardly an assignation of that magnitude!" Georgia laughed at the 'eens' predicament as well. "Don't worry, wisdom and knowledge about the fickleness of men comes with age."

"He said he would wait, but what a cad!" Charlene voiced her disappointment as well.

"Hakan the assistant, said that he had taken off on a quad bike. He didn't say much more and I had the feeling that he didn't really know that. Just that a bike had gone and who else could have taken it." Colleen informed everyone who would listen.

"And that he was angry. Faruk was very angry about something. Hakan's English is not so good, but it seems as though something happened. Hakan was mumbling about some guy named Malek. Do any of you know Malek and where we might find him? I'm not sure I want to chase around Goreme looking for him. But Hakan did mention that." Charlene added.

Everyone shrugged. The police had finally convinced Recep to let Mrs. Ted Baxter to come with them. Both Recep and Kemal offered to go, but she told them it was fine, she could cope by herself. Recep offered the services of his wife, but those too, were politely declined. The policeman who had come to Aladdin's Cave spoke to Mrs. Ted Baxter in English, promising that the identification procedure would be quick and she needn't sign anything just yet, that a verbal identification was good enough for the time being.

Barbie stepped forward. "Mrs. Baxter, I would be glad to accompany you. If you need any help, if you feel tired or anything, it would be better if someone went with you."

"No, no, I'll be fine. You are all so kind." She stood and retrieved her small bag and a light jacket. Barbie thought that it was a bad idea for her to go alone with the police, as she feared that they were totally inept and may make some horrible faux pas with a foreign woman. But Mrs. Ted Baxter had just given an indication that she was strong, independent and not about to let these flat-foots get the better of her. Barbie thought that she might just take a swing at them with her bag if necessary.

The police and Mrs. Ted Baxter left and the 'eens' slumped into the vacated chairs. "Jerk, bastard, idiot, never to be trusted," were phrases that escaped their mouths as they got up and slowly headed to their room. Maureen turned back and complained, "And I don't understand what Hakan said about some American? Something about Malek the American. Isn't Malek a Turkish name?"

Recep interjected, "Actually, it's Arabic, but very common in Turkey as well. Normally you don't find Americans with a name like that. But of course, there is always the Turkish-American with an ethnic name. Literally, Malek means 'angel' and it can also be a woman's name. In fact, I don't know many, or any, men with Malek as a name. But it's a common enough woman's name."

"So maybe it was a woman!! That sneaky bastard." Charlene did a good job of pretending to be a jealous woman.

Colleen and Maureen laughed at Charlene. "So, a simple case of someone selling to a higher bidder. Let's go rest, get set up for a big shopping trip later. Keep the home fires burning," Colleen said and they moved together towards their room.

Recep and his wife walked upstairs and suddenly the lobby was quiet and empty. Barbie sat back and admired the wall paintings. In front of her, on the wall just inside the entrance, was a portrait of a man dressed in robes and an elaborate turban, with half a dozen tortoises roaming at his feet. She had seen mention of it before. 'The Tortoise Trainer' was a famous painting that depicted the corrupt and ineffectual Ottoman Empire. In the twenty-first century, the phenomenon would be called, 'herding cats'. Was this supposed to be a statement about modern day Turkey as well? Or was it just a flavor of the old times? Other paintings were scattered around the lobby as were designs on the walls: flowers, vines and symmetrical curlicues. It was a busy lobby, with the kilims, antiques and all, but homey thought Barbie.

Feeling lonely, Barbie stood and started to mount the stairs. She heard a commotion and started walking faster. At the top of the stairs, Barbie met Recep's wife coming from the children's room holding a small jacket that belonged to Bunyamin. Recep appeared behind her and touched her shoulder. Barbie staggered back at her expression.

The woman that Barbie had seen as a stalwart backbone of the family, the silent, all-caring mother, the woman who effaced herself for her husband and children, now had come into her own. She wore an expression that told of pain, wild anxiety and uncertainty on a vast scale. Recep spoke a few words and she croaked out one and two syllable answers.

Recep turned to Barbie. "You were downstairs, right? Did you see Bunyamin leave?"

"I haven't seen him since lunchtime. When I came through the hallway up here, the door has always been closed, no sounds, no sign of either of the kids." Barbie looked at Recep. "Is something wrong?"

Recep's wife threw back her head and opened her mouth. A high-pitched scream began to emerge from her throat and forced itself out of her mouth which was held in a tight 'O' shape. The cry, born of an animalistic pain so elemental that it could not be described as human, grew in strength, volume and pitch. It shot into the air and filled the space, expanding into the hallway, down and up the stairs and out into the town. Wild, incredibly loud and uncontrolled, the cry escalated into a crescendo that abruptly stopped when Recep's wife ran out of breath.

When at last the cry abated, Recep grabbed his wife's arm and attempted to quiet the noise, the pain, and the forces that gripped his beloved.

"Recep, what's wrong?" Barbie asked quietly in the space that appeared between the wild cry of grief and the heaving sobs that replaced it.

"Bunyamin's gone. And it was not by his choice."

"How can he be gone? Someone must have seen him leave?"

"My daughter says that a man came, she knew him. He was talking about Malek. Something about a woman and Malek. And Bunyamin went with him."

"Could he have gone willingly, if he knew the man? That would make sense." Barbie argued.

"No, he would not have done that. He left his jacket and he was only wearing one shoe."

"Well, lots of kids get excited and forget something like that. What did your daughter say?"

"She was very upset, and she thinks that he did not want to go, although he said he did."

"Why are you so sure that he didn't want to go?"

Recep looked at Barbie with exasperation. "Bunyamin is not like other children. He would never forget to wear both of his shoes. Even in an emergency, he would stop to put his shoes on and tie them. He is a very special child."

Recep's wife continued to sob, protest, ask for her son, and express worry about his safety.

"Maybe he was wearing another pair of shoes?" Barbie suggested.

"No, he wasn't, here they are." He dragged Barbie just inside the door of the room. On the floor, toes neatly pointed towards the back of the bed, tidily put together, was a pair of sandals. One left shoe, pink, yellow, blue and green, sat beside them. The bed was made, and hardly wrinkled on top. Clothes were hung on hangers and placed neatly in the open wardrobe. The other bed, in sharp contrast, was lost under a flurry of blankets, pillows, frilly pink socks, dirty tights, shoes that seemingly had no mates and three little ponies, their long blond hair wild and uncombed.

Barbie remembered the obsessive-compulsive behavior of the little boy, straightening the forks and knives on the table and tucking in his shirt until it was perfect. Recep was right, Bunyamin was special.

Bunyamin's sister stood still, tears rolling down her face, terror writ large on her whole body.

Recep stressed his earlier point. "Bunyamin would never go without both of his shoes. He did not go willingly. He was kidnapped!"

Chapter Seventeen: A Trip to Love Valley

"Kidnapped?" Barbie stared, unwilling and unable to believe Recep. "Are you sure? Why would someone kidnap Bunyamin?"

Recep looked around. The balcony and stairs were crowded with people. His wife continued to weep, but the howling had ceased as abruptly as it had started.

Barbie snapped out of her trance and forced herself to think. This had something to do with Ted Baxter. It all had to do with Ted Baxter. Who, where, how, what was the plan; all of these questions swirled through her head. Stop, she told herself, think logically. No one here really knows as much as you. You have been the target before, why now Bunyamin? Maybe it was because he was close, available. But what could anyone do with him? Demand ransom? That made sense, but at the same time, it didn't.

"Everyone, sit down. We need to figure this out. When did this happen?" Barbie spoke quickly as the inhabitants of Aladdin's Cave took seats, where they sat for breakfast in the mornings. Barbie glanced around, and looked carefully at each of them. The 'eens', Georgia, Geoff, Recep and his wife, with their daughter now hiding behind her mother's skirt. Kemal and his sons sat as well.

Just as Barbie started questioning everyone, a commotion erupted downstairs. Silence fell and everyone listened. Mrs. Ted Baxter had returned. Kemal dashed down the stairs to bring her up. Everyone strained to hear the conversation. Sound bites drifted up the stairs, but no one seemed to comprehend why she had returned so quickly.

When she appeared at the top of the stairs, Mrs. Ted Baxter announced her annoyance. "A holiday, they said, it is a holiday. No one would answer the phones, unlock the offices or anything else. So far, this trip has been a debacle. I can't think of any other word for it."

"We have a missing child. Bunyamin, Recep's little boy has gone. We think it was not of his own free will. Do you have any ideas?" Barbie boldly stated.

"I have no ideas about anything. Obvious to all, Ted Baxter and I were not living together and I really didn't know much about his life here in Turkey. We did not always see eye to eye on things and it was better if we weren't in each other's pockets all the time. We were better with more space between us. A couple of continents, actually." She looked distressed as she said this. "I have no idea how any of this happened, or even why he would walk around in the middle of the night, drunk… Or rather, I guess I do."

"Were you separated, getting a divorce? I know that his death was not suicide, but could he, maybe he was involved in something you didn't know about?" Barbie asked timidly, trying hard not to sound pushy, even though that is what she wanted to convey. She needed some more information. It was no longer the time to be nice and sympathetic. Bunyamin was missing and it was quite likely that this whole mess was connected.

"You know, he was always getting involved in 'get rich quick' schemes. He always believed that the developing world held so many opportunities and that is why I think he gravitated to working in countries that were going places. Turkey was that for him. A booming economy, opportunities everywhere. And he knew some Turkish students, that's what brought him here in the first place. He always saw himself as an 'angel', bringing the money, the financing needed to bring a booming economy to places. I mean, he was a bit silly that way; he never did make money. He was always the dreamer, the entrepreneur, but it just never worked out. The man was forty-six years old, and nothing, nothing left of his life. A liver that was probably afflicted with cirrhosis, angry women that he propositioned, students that didn't get the grades they deserved. Whatever, Ted Baxter was a loser!"

The diatribe threatened to go on and on. Barbie interrupted. "Sorry about all of this. But I think there was something not quite right about his death, Ted Baxter's death I mean."

"It wasn't an accident, you mean?"

"Yes, that is what I mean. I think he was, well, he was murdered." As Barbie said this in public for the first time, she felt frightened. If it was in her head, she felt as though she could dismiss it. If she said it to Penelope, then it was telling someone who was so far away that it made no difference. But when she said it out loud, to these people, who were Ted Baxter's colleagues and who had found his body, it made it more real, and more dangerous. She thought of Bunyamin; his small arms that were always akimbo, the glasses that he constantly pushed up on his nose, his teeth too big for his mouth, his gangly walk and his innocence.

She looked at the balcony full of people. Those she may have suspected were there. Georgia, red hair flaming in the afternoon sunshine, was not a fan of Ted Baxter, but was not a killer. The same with Geoff. He was a bit off-putting a lot of times, not the best colleague, but not a killer.

Who was not here? Who had opportunity, means and motive? Motive was always sex or money, wasn't it? Ted Baxter had interest in sex, but Barbie couldn't see anyone having an interest in him. Money?

"Angel, you said he was an angel," Barbie leaned into Ted Baxter's wife's face. "He liked to be an angel for struggling businessmen, investing in their businesses. He hoped to make money that way. Did he call himself an 'angel', is that the term he used?"

"Yes," Ted Baxter's wife whispered. "That's what he liked to call himself. Not that he had a lot of money, but he had inherited some and he liked to see himself that way. Why? Does this have to do with his death, his murder?" This wife was as quiet as the other wife had been loud in her grief and anxiety.

"Malek, the lady malek, the angel's lady," Recep said.

Barbie looked around, hoping against hope that he would be there, appearing as he always did, unexpectedly, smiling, laughing, and trying to cajole them all into a quad bike ride.

"Faruk," she spat. "Faruk. Ted Baxter was his 'angel' and the business wasn't doing well. Money, money, money, the root of all evil. Where is Faruk?"

The group as one scanned the assemblage, then realized what must have happened. It didn't make sense; what did Bunyamin do to deserve this? He wasn't part of any of it. But maybe a crazed mind will leap at anything.

Barbie quickly ran up the stairs, staring at the floorboards, which were always slightly dusty due to the swirling wind that came off the desert on a daily basis. On the roof, she marched purposefully to the short wall that separated the roof from the hillside behind the hotel. Faintly visible smudges marked the lowest part of the wall and the easiest point to enter or leave from the rooftop. The sand on the hillside appeared disturbed. Barbie leaned further out, and saw the footprints in the sand. It was impossible to tell when they had been made or by whom. There were no sole marks to identify the shoes of the person who had climbed down from this point. Barbie raced over to the other side and looked down into the side street. Nothing there, no marks, and certainly no car, motorcycle or quad bike.

Barbie realized that she was wasting time trying to find minute evidence. It was time for speed, a time to find Bunyamin. "Bunyamin!" she called out once. She cupped her ears but heard nothing in return. No, if Bunyamin were here somewhere close, or if he had not been kidnapped, he would have come home. The conclusion that Barbie made was the same one that Recep had. The small boy had been kidnapped, taken against his will.

Barbie quickly descended the stairs where everyone still sat and talked about what she had said. The word 'murder' raced around the room and elicited responses from everyone.

"How do you know it was murder?" Georgia asked Barbie as she reappeared among them.

"Don't have time for that, but basically I went to the scene of the 'accident' and found evidence that there may have been another rock, other than the one that was obvious. I was then followed into Pigeon Valley. Scary. Then there was the potted plant that just 'accidently' fell last night. And today, that woman who was hit with a rock? That was no accident, the rock was thrown. And she was wearing a blue jacket just like mine."

"But just because she had a blue jacket on doesn't mean anything. I know the one you mean, everyone has one like that, they sell them everywhere." Charlene said.

"What you didn't see that I did, was that she had blonde hair just like mine. So from the rear, she looked just like me. No time for chat," Barbie declared. "Bunyamin is out there. He was taken, over the roof wall and down the hillside. We need to find him, before he is hurt or… We need to find him."

"Where is he? The countryside is vast and wide," Recep said, his voice tinged with fear.

"Kemal, how do we get to Love Valley?" Barbie demanded.

"Love Valley, why do you want to go there?" Kemal asked.

"Because that is where I think Faruk has taken Bunyamin. It's not as popular as the other places nearby and he needs time to get away, figure out a strategy, ask for money, whatever the reason it was that he kidnapped Bunyamin."

"Why don't we just call him?" asked Colleen.

"Maybe, give it a try," answered Barbie. Then she turned to Kemal. "I am not joking, I really think that is where we need to start looking." She turned to Colleen who shook her head, no answer. "Try the office? Do you have the number?"

"Kemal, call the police, they need to help us. Faruk might be very dangerous, but we need everyone we can. Recep, help us. Do they have sniffer dogs here do you think?" Barbie asked the increasingly distraught Recep as the concept gradually sunk in that Bunyamin had actually been kidnapped.

Georgia weighed in, "We should try to get quad bikes. If Faruk is on a quad bike, then we could follow more easily with the bikes."

"That frankly gives me the creeps! I don't ever want to see or hear about quad bikes ever again," declared Maureen.

"Everybody, get your water bottles, snacks, jackets, good walking shoes, small backpacks to carry it all in. Flashlights for everyone." Georgia said this at a run to her own room to outfit herself. Barbie, thankful for the list of things to take, ran to her room and scooped up the items. She found two granola bars that she shoved into her pack.

Within two minutes she was back, and along with Georgia was organizing water and apples from the fridge. Recep settled his wife and daughter in the lobby. They were too frightened to stay in their room alone. Mrs. Ted Baxter joined them.

Kemal and Recep consulted in Turkish; a phone call was made to the police. "We can take the small van. It can carry many people. We can all go together."

Just as the PAEA teachers finished their preparations, the police arrived. The police chief was accompanied by one young policeman. The police chief seemed to think it was a hoax, a runaway child, but offered the one young man. "We have a holiday. We cannot give you more than this. If this child is not back by morning, we can invite more and maybe people from the town. But now," he shrugged. "You are lucky to have this one. So many problems."

Georgia urged the 'eens' to be quick and collect the items needed. She seemed to have acquired a commanding attitude that made everyone do what she said. Her voice had a deeper, more forceful tone and the rest of the group let her take the lead.

Kemal turned the van around and they all squeezed into it. Kemal sat in the front with Georgia; Barbie, Charlene and Colleen sat in the middle seat, and the three men and Maureen squeezed in the last seat in the back. They felt squeezed in, but the alternative was to try to find other vehicles. The police chief, sitting in the back seat of his car, watched them all leave.

He even waved as they started down the hill. He called something out the window as they went by. Kemal stopped, leaned out and had a brief conversation. He then translated for everyone. "He said he would have a man at the Uchisar end of Love Valley in case there was a person there. He also said he would telephone the farmers there. But there are no farmers there anymore. All the farmers have gone away. They work in Goreme now. There is no money in growing grapes, so they work with tourists. Hotels, restaurants, shops. No one makes wine anymore either. We have a religious government now too. No farmers in Love Valley."

They had to pass Faruk's quad bike stand on the way out of town towards Love Valley. Hakan the assistant was there, sitting in the kiosk. Kemal stopped and leaned out the window to talk with Hakan. A brief exchange between the two men was quick and inconclusive. Within thirty seconds they were on their way again. "No Faruk, no calls, no one knowing where he is. We go to Love Valley."

The van raced out of Goreme, passed the bus station and turned left at the next corner, the road to Avanos. The van roared as it sped down the road with its full load. Within a few minutes a road appeared that veered off to the left, which Kemal took with no delicacy in his speed or care around the corner. Within a minute, they approached another turning to the left, a smaller road with only the vague traces of paving. This was the entrance to Love Valley, announced by way of a small, rusted sign.

At this point, the road deteriorated into a one way dirt road, gradually becoming narrower and more rugged as it entered the Valley. It was another three minutes until they came to an empty open space where cars and buses had parked. Above them on the hillside sat a modest open air tea house. The van screeched to a stop and Kemal leaped out, heading for the tea house.

As the group watched Kemal speaking to the owner, a middle-aged woman, they stepped out and consulted with one another.

"It might have been one of us," said Charlene. "He could have gotten us here on bikes and then, forced one of us with him. But poor little Bunyamin, that's not fair. Why? Why did he do that to a child? A helpless child?"

Geoff said, "It's been that way forever. Men prey on the small, the weak, the old and women, because they are usually smaller and weaker. Throughout the ages, hostages have been chosen for their value, their treasure for the kidnapper. Money, power, negotiating chips in war and criminal activity. You are right, poor Bunyamin. Poor kid."

Kemal, after consulting with the tea house woman, dashed down to the car in a flurry of dust. He stood staring at them while he caught his breath.

The wind had momentarily died and the leaves on the trees overhead suddenly stopped their spinning and rustling. The cloudless blue sky began to take on the tinges of evening blue, the subtle change that came in late afternoon to herald the end of the day. Above them towered enormous chimneys, thick in their bodies and many clustered together in groups. The layer of hard rock on top was a deep rich red and extended for many feet into the air. These caps were thick and sat squatting on top of the massive chimneys. Barbie remembered the photos of these massive phalluses.

"We are in the right place. This is right. Barbie knew where to come. I don't know how, but this is right." Kemal said.

"But what is right? Is he here?" Colleen asked.

"Yes, Faruk is here. The woman in the tea house saw him. About one hour ago. He was riding a quad bike very fast. He didn't stop. But the woman knows him. He always stops for a drink. She has orange juice and nar juice, you know, pomegranate. He always stops. But today, he didn't stop. But she knows that it is him."

"Bunyamin, what about my boy Bunyamin?" Recep asked frantically.

"Yes. The woman said that she saw Faruk with a small boy on the bike."

Chapter Eighteen: The Search in Love Valley

Barbie heard the news of the sighting of Faruk and the boy, presumably Bunyamin, with a sinking heart. She stared up at the majestic, strong chimneys. Could they tell how and why the boy was taken? Could they show where he was? Could they tell if he was still alive? She knew that time was of the utmost importance. All of the nonsense about attraction and possible love just flew out of her head. What could she possibly have seen in him? Something of much greater importance now occupied her thoughts.

They fell silent with the news. Geoff cocked his head as if he were trying to listen for the rattling hum of a quad bike. The 'eens' stood stupefied. Until this time, they had never exhibited any outward signs that they felt Ted Baxter's death was anything but an accident that was sad, but was just a part of life. Everyone has to die. Recep began to shake, with fear, grief, hatred for whoever had taken his son. Kemal stood shaking his head, seemingly at a loss at what to do. Barbie noticed Georgia searching in her day pack for something. Of all those gathered, she alone seemed to have some idea of what they should do.

The tea lady was packing up her kitchen and bringing chairs back inside the canopy. Barbie asked Kemal about her, "What is she doing? Leaving?"

"Yes, she is going home. There is no one here. All the tourists went home. When anyone comes here, she notices. And then when they leave, she notices. Everyone except Faruk left. Of course, there are many ways out, but only local people would do that. The tourists always come back to this place. They park their cars here, or bicycles or even the quad bikes. But you cannot go far on quad bikes here. The trails are small and the way is steep," Kemal explained by pointing up the valley. The trail disappeared almost immediately into the brush and there did not seem to be any more views of it from this vantage point.

Barbie asked Kemal, "How do we search?"

Before Kemal could answer, Georgia stepped in. "What we do is this. We break into teams. Recep, Kemal, what are your phone numbers? Make sure everyone has everyone else's number. Do we get reception here? How good is it? Where are the police? I thought they were coming? Where will they be? Where are they now? I know we have one, but this is pathetic. Are there guns involved in this?"

Barbie stood hypnotized as Georgia organized phones and numbers. They discovered that the policeman who had been assigned to them had a phone, but no other equipment; not even handcuffs or a weapon of any kind. Barbie thought that this might be for the best, although it would obviously have been better if there had been something more than cell phones to counter a man who had murdered a man and kidnapped a boy.

"We go by twos. No one goes alone, ever. You, you, together; you, you, together." Georgia took charge. She assigned team partners, made sure that everyone had water, flashlights. She parceled out the three maps to those who were unfamiliar with the terrain. She instructed them on calling headquarters every 15 minutes. "If you are stuck in a depression or can't get a signal, climb higher, get a signal. It is very important that we know where everyone is at all times." The efficiency with which Georgia assumed leadership and control of the situation was a surprise, most of all to Geoff.

"What's with the 'do it this way' stuff, Georgia? Why should we be doing what you say?" Geoff whined.

Georgia looked askance at him. "Because I have experience," she growled. "I don't have time to read you my CV or 'show' you my credentials. Just for once, do as you're told!" Georgia turned to Kemal and the young policeman, who showed his nervousness at the Jekyll to Hyde transformation of the fiery red-headed woman.

The young man huddled close to Kemal and whispered to him, nervously fingering his only weapon, his phone. Kemal laughed and slapped him on the back. Kemal was used to Western women and their vast knowledge and capability. He had been corrupted out of his male arrogance of assuming that any man is better than a roomful of females. He said as much to the policeman, making sure that the young man had something important to do. Mainly, Kemal needed to stay here and tell the police where they were and what they found.

Colleen tentatively asked Georgia, "What if he has a gun? What do we do then? I mean, he is really dangerous, isn't he?"

Georgia snorted in impatience. "Bunyamin has been kidnapped. Think of him. The sooner we find him, the better chance he has to live through all of this. Kidnappers don't hurt their precious tickets to freedom until they become too frustrated. Let's find them before that happens. Don't think of your own safety too much. If you see him or find out he has a gun, then call back here, or come back here. Don't try to be a heroine."

Barbie's heart fluttered. She remembered the gunshots at night in Cairo during those days of the Revolution. She remembered the young man in the alley, red liquid oozing from his body. She shut her mind to these thoughts. Dwelling on them would do her no good now, she thought. She needed to concentrate on the present. Guns scared her and they didn't. She and her dad, in a stolen moment of father-daughter bonding that was ever afterwards kept from her mother, went to a hunter safety course one Saturday. Her grandfather had hunted deer in his younger days, proud of his ability to 'bring home a buck' and not the dollar kind. But he had also seen bloodied bodies of Japanese in the Pacific Islands during the War and had passed those ideas of the preciousness of human life to his son and granddaughter. Barbie, the child of dyed-in-the-paisley 60's hippies, knew how to shoot a gun. And she respected those who wielded them.

Barbie found herself with Geoff. She looked at him, realizing that she did not know him. She had suspected him of murder, and not that long ago. She did not know if he was a whiner or a stalwart companion. She did not know if he cringed at the sight of blood, or would back off from confronting danger, especially if that danger presented itself with a steel barreled gun. Would he panic if shots were fired at him? Would he run away if it got too hot to handle? At this point, Barbie had no time to test him out, and no time to change her mind.

They were assigned to the 'middle of the valley'. The other groups had been assigned to the right and left hills. It seemed to Barbie that the 'middle' was easier than the sides, less explicit as to where it started and stopped and easier to navigate, at the same time more nebulous. Well, thought Barbie, do the best you can, and glancing at Geoff, with the best you've been given. Barbie studied the map. Pathetic, not at all useful and perhaps a complete waste of time. Maybe google maps were better? She now cursed herself for not having the latest in phone technology. She reminded herself to come out of her dinosaur mentality and upgrade her telephone as soon as this was over.

"I've got Google maps" Maureen called out. They crowded around, Barbie now finding herself jealous of the bearer of the updated phone technology.

As they peered over Maureen's shoulder, the image faded away. Maureen stroked and petted her phone until the fuzzy gray image reappeared. She stroked it until they saw the road from Goreme, the left hand turning, the next left hand turning and the narrow road leading into the valley. Just as the screen began to show the place where they stood, a small dialog box appeared, "Battery is running low. Please recharge now."

Maureen groaned, Barbie silently snickered and the group broke up. They prepared for the search.

Kemal stood smoking a cigarette, the pungent smoke wafting around them. Charlene turned to him with a frown on her face. "Put that thing out! Have you no sense? How can you smoke at a time like this? Gosh," she murmured to herself. "Men have NO brains."

Kemal was chosen to stay at the tea house headquarters to coordinate. He was the only one with local knowledge who spoke both English and Turkish well enough to translate and understand on the telephone. The others were teamed up with stronger and weaker members. Barbie tried to figure out the logic, but noticed that males were matched with females except in the case of Charlene and Georgia. Charlene was the weaker member, being shorter, overweight and prone to stereotypical female giggles and flutters. Barbie looked at her partner and felt they were a particularly strong team, in light of the other teams.

Two by two, the four groups who were searching spread out and began to walk south from their position. Within forty-five seconds, they had disappeared from each other's sight. Barbie stopped as soon as she realized this, to listen to them. She heard nothing. It was as if they had never been accompanied by anyone into this valley.

Geoff stopped at a wide spot and turned to Barbie. "I take it that we are looking for any evidence that Faruk and Bunyamin have been by this way. Tracks, discarded bits of paper, broken branches of trees."

"Yeah, and scat, bits of hair…"

"What?" Geoff stared at Barbie.

"Just joking. I'm assuming that we want to keep as close to the center of the valley as possible. As the others are looking at the sides, and Georgia and Charlene are heading for the higher hill to the west, we want to scour this area, not to miss anything. Yes, I think you are right, we want to see if there is anything that can identify those particular two. But there must have been others here today, how can we make sure that the tracks we see are the ones we are looking for?" Barbie began to despair a little as she said this. Unless they could actually find the two of them, what good would it do to find a paper wrapping from a piece of gum? A set of tire tracks in the sand? A cigarette butt?

They walked on silently for five minutes, stopping frequently to take measure of the surroundings. At one point, Barbie saw what she thought was Georgia on the ridge to their right. She then disappeared behind a large chimney. Soon the trail began to rise, and they went with it. To the left, a puny muddy patch delineated the floor of the narrow valley, or a place where ground water had seeped into. She glanced at the mud, and then looked again. As she walked towards the mud, she called out to Geoff. "Look!" She pointed to a tire track in the mud.

Geoff had forged ahead and had to slide back down to the wet ground area. He squatted down and reached his hand out to the spot that was definitely the tire track of a small vehicle. It was NOT a bicycle, or a motorbike, it was too large for that. But smaller than a car tire. Quad bike.

"We'd better look this way. It could have been made this morning. I'm not sure about tire tracks and how fast they dry out, or when this was made, but this is the best we have for now." Barbie looked to Geoff for confirmation, although she did not wait for him to give it.

"Better see if we can phone." Barbie pulled out her phone. "No signal," she announced.

"Keep going this way, it's the only thing we can do." Geoff stood straight, squared his shoulders and marched off the way the tire tracks pointed.

Soon the trail split. It was hard rock here, no signs to guide them. Barbie pulled out her water bottle and took a short drink. She glared back at Geoff as he made a 'aren't you the wimp' face at her and then looked up to scan the top of the hills. They stood quietly and listened. There were faint noises coming from their right, scrambling noises and small screeches as someone slipped. It was definitely female. One of the 'eens' Barbie thought. They went on, a bit more slowly now as the grade became steeper.

Ten minutes later, Barbie stopped to catch her breath. Geoff pushed on a bit, then stopped as well.

The light had begun to fade from the valley floor; it was almost dark under the bushes, although the sun was not behind the horizon of the hills yet. The light bathed the upper reaches of the valley in light made of spun gold. The rocks absorbed the light and tiny sparkles were sent back out. The stately phalluses around them rose majestically to the sky, as if they were aware of their antiquity, beauty and power to inspire awe. The wind stirred again and the breeze of evening began to strengthen.

Once more they walked forwards always going up. Soon they came to another split in the trail.

"We need to split up," Geoff said.

"No," Barbie spat back, "that is the worst thing we can do. What if we find them? We can't go just one alone!"

"Are you afraid?" Geoff asked sternly.

"Yes, I am and so should you! Faruk has killed a man and kidnapped a child. He is not someone to meet alone!"

"Oh, I guess you are right. But look, we can just go one minute. One of us this way, one that way. Not even far enough out of sight or out of hearing. Then we come back. If that bike has come this way, we may see more signs. But it will take forever, if we have to go this way, then turn back and then go and then turn back." Geoff looked sternly at Barbie again.

Barbie made a face and thought. It did seem to be more logical. They were not in sight or sound of the other groups at the moment and there was a lot of territory, rocks, bushes, chimneys, caves, and corners, between them and the other searching groups. Besides, the wind had begun to blow harder, sending curlicues of dust into the air at every step.

"Okay, but only just around the corner." Barbie indicated with a nod of her head that she would go left. Geoff went right. Within one minute, Barbie stopped. Ahead of her lay a jumble of tracks and in the middle of them were droppings of sheep, goats, and the paw prints of dogs. No tire tracks. She listened again. Nothing but the wind and the faintest of bird song. The animals had been taken home for the day, locked in pens. The dogs, she hoped, had gone with their masters to hunker down in kennels or be tied up by back doors.

The wind dropped suddenly just then and she listened into the silence. Nothing but her tinnitus. Then, she felt it. Fear. The familiar fingers reached up to clutch at her stomach, her lungs and her voice box. Her breath speeded up, her heart began a wild pounding, squeezing blood through arteries and veins that seemed blocked and tight. Why had she let Geoff talk her into splitting up? She stood alone, in a place she did not know. The night was closing in and she knew a killer lurked nearby. "Geoff," she whispered. "Geoff," she said more loudly. A whisper, a swish of a branch, a scurry at her feet.

"Uuurhp," she breathed in. A mouse, or some other small animal, nothing more. She closed her eyes for a brief second. She willed her eyes open, her breathing to deepen, her heart rate to slow. She turned around and followed the trail back the way she had come. It was only a few yards from where she had stood moments before in a panic. She waited at the place where they had split up, still forcing control on herself.

She looked once more at the beautiful nature around her. Nature so beautiful, humans so evil. What was she doing here, she thought. What horrible evil had man done to bring her to this place? To bring all of them here? She stood silently and then called Geoff's name again.

Feeling that the way she had gone was not the right way, she followed the trail that Geoff had taken, carefully watching for side trails or other diversions along the way. It seemed wider and more substantial than the one she had taken, until she got to an enormous chimney that blocked her way. Brush grew on both sides in the level areas, although the sides near the chimney were made of rock, softly crumbling away. Then she heard footsteps.

Fear rose again and Barbie started to step backwards, but the footsteps continued. She thought back in panic to the chase of the day before, in another valley. Willing herself not to move, she shrank back against a bush just down from the chimney. She saw a shadow pass lightly on the other side of the massive rock, elongated because of the angle of the sun. The grotesque being grew larger, then shrank and disappeared. Barbie felt like crying. Why, why was she being targeted like this?

"Where can she be?" came a whisper.

Barbie held her breath and listened. Was it Geoff? Or Faruk? She shrank back further.

"There you are!" said Geoff louder.

"Oh, it's you. You scared me. Where were you? You left me, and I called to you." Barbie spoke rapidly and breathlessly.

"Don't get yourself tied into knots. We're together again. We can start looking now." He approached Barbie and grabbed her arm. "Look what I've found."

He dragged her a few yards until Barbie shook him off. "I can walk by myself, thank you." Barbie straightened, her fear vanishing in the presence of Geoff.

"Be quiet, he may still be around." Geoff continued quietly but quickly along the path.

Suddenly Geoff stopped and motioned Barbie to get back. They pressed themselves into the middle of a stunted clump of bushes, branches of which came out to poke and scratch them. Cautiously Geoff pointed to another clump of bushes ahead and to the left of where they tried to hide.

Tucked into the gray-green bushes was a bright red quad bike. It was dusty and scratched, but was new and shiny under the coat of desert sand.

Barbie noticed the silence where they crouched, but heard distant bird calls. The sunlight became more golden on the weird giant sculptures surrounding them. Nature was never more beautiful.

Chapter Nineteen: Sunset among the Chimneys

Barbie and Geoff stared at the dust covered bike for a few moments, trying to absorb the meaning. Was it Faruk's? It looked just like the others lined up along the main street in Goreme. This is what they were looking for, and they must believe that it was what they sought. The shadows moved again, the dark spaces became darker under the bushes. The sky was still light, still exuding a golden haze and still bright enough to see. Barbie took a deep breath, choked momentarily on the dust, and then sneezed.

"Shush," Geoff whispered.

Barbie countered, "Can't help it. But one thing is sure, we have found the bike. But we haven't found them, yet. This place is honeycombed with places to hide, places small enough to fit one man and a child. It's getting dark, harder to see anything. And this only tells us that they came, or at least 'he' came this far. They may be very close, or they could have walked a long ways. It's been hours since they went missing."

Geoff fussed with his phone. Disgustedly, he shoved it back into his pocket. "No signal."

"Which way did he go? He could easily have gone up and over the edge, be long gone, half way to Istanbul. On the other hand, he could have just holed up near here." Barbie's voice dropped to a whisper, "They could be just around the corner. I think that stealth is on our side."

"Stealth?" Geoff snorted. "With the 'eens' giggling and slipping and sliding. Voices echoing all over the Valley. He must know that we are on to him."

"So, are you insinuating that he has gone, or that he is in hiding?" Barbie whispered.

"Don't know."

Barbie settled deeper into the bush, which she now discovered was on an incline. The muscles in her feet cramped and she tried to ease herself into a better position. In doing so, she bumped into Geoff, sending him skittering forward, into the open.

He scooted back and muttered a curse under his breath. "That's right, let's make lots of noise, flush him out from his hiding place. How do we know he is hiding? Do you think that we should go back? Now?" Geoff was thinking out loud as neither of them had gotten any instructions on what to do if they actually found something.

"I don't know. I don't think we are supposed to face him alone, but there are two of us." Barbie turned her neck into a pretzel in order to whisper into the nearest of Geoff's ears. "We've got to think of Bunyamin!"

"Let me try going up a little ways and try phoning again." Geoff carefully stood and looked at his phone as he walked. Just before he went out of sight, he turned and shook his head. No signal. "I'm going this way," he mouthed. "Go that way", he pointed in the opposite direction.

Carefully, Barbie chose a small path to her left as she watched Geoff go off towards the right and the ridge that they could see above their heads. Trying to keep Geoff in sight, she followed the small path cautiously, looking for any signs that someone had passed here not long ago.

Suddenly she stopped and swiveled her head. She had lost sight of the red quad bike in the bushes, lost sight of Geoff and found herself on a dead-end trail. She stood on a narrow saddle between two large chimneys. She had clambered up a relatively easy slope, but what faced her on the downwards side was much, much steeper. Although she could see for hundreds of yards around her, she realized that she could be seen by anyone who watched, including someone in a crevice, a cave or inside a carved-out chimney. She ducked behind one of the giant towers and checked her phone. No battery life! Was this place haunted? Sucking energy from phones? She hoped that Geoff's phone hadn't been similarly affected.

Cursing herself, she looked again for Geoff. All around her the tall chimneys rose, and at her feet were waves of hillsides that undulated off into the distance. Bushes grew, grayish green and lumpy, dispersed randomly on the hillsides and down in the watercourse at the bottom of the gully. Sparse fields of grapevines dotted the slopes near the bottom. Most of them looked abandoned and overgrown, the result of tourism that brought better money than tending to the stunted vines. The sun dipped lower, and no longer shone down into the valley. Only the top of the eastern ridge was still alight. Barbie tried to scan the ridges, the hillsides, the valley. No one. Nothing. Not a sound but the softest breeze and distant birdcalls of sunset.

She slid down the hillside. She thought as she went that Geoff should have been with her, not off on some scheme to make a phone call. But the thought of little Bunyamin made her angry and she did not stop to think clearly. At the bottom of the small hill, she again entered a maze of bushes. A faint trail kept her heading in a southerly direction. Find that kid, find that kid! She said to herself. F*** the rest of them, they are just playing. We found the bike. They are here, somewhere. It is getting dark, must find the kid before we can no longer see.

A footprint. It was clearly visible in the soft dirt, with another, the opposite foot, just ahead of it. The second footprint was only a half. Other scuffs surrounded the footprint. No child prints, but an adult print. It must have been recent as the dust was soft and the print would not stay long. But was it Faruk's? Did he come this way? Or was it just a farmer's, or a shepherd's? The pattern was a modern one, not that of an old farmer's, but even middle-aged Turkish men wore modern soled shoes.

Enough, enough, she told herself. Keep going, time is NOT on your side. Then she saw the other set of prints.

There were two, child-sized, one of a shoe, and one of a bare foot, both only partial prints. If she hadn't been looking, she might have missed them. She might not have realized what they were. Now she felt certain, they had gone this way. Where was Geoff?

She caught herself before she called out. No, quiet, she told herself. Should she go back? She turned and examined the steep hill that she had slid down. She wasn't sure she could climb up that way. Was there another way she could go? The weight of darkness bore down on her. She crept forward.

The scene expanded and she looked again for Geoff, for anyone. The difference between the valley floor and the sky sharpened. The sixty million old towers of tuff rose around her and impeded her view. What was behind that one to her right? What about the cluster in front of her, only fifty feet away? What did those chimneys hide? A carved-out church, like in the Valley of the Pigeons, or did they hide a slim cavern, a hiding place for a criminal and a small boy? Slowly, Barbie sank down on her haunches and extricated her water bottle. Think, she tried to tell herself, think like someone trying to hide, to cover up tracks. Where would I go?

And where was everyone else? There should be noises out there! There were four groups, plus police that were supposed to come. Why aren't they here? Why can't I see them? The valley appeared wide, yet full of puny hills, large chimneys, small caves and waves and waves of eroded tuff. Barbie put her head down and slowly moved forward. To her right now, she saw a series of caves that undercut the hillside. A few of those had stick fences and primitive doors or gates as if they were used, or had been used, as paddocks for animals, or primitive overnight accommodations. They looked abandoned now. No smell of recent use, no animals in any of them. Barbie suddenly wished that the tourists had not come to Goreme; that these little corrals were still being used for sheep and goats and small donkeys...

She slowed her breathing and her movements, scanning the caves. Then she saw it.

A faint glimpse of a knee covered in denim. Was it just a piece of a pair of abandoned jeans, or were they covering a man trying to run with a small child? Barbie pulled herself back into the shadow of a giant chimney. If it was Faruk, what could she do to make him come out? She couldn't just run into the cave and grab Bunyamin. She also didn't know yet if Bunyamin were there. What could make him reveal himself without her telling him where she was?

Barbie had practiced for years throwing her voice with her father as coach. Her father, the hippie, the alternative job seeker, had practiced magic tricks, pulled coins out of little boys' ears, made balloon animals and perfected his ventriloquism. When her parents discovered that Barbie had been born with a 'voice' that caused her parents and her parents' friends to gasp in wonder, some had urged her parents to capitalize on this gift. But they had demurred, not wanting to make a 'pet' out of what could have been a child prodigy. Instead, Barbie's father had taught her to throw her voice, to use it for casual magic tricks or just for fun. She had done that this morning and now thought about how she could use this trick with the chimneys. How could she make her voice sound like many voices? How could she make it sound as if the voices came from many unknown directions?

She glanced around, choosing her target carefully, a rock niche that would deflect the sound away from herself and diffuse it over a wider area. She started with a whisper, "Bunyamin, Bunyamin."

The sound went out, swirled with the wind and echoed back towards herself and the cave just to her right. She realized that she might be able to use the sound to cover the noise of her footsteps and move closer. And she also understood that if she moved, the sound moved and she could give the impression that a multitude of people were here, calling, looking, searching for a small boy.

She began slowly and softly, gradually reaching a crescendo. "Bunyamin, Bunyamin, Bunyamin, Bunyamiiiiiiiiiiiiin."

Immediately after this last call, Barbie moved stealthily closer to the caves. She stopped when she heard small rocks falling into the valley, and trained her eyes on the place where the pants leg had appeared. Definitely a pant leg, attached to a moving leg. The wind started up again, blowing puffs of dirt and dust into the air. Could she make him believe he was outnumbered and surrounded?

Quickly she shrunk back into the shadow. She waited until there was another lull in the wind and called louder this time, "Bunyamin, Bunyamin," sending the sound bouncing all around this section of the valley, creating a confusing, overlapping horde of ominous, anxious voices. She peeked out to see the result of her trick.

A head poked out of the cave, looking, scanning the landscape. Barbie watched mesmerized as Faruk's face peeked out and turned from side to side. His gaze settled on her and he peered into her eyes. His dark eyes bored into hers, and she felt like a scared rabbit looking into the evil slit eyes of a venomous snake. His face was warped with a grimace that contorted his lips. She recognized the man she had met just days before, but now the monster in his soul shown through, so different from the Faruk she had imagined in her sexual yearnings.

A huge knife flashed in the dying light. In his right hand, Faruk held a massive kitchen knife and in his left, he held a quiet boy. Two large eyes looked at her and filled with tears that ran down cheeks in dirty runnels. Bunyamin mouthed her name, "Barbie."

She heard no sound, but the sight of one small boy precipitated courage – or foolishness.

Barbie stood and walked towards the two in the cave. She stopped about twenty feet away and stared at Faruk. "Let him go, Faruk! How can you do that to a little child? Take me instead. He has done nothing to you. Can't you see how scared he is? Frankly, I'm a better hostage. Blonde, American, what could be better than that? Look, I've got nothing with me, no weapon. Even my stupid phone doesn't work. I'm alone. Let him go!"

While Barbie spoke, Faruk rose and gingerly moved out of the cave, tightening his grip on Bunyamin. He looked directly at Barbie, his eyes dark pools, hair falling over his forehead, a twisted smile on his lips. He said nothing. Bunyamin wiggled slightly and Faruk let him wriggle slightly out of his grasp, the knife falling farther away from the slight body. Bunyamin's tears increased. Barbie held Faruk's gaze. Sunset came closer and the light faded even as they stared at each other.

Barbie leaned forward and whispered to Faruk. "Recep will never let you go with him. He will fight you, the police will force you. But I can talk with them, I can convince them I'm going of my own free will, that I am a willing hostage. They don't care about me, but they will care about him." She nodded towards Bunyamin, now standing quietly, one of Faruk's arms encircling him.

Barbie noted that Faruk was tired, maybe thirsty, not thinking clearly. As the sun began to die, Barbie thought he, too, was at a low ebb. It had been two days since he hit Ted Baxter over the head. Two days of hiding, perhaps not sleeping, watching every step he made, every word he spoke, every facial expression he showed. His mind must have churned, torturing him at every turn. He was tired, she told herself. Capitalize on that.

"It'll be over sooner if you let him go," she whispered, trying to be as calm as she could. "Let me take his place, let him run away. We can get out of here quickly." She looked directly at Faruk, with a look that she hoped spoke of sympathy and hope. She smiled at Bunyamin, who attempted a tiny smile in return.

Faruk shifted with a grimace. A cramp, thought Barbie, maybe he had been uncomfortable in that position for a while. Running, dragging a child, tired, thirsty.

"If you want, I have some water," Barbie offered cautiously. "Let him go. Take me."

Faruk stood upright suddenly. "Yes, you are right. You are more valuable. I'll take you." He grabbed at Bunyamin more tightly as he said this, wrapping a strong arm around him. "But he doesn't go until I have you!" he spat. "Come here, slowly."

From her half-crouch, she cautiously began the twenty-foot walk towards the pair. She had to glance down a few times to check her footing on the sloping hillside as some sandy patches needed careful negotiation. A small fence, broken and abandoned now, separated them at one point and she carefully stepped over and around the pieces. As much as she dared, she looked up, at Faruk and Bunyamin. She realized the danger in which she had put herself. Bunyamin was still a hostage, he may have been injured and she was approaching the kidnapper, a murderer, with the idea that she would be his hostage. She continued walking forward until she was within five feet.

"Turn around!"

Barbie looked at Bunyamin once more with a small smile and turned slowly. She heard a noise, a scuffle, and then her right arm was jerked up and twisted behind her. An involuntary grunted scream left her mouth. "Quiet, or this knife will find a nice soft place." A strong arm reached around her chest and held her tightly, pinning her left arm against her body. She felt a little movement at her left thigh and a small body ducked out from behind her. A petite pinched face stared up at her.

"Run, Bunyamin, run," she called loudly.

A jerk on her arm and a tightening around her chest choked off her words. She felt the coldness of the knife before she felt the blade against the skin on her neck. "One more word and I'll…" came the hiss from behind her head.

Barbie and Faruk watched the small figure dash down the hill. He had one bare foot, while the other was clad in a sneaker that was bright pink, yellow, green and blue. He jumped over the little fence in a single running leap and then tumbled down the slope beside one of the giant chimneys that hovered over the rapidly running small form. Within seconds he was out of their sight. When they could no longer see him, Faruk tightened his hold which had loosened as they had watched the escape.

Feeling alone, and suddenly questioning her reasons, Barbie whispered to herself, "Run, Bunyamin, run."

The last slice of gold light slipped from the escarpment on the east side of Love Valley.

Chapter 20: Love Found

Barbie watched the small swirl of dust as Bunyamin disappeared from view down the hill. She hoped that Geoff and or the others were nearby and that he would not get lost.

But these thoughts were quickly quashed by the reality of the cold blade at her throat. Barbie sighed; Faruk grunted. "Little one gone."

"Why, Faruk? Why little Bunyamin?" Barbie asked quietly, trying to create an atmosphere of calm and friendliness, if that was possible.

Faruk heaved and a long hiss marked the release of breath and tension. "I thought it was going to be easy, little kid. But I didn't think it through. I haven't thought anything through. That's Faruk, never thinks anything through. I can just hear my dad now. Never going to make anything of yourself, always going off and never planning anything, never thinking about what it will mean."

"But why? Why all of this?" Barbie dared to ask.

Faruk snorted ironically. "It was an accident. It was all an accident. I never meant any of it. I never, ever meant to hurt anybody."

"But you did. You hurt more than one."

"It was an accident," Faruk pulled harder on the knife. "You need to understand that. I never meant it. But he didn't deserve it. He didn't deserve to have the money. He never earned any of it. He never sweated for anything. He lied and cheated for his money. All the time I knew him, all the years that we worked together, on this scheme and that one. He never worked for it, I did."

"You knew him for years!" Barbie breathed this statement quietly, as if she didn't believe it.

"Yeah, since he worked in Denver and I was his student. He was a terrible teacher by the way. Always hitting on the girls, disgusting dirty old man. And never once did they catch him. He fawned on the administration. Always telling the secretaries how beautiful they were, bringing presents to the head teachers, the bosses. They didn't notice what a jerk he was. A really awful teacher."

"He couldn't have been a really bad teacher, your English is excellent."

"Well, thank you ma'am. But he didn't teach me this English. I learned it on the streets and in the movie theaters. I am an actor, you know, I spent a long time working on accents and phrasing. It hasn't been easy. No, Ted Baxter was not worthy to live."

"But you said you had worked together for years." Barbie was amazed. It was not obvious, no one knew. No one had ever mentioned to her that Faruk and Ted Baxter had known each other, and that they had known each other for years, and, it seemed, had been business partners. Well, she thought, Georgia did tell her something.

"He lent me money to get started in various things. Then, when it began to take off, when the store started to make money, or the IT business was sold at a profit, he would take over, kick me out, tell me to move on. He treated me like a gofer, worse than that, like a nasty rat that had somehow gotten inside without doing any work for it. He sneered at me. He looked down his nose at me. He treated me as if I had done nothing and he had done everything."

"You didn't get paid?"

"Oh yes, I was paid, but only enough to live on. He always said that we had to start small, that we needed to not spend beyond our means. That we had to share the hard times. I didn't see him sharing any hard times with me. When I pointed out that he always had a nice house, later a wife, whom I had only met a few times, by the way, he was quick with an answer. I was one of those, one of those with darker skins, I didn't deserve to live well. He said he was the one with the capital, he supplied the money, he needed to look successful. He always did the 'front man' work, so he needed to appear successful. I didn't like that at all. He manipulated people!"

"I can see why you would be upset with him." Barbie tried hard to remember her listening skills from counseling training. She thought about what she should say to keep him going. Let him talk, explain himself. She needed to appear to be on his side. She thought that in reality, she was in great sympathy with Faruk.

"He sneered at me. The way he looked at me, as if I didn't really count. He looked down his nose at me. Just like this."

Barbie felt Faruk shift behind her, loosening his hold on her. She turned briefly and saw that Faruk had struck a pose, holding his head back, pretending to look down his nose. She felt a giggle bubbling up and she quickly quashed it. Don't laugh now, she told herself.

"But the rock? How did he hit his head?"

"You are a fool as well. I did it. It was about time. But I didn't mean to hit him so hard. It was only to scare him. He got in the way of the rock that I was holding. Hah! All of you thought he was just drunk and fell down, cracked his head on a rock. I like that. That's how it was. That's what it really was. His head and a rock. Poor fool."

"But you were holding the rock?"

"Fools, all of you are fools. You don't understand, he didn't deserve it. He didn't deserve all that money. He had cheated me for years. He cheated all of us who helped him get money. He was always going on and on about how hard he worked. But I know who took the chances. Moving money from country to country hidden in their underpants or in false bottoms to their packs. That was risky. Did he ever care? Did he ever take those chances? Never, not once. But he benefited. Oh yes, he benefitted."

"You mean he smuggled money? He was breaking the law?" Barbie was aghast.

"You thought he was such a goodie two-shoes, huh? No, be honest, you didn't like him or trust him either, did you? I can't imagine why that woman married him. Maybe she was desperate too. We all believed his lies, his filthy lies. He was always promising, promising and never delivering."

"So, you killed him," Barbie whispered.

"Oh, you can call it killing, but it was justified. And I didn't mean it, it was only to scare him. He wanted the money back you see. I had made money for him for years, and this time, this was MY business. This was MY chance. I deserved that money and he didn't. He wanted me to pay him back, can you imagine?"

"But why did you chase me, why did you push that planter off the roof?" Barbie was now pushing the limits of her 'listening training', but she didn't care. She wanted to know.

Faruk threw his head back and laughed. A guffaw, a belly laugh that shook his whole body. "Ah, Barbie, what a cute name. Who named you that? It is dated, but a wonderful name. So much like one of those dolls. That pretty blonde hair, that wonderful squeaky voice and that look of surprise. What, a world out there? Not connected to me? You make such a good target. And why are you curious? What makes you want to sniff around, like a snooper dog at the airport? Going to the scene of the crime, going around poking your nose in where it does not belong. I was just making sure that you didn't keep doing it. No harm done, was there?"

"But the girl at the Museum. She was hurt. That was you, too, wasn't it? Trying to stop me, but you got the wrong person." Barbie felt indignation well up, but she stopped herself from making things worse by showing it. "You hurt her," she said softly. "It wasn't fair, for her. She was totally innocent."

"A mistake. Collateral damage. She's okay though, isn't she?"

"Yes," admitted Barbie. "But little Bunyamin? You didn't hurt him, did you?"

"Ah, that was another mistake. Mistake Faruk, that's all he does. But he's okay, you saw him run off? Not hurt." Faruk laughed ironically, a fake villain laugh.

"What about Ted Baxter's wife?"

"Hah, do you really think she is sad to see him go? Are any of you sad to be rid of him? Did any of you like him, respect him? Hah, I thought not. I heard you, all in an undercurrent. You were blaming each other. 'Who liked him? Isn't it sad about Ted Baxter?' Everyone had a grudge against him. Those who knew him longest, those who had worked with him, none of them cared. Some of them hated him. But no one would admit to the hate, would they? Then someone would suspect them. But me, none of you suspected me, did you? Only her."

"No, how could we suspect you? We didn't know you knew him. It was later, Georgia said, but frankly, I didn't believe her. No one ever connected you two together. Not to my knowledge. I mean, I didn't ask anyone directly, 'Does Ted Baxter know Faruk?' But we did not like him, that is true."

The silence filled the air. Barbie had hoped that if she could keep him talking, that sooner rather than later Bunyamin would be found and a rescue party would come for her. The sun had set from the valley and only the very highest of the chimneys had a faint glow on them. The birds could be heard in the distance, none close to her and Barbie wondered why. Did birds know about anger, danger, avoid bad vibes? Certainly, a lot of bad vibes came from her position. She shifted to ease tension on her calf and the steel blade touched her skin, cool metal close to her face.

Barbie's head twitched with a thought. "Her, who is 'her'? Georgia?"

"What?" Faruk also moved into a different stance, still holding the knife tight against her, pulling on her twisted arm.

"Her, you said, 'only her'? Who is the one who would suspect?"

"Her, Missus. Ted Baxter's wife. She knew me, she had seen me before, and I think she may have suspected me. She didn't know the rest of you and though she may suspect, I was sure she would remember me. We knew each other."

Barbie thought of the Biblical 'know.' Had they had an affair? Was there a reason for Mrs. Ted Baxter to suspect Faruk of having killed her husband? Even if there was not such a close 'know', 'acquaintance know' may have been enough. Surely, she knew about her husband's nefarious schemes? And if she recognized Faruk as an old student, old acquaintance, old business partner, she could have fingered him.

"But Bunyamin, how could you have done that? How could you have kidnapped him? He liked you. Come to think of it, we all liked you. So why Bunyamin?"

"He was in the way, he was there, he was easy. I was desperate. Actually, now that I have you, I think that you are better. A better hostage."

"Actually, Faruk, there is no one as good a hostage as a kid. Especially one that is so obviously precious to his mother and father. Maybe you should have kept him." As soon as the words were out of her mouth, Barbie felt like swallowing them back. "No, you are right, dumb blonde Barbie is better."

"Dumb blonde? You are far from it! No, you are a piece of work. You figured it out. That's why I had to try and get rid of you. Not kill you, I never did anything that would kill you, just get you out of the way. But it was her. When I knew that she had arrived, then I knew I had to do something. I had run out of time, you see."

Faruk, still keeping a tight grip on Barbie, shifted around in the small space which Barbie suddenly realized was a sheep pen. This one looked like it had only recently been abandoned. It was a cave with a wide opening, straw underfoot, and the fence that Bunyamin had tripped over in his flight. Faruk suddenly pushed her over and Barbie landed face down in a pile of dried sheep droppings. She lifted her head and spat out the pellets, but before she could stand, Faruk was back at her side. He had a short length of rotten old rope in his hand with which he proceeded to wrap her arms.

"It's over now," he said as he tied the rope the best he could, given that he needed to keep the knife close at hand and one eye on Barbie. The rope was a pathetic sample of a rope to tie a hostage.

Barbie thought about what she needed to do in this situation. She went slack as he pulled the rope around her hands. Or was she supposed to tense up? Never mind, she thought, this was not going to be difficult to get out. That is, if Faruk was not going to kill her like some sort of Inca sacrifice in situ.

"But this is it, this is the end. There will be no more debts, no more creditors, no more balancing this way and that, who owes whom. No more asking, no more pleading, no more holding back, wanting to fight back. There is no more fight. There is no more bad luck. Luck is gone, run out. I'm going and I'll never come back." Faruk pulled the last knot tight.

Barbie leaned over to look at him, her eyes bored into his, bold now in her hour of terror. "But can you always outrun them? Where will you go? How can you know?"

Faruk stood over her, handsome, strong, and certain; his dark eyes were pools that held depths that could not be read. He breathed heavily with a fierceness of decision and certainty. "No more," he whispered.

He pushed Barbie down into the straw and then he was gone.

Barbie struggled upright and strained to see where he had gone. The shadows had swallowed him up. She stopped breathing and listened. She heard the sound of footsteps quickly moving away from her. Above the sky had turned a deeper blue, but it gave no sense of which direction Faruk had fled. She struggled for only a minute, pulling at the ropes, and then found herself free of them. Quietly she listened again. There was a noise further up the valley and to her right, away from the direction she had come.

She concentrated on trying to place the figure she knew was there, running away from her. What was it that she hoped to do, follow him? Persuade him to surrender? She searched the scene in front of her, trying to pinpoint the direction from which she had heard the noise.

His lithe figure appeared, dipped down into a culvert and then reappeared on the opposite side. He ran easily, smoothly, not as if he were frightened or being followed. He did not look around, just moved on smoothly, as if he had a destination. He slipped behind a gigantic chimney, only to reappear as a black form against a quickly darkening background. Finally, he reappeared on a ledge between two of the phallic giants.

Stupefied, Barbie watched as he began to climb. The angle seemed impossibly steep, but the closing night made the shadows waver and shake as if the wind tossed the figure of the man about. There seemed to be some sort of handholds, or rocks sticking out. But he ascended so quickly and efficiently, Barbie had no time to see how he did it; a real 'Spiderman.' Suddenly he was near the top and only a few feet separated him from the cap on top of the giant chimney. Barbie held her breath and could just faintly hear heavy breathing. A burst of speed that seemed surreal brought the figure to the top of the cap. He stood.

Silhouetted against the sky, he could be seen quite clearly now. He no longer held anything in his hands and his elbows stuck out at angles from his waist. The slight breeze ruffled his hair, whispered along his shirt and flattened his clothes to his body. Barbie saw the young, virile man who had made her heart flutter just two days ago. Why did she do this? Why did she fall for the broken ones, the flawed ones? Why was she always attracted to the 'bad boys', the wild ones? In her mind flashed a scene from that old movie with Marlon Brando as the outlaw on a motorcycle. She was only fourteen but she knew at once what lust and desire was. It was the same thing that she had felt for this man. And now he stood on the top of an enormous chimney. Could he be talked down? Who could she find to try and talk some sense into him? What did he mean to do up there? Fly?

The cap was dark red basalt and flat on top. Slowly Faruk strolled to the edge. Barbie now understood what he planned to do.

In the background a rumbling noise could be heard. Noises, voices, shouting, but in the distance, from the north, where she had come from. Now, had they finally figured out where she was? Or were they still just looking, but now closer? She saw Faruk lift his head and turn it towards the racket.

Barbie loosened the last bit of rope, letting it fall at her feet. She moved out to the edge of the cave where she had a view. Should she call out to him? She could not open her mouth. Time passed slowly, as if she were drugged or in a dream. Barbie saw it all. She saw Faruk walk slowly and deliberately to the very edge of the cap where it jutted out over the thick base. She saw him raise his hands and then she saw that the knife was still there, clutched in his right hand.

The sound of people running and shouting came closer. She began to hear the clear shouts of men and thought she could hear Kemal's voice speaking loudly in Turkish.

Faruk leaned his body over the cap, his arms outstretched still and he pushed himself out and off into the void. It was slow and beautiful, like a feather falling through the air. His body turned slowly so that his head led the fall, like a well-practiced dive. Only there was no deep pool of water under him.

The cry came on the breeze, the baritone starting deep and rising, rising in pitch and volume until the sound reached Barbie where she stood as a full scream of terror and defeat.

Barbie watched hypnotized as the body in its swan dive disappeared into the blackness beneath. She averted her eyes at the last minute, not wanting to see the final end. She also heard another scream, a higher pitched one. It came from her own throat as she tried to block out the sound of Faruk hitting the ground beneath the chimney in his certain death.

Chapter Twenty-One: What to do about Ted Baxter III

They gathered in the downstairs dining room of Aladdin's Cave. A painting had appeared on the wall one day, Kemal said. Actually, it was over three days, and he hadn't given permission for the artist to paint it, she just took the initiative. Religious in tone and content, it mimicked the church paintings that the guests see every day as they explore the churches of Goreme and the surrounding area. A Christ figure was at the centerpiece of the work while his disciples gathered at his feet, looking up at him. He had his arms stretched out as if he were hung on the cross and yellow rays of sunrise, or sunset, or holiness, radiated from behind him. Barbie sat facing it, could not take her eyes off of it, could not imagine seeing this scene and seeing in her mind's eye anything other than what she had seen in Love Valley just hours before. It was as if the artist had seen what she had seen and flipped it into something else.

The clock on the wall read 11:00. The police had finally left. All were exhausted, but too tightly wound up to sleep. They had talked, they had laughed, they had drunk deeply from the bottles of beer, they had fallen silent, they had cried, they had asked each other why and how.

Bunyamin sat amid the hubbub wedged between Barbie and his father, Recep. He clutched Barbie's hand tightly, resisting if she threatened to let go or move away. Over the last hours, Barbie had grown accustomed to it, and wondered when she would be able to pry herself loose.

The police had questioned everyone, starting with Barbie. She was only able to persuade them to listen to the description of Faruk climbing the chimney and throwing himself off. They were not at all interested in long explanations of what he had confessed during the time he was with Barbie. She had told them he had confessed that it was an accident, but that he had been responsible for that accident. That was all they needed to know. They had Kemal identity the body, easier that way. They needed nothing more than an open and shut case. One foreigner dead, a suicide of the one who had murdered. Besides, as far as they were concerned, Faruk was a foreigner too as he had a US passport in his office. Foreigners having arguments with other foreigners were not part of their business. After all, they relied on the tourist trade as much as anyone and bad publicity about foreigners dying was bad publicity for Goreme. They could now go back to their comfortable desks and shut the case up tight. Bunyamin was safe, Barbie was safe, and psychological scars were not their business. They wanted the case to go away very quietly.

Ted Baxter's wife joined the group now. She had followed the police out the door to ask about details, but they had brushed her off. She approached Barbie.

"Thanks for all you have done today. I'm sure that little Bunyamin and his family appreciate it. You have been brave. And you solved the mystery. This is important too." She smiled sadly at Barbie and Bunyamin.

Barbie couldn't help but notice that her clothes were clean, neat and smelled nice. Unlike the rest of us, thought Barbie. When did she have a chance to have a shower and change clothes? Don't be catty, Barbie thought to herself. She smiled sweetly, and she hoped sincerely, up at Mrs. Ted Baxter.

"I wonder if they will let me cremate him and dispose of his ashes somewhere around here?" she suggested.

The 'eens' looked at her startled. "Around here?" Colleen asked incredulously.

"Perhaps not." She grimaced. "It's just that I don't really care to have much to do with all of this. I mean, the relationship ended a long time ago and I don't think there is much of an estate and there are no children, so I don't see the point..." She twisted her lips in distaste.

Barbie suddenly felt sorry for her. She wanted on one level to tell her that the reason why Bunyamin had been kidnapped was that her presence had set off Faruk. He would have felt much safer in his secrets except that she had appeared and frightened him into the horrible panic that had ended in kidnap and suicide. On the other hand, she understood the standoffish behavior. If they had not been close, she may very well have had little interest in Ted Baxter or his current life. But...

"Well, I think you have been a very devoted wife, flying out here at a moment's notice. This has been a traumatic thing for you." Barbie tilted her head just a bit, a subtle signal of womanly camaraderie.

With a stoic voice, Mrs. Ted Baxter answered, "Yes, it has been traumatic. You have all been very nice to me."

"But you did know Faruk, didn't you?" Barbie couldn't hold her tongue.

"You know, it has all been so long ago. I'm not sure I would have recognized him. And Ted Baxter always had students around, he was so popular with them. I really didn't know any of them well. We had really led rather separate lives for years, seven or eight. I mean we had a house together, but he was abroad so much and I didn't know any details about his businesses."

Barbie listened to this pathetic explanation and wondered where the truth lay. She wondered if Faruk's business would continue, who might run it and if that money would have done someone any good.

"I guess you could say that we were too lazy to divorce and there was no reason to, was there? I had my job, he had his. I didn't know much about these outside businesses. I mean, he was a teacher, always had a job and I thought that was what he got along on. He was never really extravagant. And there was a small inheritance that he tapped into occasionally. I just don't know about all of this. I mean, the police are all finished? All through? No more questions? I guess we can go home now? But I just have one question, what are we going to do about Ted Baxter?"

The group around the table stared at her. They had spent the last two days since his death wondering what they were supposed to do. When Mrs. Ted Baxter appeared, they had been relieved as it then became her job. Now she was asking them what to do about Ted Baxter.

"Dinner!" Kemal's son brought in bags full of Styrofoam boxes. The smell of roast chicken, grilled shish kebabs and fried potatoes suffused the room and they crowded around to watch the boxes being opened. Kemal organized cutlery and handed around drinks from the fridge.

"Ah, I have it here. A bottle of local wine. Made from plum. Who wants a glass?" Kemal held up a plain glass bottle with no label.

"Well," chirped Maureen. "It looks very local. We need to try this. Go all the way, experience life!" And she jumped up to help Kemal find glasses for everyone.

Bunyamin turned to his father and asked a question in Turkish, looking shyly at Barbie as he did so.

"Okay, Recep, what did he say?" Barbie asked, trying once again to loosen the death grip on her hand.

"He wants to know if he can bring you home with us."

"Bunyamin," Barbie stared at him. "I have my own house. But we can ride back to Ankara together on the bus and I can see you whenever you come by the school. Or maybe I can come to visit you. I will see you again. I'm not going anywhere!" She smiled broadly at him, hoping he could see her sincerity.

"You saved me. You saved me from him," Bunyamin said in English.

Barbie hugged the small boy whose shoulders began to shake with the first emotion he had expressed that evening. Tears rolled down his cheeks and soaked into Barbie's filthy shirt. "Yes, you are safe now."

Barbie's stomach roared at that moment, causing Bunyamin to giggle. Mercifully, he let go of Barbie's hand long enough for her to grab a couple of trays of food and a fork. "Yeah, I'm hungry. Aren't you?"

Bunyamin nodded and started on a pile of French fries.

"I almost forgot. Photos!" Kemal said. "They came while we were gone. Photos of the balloon trip. Look! I said that I was sure you would like them. Everyone wants photos of balloon rides. Don't you?" He produced a large envelope and those with non-greasy hands crowded around, trying to find photos of themselves.

"OOOOH!" squealed Charlene. "Look at that expression! And wow, you can really see the landscape in the background behind the balloon. These are fabulous. Because we are IN them, not taken by us. And see, in this one, the basket, fabulous, you can really see the branches all twisted around, a real, true basket. Oh, what fabulous souvenirs."

Mrs. Ted Baxter leaned over to look, taking a few in her hands. A wistful, or was it cautious, expression crossed her face. "I don't suppose there are any of..."

"No," Barbie said sharply.

Georgia glanced crossly at Barbie and said more softly, "No, you see, he didn't go with us."

Barbie looked apologetically at Mrs. Ted Baxter. "I mean, he was already... We saw him from the balloon."

"Oh, I see," she said, handing the photos back to Kemal.

Georgia moved to sit next to Barbie. "Why so snippy? Tired, I suppose, we all are. Well, what's next for us?"

"I heard from my friend Penelope. She is trying to get a job in Istanbul. Right now, she's in the States, so who knows when she'll get here. Soon I hope. She is really one for adventures. We were in Cairo together, you know, during the revolution."

"Great, does she like to travel?" Georgia grinned.

"What a stupid question," Barbie retorted. "Have you ever met an English teacher that didn't like to travel? Isn't that why we do it?"

"So, are you up for Morocco? Next break? Or maybe in the spring? And could I ask you not to bring along trouble with you? No more dead bodies," Georgia's voice fell to a whisper. "Umm, I really came over here to ask you about Faruk. Did he really tell you why he kidnapped Bunyamin?"

Barbie stared at Georgia, but found trouble trying to erase Faruk's face from her mind. How long would it be before she could even think of him without seeing those dark brown eyes, even white teeth surrounded by soft lips spread wide in a smile, half warm and generous, half lascivious? Even now, exhausted physically and emotionally, she felt the warm feeling of attraction. It was age-old, timeless, it was that feeling that had gotten so many in so much trouble over the years. Wars, kidnapping, murder. And she had not been immune. It had led her astray, this attraction. Barbie quietly told Georgia the outline of what Faruk had said, leaving out the angriest details of feeling cheated by Ted Baxter and the world. Money was not mentioned except obliquely. "He sounded bitter, as if life had dealt him a raw deal. I have had a few setbacks in life, but I never dreamed of knocking someone over the head with a rock, or pushing potted plants off of rooftops or throwing rocks at someone just because they looked like someone, or heavens, kidnapped anyone. That was too much."

"Wait, Barbie, just a minute," Georgia said, leaning closer. "What is this about potted plants? Or throwing rocks? Did he do that, when, how?"

Barbie filled Georgia in. She hadn't mentioned any of this to the police, it didn't seem relevant. She had only let them know that Faruk had confessed to hitting Ted Baxter over the head with a rock and left him lying there as if it were an accident. And the kidnapping was public knowledge. But the other incidents, well, Barbie thought, now she could tell them discreetly to Georgia and then everyone would find out, but it would be rumor, after the fact and not important to the police. Being chased in Pigeon Valley by a pair of multicolored shoes was simply an embarrassment that Barbie wished to leave out.

Geoff materialized suddenly in their midst holding a box that looked remarkably like a shoe box. He cleared his throat, loudly. "Well, Barbie, we have finally found them. It was supposed to be a surprise for all your work in organizing this trip and so our dearly departed member of staff had these for you. I thought it only fitting that you take them. A last gift." He handed the box to Barbie.

As she lifted the box, Barbie tried not to shudder. She had a premonition of what was in the box and she was right. Nestled in multicolored tissue paper was a pair of pink and yellow and green and blue shoes, the matching pair to everyone else's. She pasted a sick smile on her face and looked at Geoff. She narrowed her eyes and practically hissed, "You really think I should wear these shoes? You really think I want these shoes?" To herself, she simply vowed to leave them in Goreme. Maybe there was a charity for local kids with no shoes.

Geoff shrugged. He turned to Recep, "Well, what are we going to do about Ted Baxter?"

Recep's face registered surprise. "What do you mean? The police... the body...his wife will see to that, what should I do?"

"Well, are you expecting all of us to do extra classes? I mean, someone has to take over Ted Baxter's classes, don't they? Are you expecting double time from us?"

Recep sighed, "Oh, is that what you mean? Well, that would be wonderful if everyone helped out."

The 'eens' groaned. And Maureen voiced what they were all thinking, "I don't really want to try to 'step into his shoes' with those students. Maybe we could ease them into other classes???"

"Never those two Seymas in one class again" Charlene groaned. "I just taught them in the class before Ted Baxter got them. I've never been so happy to pass students along as those two. I won't do it again. I've never met two pains like those!"

"Well, does anyone know of an English teacher that is looking for a job?" Recep said hopefully, looking around the group.

Georgia looked at Barbie, "Penelope?" she mouthed.

Barbie bit her lip and looked frightened. Vivid thoughts of running down the streets of Cairo, tear gas following them and indistinct figures huddling in darkened doorways sprang to Barbie's mind. "Well… I do have this friend that is looking for a job. I guess I could ask. I mean, lightening doesn't strike the same place twice, does it?"

"More tea, everyone," Kemal announced as he brought a tray of tiny tulip glasses filled with amber liquid. "And for Barbie, some fresh Turkish Delight!"